P9-DFT-396

VANDERBILT MEMORIAL HOSPITAL

Record Of Birth

Child's Name: Moore, Christopher

Date of Birth: June 7

Mother's Name: Moore, Annie

Age: 17

Address: WHEREABOUTS UNKNOWN

Father's Name: Unknown

Age: ?

Address: WHEREABOUTS UNKNOWN

Attending Physician: Dr. Anthony Petrocelli

Nurse on Duty: Bethany Kent, R.N.

Remarks: Infant appears healthy. Prognosis excellent. Contact Social Services re: foster care. Alert precinct re: mother's abandonment.

> *Bethany—*
> *Here are the records you'll be*
> *needing for the adoption proceedings.*
> *Now all we need to do is make our*
> *wedding plans—STAT.*
> *How about dinner?*
> *Tony*

Dear Reader,

Sometimes your life can change in a heartbeat. For the residents of Grand Springs, Colorado, a blackout has set off a string of events that will alter people's lives forever....

Welcome to Silhouette's exciting new series, 36 Hours, where each month heroic characters face personal challenges—and find love against all odds. This month, nurse Bethany Kent enters a marriage of convenience to gain custody of the baby she helped deliver. Dr. Tony Petrocelli seems happy with the arrangement—until he starts falling for his "in name only" bride....

In coming months you'll meet a rough-edged cop who could mean the difference between life and death for a woman unjustly accused; a secretary who discovers she is carrying her boss's child; and an estranged husband and wife who have just one chance to save their marriage. Join us each month as we bring you 36 hours that will change *your* life!

Sincerely,

The editors at Silhouette

36 HOURS

MARRIAGE BY CONTRACT

SANDRA STEFFEN

Silhouette Books

Published by Silhouette Books

America's Publisher of Contemporary Romance

If you purchased this book without a cover you should be aware
that this book is stolen property. It was reported as "unsold and
destroyed" to the publisher, and neither the author nor the
publisher has received any payment for this "stripped book."

Special thanks and acknowledgment are given to
Sandra Steffen for her contribution to the
36 HOURS series.

For our Godchildren—
Jeff Thelen, Rachel, Brandy and Dusty Rademacher,
Brett Whitmore and Marc Hufnagel.
Blessings really do come in many forms.

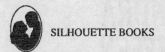 SILHOUETTE BOOKS

MARRIAGE BY CONTRACT

Copyright © 1997 by Harlequin Books S.A.

ISBN 0-373-65013-2

All rights reserved. Except for use in any review, the reproduction
or utilization of this work in whole or in part in any form by any
electronic, mechanical or other means, now known or hereafter
invented, including xerography, photocopying and recording, or in
any information storage or retrieval system, is forbidden without
the written permission of the editorial office, Silhouette Books,
300 East 42nd Street, New York, NY 10017 U.S.A.

All characters in this book have no existence outside the imagination of
the author and have no relation whatsoever to anyone bearing the same
name or names. They are not even distantly inspired by any individual
known or unknown to the author, and all incidents are pure invention.

This edition published by arrangement with Harlequin Books S.A.

® and ™ are trademarks of Harlequin Books S.A., used under
license. Trademarks indicated with ® are registered in the United States
Patent and Trademark Office, the Canadian Trade Marks Office and in
other countries.

Printed in U.S.A.

Sandra Steffen

Sandra Steffen saw her first novel published in 1992. Since then fifteen of her heartwarming books have graced the shelves of bookstores everywhere. This award-winning author lives in Michigan with her husband and their four children.

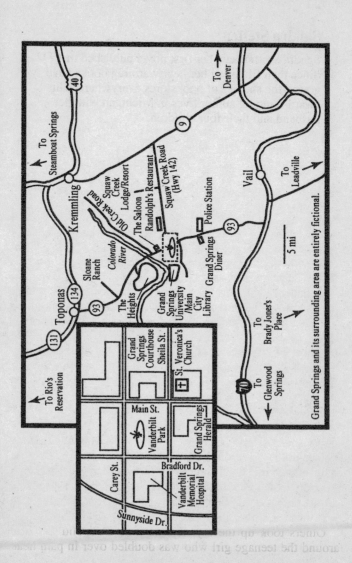

Grand Springs and its surrounding area are entirely fictional.

Prologue

"Somebody help me. It hurts. Make it stop. Please, make it stop."

Bethany Kent placed an ice pack on a patient's swollen wrist, her feet already moving in the direction of the quavering voice. Wheelchairs and gurneys blocked her path, and men, women and children all looked up as she passed, worry and pain and shock in their eyes.

It had been almost three hours since a mud slide took out the power in Grand Springs, Colorado, and the rain had yet to let up. Most of the people were here tonight because of car accidents due to the mud, the driving rain and the absence of street and traffic lights throughout the city. Some had sustained injuries from falling down stairs or tripping over furniture. Even the mayor had been brought in—the victim of an apparent heart attack. Beth was nearly asleep on her feet, and there was no end in sight.

Thunder rolled in from the mountains, rattling the windows and stirring up the overwrought patients huddled together in the emergency room. The lights dimmed, sending a hush from one end of the room to the other. An old man's gravelly voice cut through the tense silence. "The generator's going out. Without lights, the doctors will have to wait until morning to fix us up."

Others took up the cry. By the time Beth slid her arm around the teenage girl who was doubled over in pain near the door, some of the patients were rocking back and forth, others were starting to wail.

In a voice as sure and steady as her hands, Beth said, "I've worked in the ER long enough to know the ins and outs of the generators Vanderbilt Memorial uses during emergencies such as this one. And believe me, the lights are *not* going to go out."

Turning her attention to the girl who was moaning softly, she ignored the sheen of perspiration dampening the hair on her own forehead, and placed her hand on the girl's abdomen, which was taut with another contraction. "Dave," she called to a clerk near the desk on the other side of the room. "Find Dr. Petrocelli. Stat. Tell him we have another mother in labor."

The girl tried to straighten but couldn't. "I can't have the baby yet. It's ten weeks early."

Beth did her best to hide the anxiety twisting the knot in her stomach as Dr. Amanda Jennings joined her. A baby born ten weeks premature would be tiny, its lungs dangerously underdeveloped. As the two women helped the young mother to a vacant wheelchair, Beth had her first glimpse of pale skin, big eyes and a narrow face framed with a tangle of wet, dark hair sticking out of a tattered baseball cap. Sweet heaven, the girl was just a baby herself.

"What's your name?" Beth asked as they wheeled her into a trauma room and prepared to move her to the examining table.

Blue eyes rose to hers. "Annie. Annie Moore. Will you help me?" the girl pleaded, looking from Beth to Amanda Jennings.

Beth had seen lives saved, and she'd seen lives lost. Neither ever failed to move her. But nothing in all her thirty-five years had ever touched her more deeply than the entreaty and the unusual flicker of bravery in Annie Moore's eyes. Blinking back the tears that always seemed close to the surface these days, Beth nodded. "We'll help you."

The girl folded over as another contraction racked her thin body. Beth didn't like the looks of this. The pains were coming fast and furious with little time in between.

She was in the process of helping Annie into bed when Dr. Tony Petrocelli pushed into the room, past Dr. Noah Howell. Dr. Petrocelli's scrub suit was clean, and a face mask and stethoscope hung from his neck. The black stubble of his day-old beard was testimony to the fact that he'd been here for twenty-four hours, at least.

"Hello," he said matter-of-factly. "Who have we got here?"

"*We* don't have anyone. I'm here by myself. And my name is Annie. Am I going to die?"

Dr. Petrocelli glanced at the girl, obviously taking her terse words in stride. "No. I'm Dr. Tony Petrocelli. It's nice to meet you. How old are you, Annie?"

"Seventeen. How old are you?"

An arched eyebrow was the doctor's only indication of surprise. "I'm thirty-six. Nice night to have a baby."

The line creasing his lean cheek and his notorious half smile didn't seem to faze the girl. Squaring her jaw and straightening her shoulders, she said, "I'm not having the baby tonight. It's too early. I'm not ready. For once in my life, I'm going to do something right. So just make it stop."

Beth spared another glance at Dr. Petrocelli. She'd heard all the rumors and tall tales about the sexual prowess of the Don Juan of Vanderbilt Memorial. She'd seen him in the cafeteria, the corridors and elevators, but until now, she'd never actually worked with him. And she'd certainly never understood how a man with his image could also have the reputation for being one of the best obstetricians in Colorado. It didn't take long for her to understand.

While Beth held the girl's hand, showed her how to breathe and bathed her face with cool water, Tony conducted a quick examination. All the while, he talked to Annie, asking her questions about her pregnancy, the weather, and then moved on to about a dozen other topics. His voice was a husky baritone, his lips prone to smiling. His touch was strong and sure and was meant to put patients at ease, even through his latex gloves. "I'll be right back," he said, then motioned Dr. Jennings and Dr. Howell out to the hallway. Moments later he returned. Going around to the other side of the bed, he looked directly into Annie's eyes and said, "Your labor is too far advanced to stop. This baby wants to be born tonight. Let's get to work. Dr. Jennings here is going to help out."

Beth had expected panic, stark and vivid, to glitter in Annie's eyes, but she hadn't expected the shuddering breath the girl took or the pride and determination thickening her voice as she said, "My sister's name was Christie, so if the baby's a girl, I'm going to name her Christina. Christopher, if it's a boy. I just want you to know. In case something happens."

The girl cried out with the next contraction, and there was no time to reassure her. She groaned, bore down and cried out again, clutching Beth's hand, straining, hurting. She breathed when she could, pushed when she had to, and wept, her face contorting in pain a girl her age shouldn't have to endure. And then, after a momentary stillness, a baby's weak cry wavered through the room.

"It's a boy!" Dr. Petrocelli called.

"A boy?" Annie cried. "Is he all right?"

"He's tiny, but he has all ten fingers and toes."

Smiling around the lump in her throat, Beth wrapped little Christopher in a blanket, then held him up so his mother could see. Lord, he was small, but he was alive.

"Can I hold him?" Annie asked.

Beth placed the baby in his mother's arms for but a moment while the doctor cut the cord, then she whisked him away into a mobile incubator for his trip to the neonatal unit upstairs. Annie's voice stopped her at the door. "Promise you'll take care of him for me?"

Touching the baby gently, Beth turned. The young girl looked weak and exhausted and so alone Beth would have promised her anything. "I'll take care of him, Annie. You have my word."

For some reason, her gaze trailed to the foot of the bed where Dr. Petrocelli was standing. He was tall and dark, and looked as if he could have just stepped off a steamship from southern Italy. Even tired, his features were striking and strong—his nose, his chin, his cheekbones. But it was his eyes that held her spellbound. She knew the moment only lasted for the span of one heartbeat, but in that instant, everything went strangely still. His look warmed her in ways she hadn't expected, and didn't want to examine.

The baby moved beneath her hand, and the moment broke. With one last glance at Annie, Beth turned and left.

Tony heard the swish of the door and saw the blur of an auburn braid as Bethany Kent disappeared. He was aware of the whir of a fan, the strong scent of disinfectant and the floor beneath his feet. But he felt frozen in time, and in place. He'd delivered hundreds of babies, had been yelled at and kicked and hit. He'd witnessed countless moments of joy and tears and happiness at that first tiny cry. But he'd never felt exactly the way he had during that brief instant when his gaze had met Bethany's.

He'd seen her around the hospital and had heard rumors about a recent divorce. Although she kept to herself, he'd noticed her the way all men notice all women. But he hadn't had this gut-wrenching, knee-jerk reaction to her before. In fact, he couldn't remember the last time he'd felt so...so—hell, he didn't even know what to call it.

Telling himself the jolt of longing that pulsed suddenly in the very center of him was a result of too little sleep, too many patients and an adrenaline surge due to the emergency, he shook his head to clear it, then turned back to the seventeen-year-old girl who was crying, and trying not to let it show.

One

Bethany walked through the automatic door, her senses assaulted with the sudden burst of air-conditioning and the smell and clatter of patients' supper trays. After saying hello to the lab technicians heading for the cafeteria, she rounded a corner, her footsteps slowing to accommodate all the people milling around in front of the elevators. Too restless to wait, she spun around and took the stairs.

The exercise felt good. Maybe climbing eighteen or nineteen flights of stairs would ease the dread and disappointment dogging her steps. Unfortunately, Vanderbilt Memorial had only four floors. Beth stopped at the third.

She'd just come from the social worker's office downtown. All the deep breaths she'd taken since her meeting with Mrs. Donahue had failed to dull the sharp edges from the words still echoing through Beth's head.

"I know you love Christopher, Bethany," Mrs. Donahue had said. *"And I think you'd be a wonderful mother. But the court system prefers two-parent homes, especially in infant adoptions. I'm sorry, but I'm afraid your only hope is to get married."*

Beth was no stranger to marriage. She'd been married for seven years. The attorney who'd handled the divorce had casually dubbed Barry's quest to end the marriage "the seven year itch." Of course, the legal terminology he'd used in court was *irreconcilable differences*. Nobody had addressed the real reason Barry had wanted a divorce. But Bethany knew.

Her stomach roiled, a combination of the smell of hospital food, her dark thoughts and the memory of Mrs. Donahue's parting words. Forcing her worries to the back of her mind, she strode down the hall to the nursery.

Kitty Garcia looked up from the diaper she was changing and slanted Beth a genuine smile. "Hi, Beth. You're a little later than usual today."

"I had an appointment," Beth answered, her gaze automatically trailing to the other side of the glass. Already smiling at the tiny hands flailing over the top of the incubator, she strode to the sink, scrubbed her hands and donned a sterile gown. The sadness and despair she'd felt since her meeting with Mrs. Donahue faded the instant she took Christopher in her arms.

Lord, he smelled sweet, all talcum powder and baby innocence. She kissed his cheek, his chin and the tiny fold of skin at his neck. "Hello, sweet pea," she whispered. "How's my big boy today?"

She was almost sure she heard him sigh. Holding him several inches from her face, she smiled at him, marveling at his serious expression. He was two months and three weeks old, and he was slowly but surely gaining weight. It was a little too soon to tell what color his eyes would be, but his little head was covered with a layer of fine, dark hair a shade or two lighter than his mother's.

Nobody had seen Annie Moore since she'd left the hospital shortly after Christopher was born. With all the confusion and chaos in the aftermath of the mud slide, no one knew exactly when she'd disappeared. The girl had given her child life. She'd even given him a name and filled out his birth certificate. And then she'd left. Beth knew it was unusual for a mother who planned to abandon her child to sign the birth certificate. But Annie had...and it was definitely complicating the adoption process.

For the life of her, Beth didn't understand why the young woman had left. Maybe she hadn't planned to leave Christopher behind. Or maybe she'd decided she couldn't raise him on her own. Whatever the reason, Beth prayed that nothing bad had happened to Annie Moore.

"Take care of him for me."

At the time, Beth had assumed Annie had meant it in a temporary sense, but as the days and weeks had passed without word from the young woman, she'd begun to wonder if Annie had meant *forever*.

And *forever* was what Beth wanted with this child. As she stared into Christopher's eyes, a yearning so deep and so strong wrapped around her heart and squeezed like a fist. "I love you," she whispered. "If I was your mother, I'd make you feel safe and secure and well loved. Oh, Christopher, you really are a miracle baby, do you know that?"

Christopher looked up at her, his expression so earnest she didn't know whether to laugh or cry. He weighed less than five pounds, but his personality was ten times that big, and so was his will to live. The first two months of his life had been difficult. His lungs had been underdeveloped, and he was so tiny at birth that many people hadn't expected him to survive. The infection he'd gotten had weakened him further, but the little scrapper had clung to life by a thread. And through it all, Beth had stood by his incubator. On breaks, during her lunch hour and long after her shift was over, she'd laid her hand on his tiny body that was hooked up to so many wires and tubes he couldn't be picked up. Talking to him, reassuring him that she was there.

She'd never forget the day more than a month ago when she'd looked up from the chair where she was rocking Christopher and found Travis Stockwell and Peggy Saxon watching from the other side of the window, a twin in each of their arms. She'd appreciated their smiles and nods of encouragement, but she couldn't help noticing the differences between their babies and the child she was holding.

Little Travis and Virginia had been born the day after Christopher. Even though they were twins and had come into this world in a cab during a terrible storm, they were already chubby and wiggly and strong.

Just as Christopher would be soon, Beth reminded herself.

Barring any more setbacks, he'd be ready to leave the hospital in a week or so. She couldn't think of anything in the world she wanted more than to be able to take him home and make him her son.

"Your only hope is to get married."

The last Beth knew, husbands didn't grow on trees, although her closest friend claimed that now and then they'd been known to crawl out from under rocks. Thoughts of Jenna made her smile, just as they always did. But no matter what Jenna said, Beth hadn't found Barry under a rock. He happened to be bright and articulate and was an extremely successful corporate attorney. She'd loved him, and she'd thought he loved her. But a person couldn't love someone and then casually throw them away. She was still aching from the events of the past year, but she had to hand it to Barry; he certainly knew the ins and outs of obtaining a divorce. Beth only wished adopting Christopher could be half as easy.

She fed the baby his bottle, burped him and changed him, then stood next to his incubator and watched him sleep. She'd never experienced the joy of feeling a baby grow beneath her heart, but she knew how it felt to have a child grow within it, as Christopher had.

If only wishes made things so, she thought to herself, finally turning to leave. Too tired to stave off the sadness that had been building up inside her since Mrs. Donahue's parting words, Beth walked through the corridors, her arms folded, her footsteps quiet and slow.

A man's voice drew her from her thoughts. "The hospital board wants to promote you to head of obstetrics,

Tony, but they think it would look a lot better if you were married."

Everybody in the hospital knew Dr. Noah Howell's voice. And there was only one Tony on staff at Vanderbilt Memorial.

Suddenly alert, Beth glanced at the stairway at the end of the hall, and at the light spilling from the open doorway ten feet away. If she continued on toward the stairs, she would run the risk of interrupting the conversation between the two doctors. Glancing over her shoulder, she decided to head for the elevators.

Suddenly, an idea too absurd to contemplate froze her feet to the floor.

Tony Petrocelli took a deep breath, let it all out, then paced to the other side of the room. Shaking his head, he faced his friend and fellow doctor, but for the life of him, he didn't know what to say. He was still in a state of shock due to the latest incident during which a patient—a stark-naked, voluptuous, single patient—made a pass at him in his own examining room. He'd heard the nicknames people called him when they thought he was out of hearing distance—the Don Juan of Vanderbilt Memorial, the Italian Stallion—but the forwardness of some of his patients was getting out of hand.

Scrubbing a hand across his face, he said, "Noah, are you telling me the board won't give me the promotion unless I get married?"

"No, that isn't what I said or what they said, at least not exactly. And you don't have to make marriage sound like a death warrant."

Tony strode to the window. Staring at the parking lot below and the mountain peaks rising in the west, he knew he could have dismissed Noah's statement easily enough. After all, Noah Howell was a newlywed himself, and Tony had always suspected that married people belonged to a secret club and earned points for signing up their unsuspecting friends. He'd been ignoring his sisters' attempts for years. But it was getting more and more difficult to dismiss his parents' subtle hints about their only son's bachelor status. And these blatant come-ons from his patients were becoming more frequent. One of these days, one of them could cost him his career.

Turning around, he looked at Noah, who was lounging comfortably in a chair on the other side of the desk. Rubbing at a bothersome knot in the back of his neck, Tony said, "I suppose you're right about one thing, Noah. My life would definitely be a lot simpler if there was a wedding band on my finger."

The other man's laughter drew Tony's eyebrows down. Noah Howell had a reputation for being responsible, dedicated and serious. Until a couple of months ago, he'd been no more prone to outbursts of laughter than he was to whistling. That was before he and Dr. Amanda Jennings had been thrown together during the blackout. Tony didn't know what had been in the air that night, but strange things had been happening ever since. Some of them were sad and shocking, such as the murder of Grand Springs' mayor, Olivia Stuart. Others, like Noah and Amanda's surprise engagement and subsequent wedding, had been much happier events.

"Think about it, Tony," Noah insisted. "Amanda says there isn't a woman in this hospital, single or otherwise, except for her, of course, whose smile doesn't get just a little brighter when you walk by. Surely one of them has caught your fancy, if you know what I mean."

Tony scowled. "I always know what you mean these days, Noah, and frankly, I liked you a lot better when you had a shorter fuse."

"No, you didn't, and I'm a little surprised you've noticed that I've changed."

Tony clamped his mouth shut on the first thing that

sprang to his mind and walked straight out the door. Giving it a hard yank behind him, he spun around. And collided with a woman's slender body.

He heard a startled "oh!" and caught a glimpse of Beth Kent's auburn hair and wide blue eyes before his vision blurred. "Whoa," he said, his hands shooting out to steady her. "Sorry about that. I didn't even see you coming."

That happened to him a lot, but no matter what anybody said, he wasn't really absentminded. He simply didn't pay attention to the world around him unless it concerned him. And this sudden pulsing sensation pounding through the very center of him definitely had him concerned.

"That's all right," she said. "It was my fault."

Her voice sounded kind of breathless, and made him wonder if her heart had jolted and her pulse was accelerating, too. He knew of one way to find out, but this wasn't a private corridor, and Beth was inching away from him.

No matter what Amanda and Noah said, not every woman's smile brightened when he passed. His eyes had sought Beth's often since the night of the blackout. Although his body always did its part, his heart speeding up and his breathing slowing down, the most he'd ever gotten from her was a quick nod and a smile that didn't quite reach her eyes. In fact, this was the closest he'd been to her in two-and-a-half months.

Fortified by the memory of the brief brush of her body against his moments ago, and intrigued by the expression on her face right now, he said, "Unless you threw yourself at me on purpose, I don't see how this could have been your fault."

Beth was accustomed to taking blame, and would have liked to convince herself that the reason her nerves were standing on end was because there was no reproach whatsoever in Tony Petrocelli's eyes. Unfortunately, she'd never mastered the fine art of lying, not to others, and certainly not to herself. That meant her heart was fluttering in her chest for another reason entirely.

"Did you throw yourself at me on purpose, Beth?"

At a loss for something clever to say, Beth could only shake her head and stare. Tony Petrocelli was standing a few feet away, one hand on his hip, the other in his pocket. A white shirt that had probably been wrinkle-free when he put it on was tucked into the waistband of low-slung dress pants. His lips were full for a man's and were parted slightly, drawing attention to his mouth.

Beth's heart thudded once, then settled back into its normal rhythm. There was no doubt about it. He had the looks, the style and, oh yes, the moves to unsettle a feminine heart. The question was, did she have the nerve to unsettle his?

Good Lord, what was she thinking?

He took one long, smooth step toward her. Lifting her chin, she held his gaze and drew on every last ounce of courage she possessed. Keeping her voice quiet so that no one else would hear, she said, "Although I didn't actually *throw* myself at you, I was waiting for you."

"I like the sound of that."

Beth was at a loss for words all over again. As one moment stretched to two, his gaze left hers and trailed over her body in that anything-but-subtle way men had. Before she lost all her nerve, she took a deep breath and wavered him a smile. "I couldn't help overhearing your conversation with Dr. Howell. Perhaps I can help."

Tony felt a fast little jolt, followed by a rousing dose of pure attraction. He had no idea what Noah had to do with any of this, but he could think of one way that Beth could *help*. Moving even closer, he lowered his voice and said, "I'm listening."

She wet her lips, then glanced in every direction. Following the course of her gaze, he felt a tightening in his throat and a chugging in his chest. Doing everything in his power to let her set the pace, he whispered, "I think the coast is clear."

He could see her breath catch in her throat, could practically hear her thoughts screeching to a stop. For a moment, he thought she might kiss him, here and now. Instead, she lowered her voice to but a whisper and said, "I heard Dr. Howell mention that you could use a wife."

Tony went perfectly still, his eyes trained on Beth. Her auburn hair was pulled back, curly wisps framing a face that had gone noticeably pale. As if she read the question in his eyes, she finally said, "I, er, um, that is, I'd like to apply for the position."

Blood pounded through Tony's brain. Through the roaring din, he managed to say only one word. "Position?"

She nodded, her eyes growing more wary by the second.

"Are you telling me you'd like to be my wife?"

She nodded again and slowly lowered her gaze.

He snapped his mouth shut, but still he couldn't move. She'd knocked the wind out of him, and she hadn't even laid a hand on him.

"Dr. Petrocelli, please report to OB. Dr. Petrocelli. OB."

The monotone voice over the intercom jerked them apart like a bolt of lightning, then froze them in a stunned tableau all over again. "Look, Beth, I don't know what to say."

Beth had never heard of anyone dying of embarrassment, but she wasn't so sure she wouldn't be the first. She moved backward, holding up both hands in a halting gesture. "You don't have to say anything. I'm sorry. I don't know what I was thinking. Just forget I ever mentioned this. And I'll do the same."

When he continued staring at her, unmoving, she seized her opportunity and fled. She listened for the sound of footsteps behind her. Thankful that none came, she hurried down the stairs the way she should have done in the first place. At the landing between floors, she dropped her face into her hands. Her cheeks were on fire, and so was her pride. Mingling with her embarrassment and sheer humiliation was the deep-seated sadness that Christopher would never be hers.

"The doctors think Christopher will be ready to leave the hospital soon. Isn't that wonderful?" Beth asked as she dusted a shelf of mining supplies and trinkets in her best-friend's store.

The soft clink and jingle of bangle bracelets was the only indication Beth had that she wasn't alone in the room. "Jenna?"

At the sound of more jingling, and nothing else, she turned around. "Don't you think that's wonderful news?"

Jenna Brigante tossed her waist-length black hair over her shoulder and flipped the Closed sign in the window of The Silver Gypsy. Instead of turning the lock, she swung around, her gauzy skirt swishing around her knees. "Not only do I think that's wonderful, but I told you it was wonderful the first three times you mentioned it."

"Oh. I must be repeating myself."

"I live in an old prospector's cabin in the mountains with only crows for company much of the time. So if you think I mind hearing about Christopher, think again. In fact, if you want to tell me one more time, be my guest. And then, when you've run out of diversions, you can tell me what's really on your mind tonight."

Beth folded her arms and studied her friend. Jenna looked every bit like the gypsies she claimed were her ancestors, from her big brown eyes to her low-necked blouse, all the way to the strappy sandals on her feet. What she lacked in height, she more than made up for with personality. She said she was thirty-two "springs" old, and had an incredibly straightforward way of saying exactly what she was thinking, not to mention an uncanny ability to read every nuance of a person's expression and behavior. She was the only person Beth knew who could swear in four languages, and the only person who accepted Beth exactly as she was.

Straightening a display of silver baubles and charms and necklaces, Beth said, "I saw Barry today."

Jenna made a derisive sound. "I suppose it's inevitable. In a city of over sixty thousand people, you never run into an old friend or former classmate, but ex-husbands appear on every corner. How is old Barry, anyway?"

Setting a string of Romany wind chimes in motion, Beth said, "He seemed all right. Better than all right, actually, especially while he was introducing me to his new wife."

"Aw, honey."

"Her name is Chelsea."

"It figures."

"She doesn't look a day over twenty-five."

"What a jerk. Want me to put a curse on him? I could make his member fall off. Just say the word."

Beth almost smiled in spite of herself. "You don't have to do that on my account."

"Believe me, it would be no trouble."

Moving on to a glass case that held the more expensive silver jewelry mined and designed with Jenna's own hands, Beth said, "Did I mention that they're expecting a baby in three months?"

"As a matter of fact, you didn't. It must have slipped your mind."

Beth rolled her eyes. Subtle, Jenna wasn't.

"That Barry always was a fast worker, wasn't he?" Jenna sputtered. "Didn't even wait for the divorce to be final. Of course, this means my curse would be a little late. I could still do it, but now it would be more for enjoyment than actual revenge."

After a momentary silence, Jenna said, "Did it hurt? Running into Barry, I mean. Is that why you're so quiet tonight?"

Beth moved on to the next display. "It's nothing I won't get over, if that's what you mean. It just hasn't been a red-letter day, that's all. I had an appointment with Mrs. Donahue at Social Services right after work. She told me *she'd* love to let me adopt Christopher, but those silly old courts prefer two-parent homes."

"Geez, Beth, have you been breaking mirrors or walking underneath ladders or throwing black cats over your shoulder, or what?"

This time, Beth cracked a smile. "Actually, there's something else."

Other than the traffic outside on the city's main thoroughfare, the room became utterly silent. Without turning to face her friend, she said, "I sort of asked one of the doctors at the hospital to marry me."

Jenna broke the long stretch of silence with a loud whoop of glee. "Bethany, honey, I do believe you're finally coming out of your shell."

"It's not funny, Jenna. And I am not."

"Sure you are, and yes it is. But tell me, what did this doctor *sort of* say?"

Running her hand over the brightly colored skirts hanging on a rack in the corner, Beth said, "Actually, the only noise I heard was the thud of his jaw hitting the floor."

Beth didn't turn around. Not when Jenna made a sympathetic sound. Not even when the chimes over the door jingled with the arrival of a late customer.

"Uh, Beth?" Jenna asked.

"Hmm?"

"Did this doctor you mentioned look as if he could have just stepped off a steamboat from Italy?"

"You could say that, why?"

"Oh, it's nothing, but unless doctors have gone back to making house calls, I believe your fiancé just walked through the door."

Two

*H*er fiancé?

Was that what Jenna had said? That her *fiancé* had just walked through the door?

Beth stared at a shelf containing books of old Romany curses, wishing with all her might that she could make herself vanish into thin air. But there was no way out. She was in a corner, literally and figuratively. Sooner or later, she was going to have to turn around to see if Tony was really standing in this very store.

"Bethany?"

Her mind went blank for a moment, then scrambled like a radio picking up more than one signal. There was no doubt about it. That voice belonged to none other than Tony Petrocelli himself. She took a deep breath for courage, then turned around to face the music and the last man on earth she was prepared to see.

She glanced at Jenna, who was suddenly all eyes and ears, then slowly raised her gaze to Tony's. Although she couldn't quite manage a smile, she nodded in greeting and said, "Dr. Anthony Petrocelli, this is Jenna Maria Brigante, my best friend."

Tony heard the regal formality in Beth's voice, and wondered where she'd acquired her manners and her style. He didn't doubt that she was strong; nurses had to be—in spirit and in body. But even the grouchiest nurses at Vanderbilt Memorial could flirt with the best of them. He enjoyed playing along, but he'd never had any trouble dismissing the overtures as fun, and nothing more. Beth Kent had intriguing looks and a willowy body that rivaled any nurse's in the building. Yet he'd never seen her so much as wink at one of the doctors. She obviously didn't believe in small talk or casual flirtations. Oh, no. She'd cut straight to the quick when she'd asked him to marry her, in so many words. And he simply hadn't been able to dismiss that.

Tony cast a sideways glance at the dark-haired woman who was watching him openly. *Jenna Maria Brigante,* he thought to himself. *Oh, boy. A woman with three names always spelled trouble.* "Brigante," he repeated. "Is that Italian?"

Her eyes danced with a peculiar light, her hair swishing as she shook her head. "Romanian Gypsy."

He cocked his head slightly. "That would explain how you knew that I was a doctor."

The woman stared at him, then burst out laughing. "Bethany," she exclaimed, "I do believe your taste is improving."

Jenna Maria Brigante obviously didn't let a man's size intimidate her. She raised her chin and stared him down, pointing one red-tipped finger directly at him. "Since you and Beth undoubtedly have a lot to talk about, I'm going to let her lock up here and I'll leave you two alone. But I'm warning you. If you hurt her, you won't like the repercussions."

He looked her straight in the eye. With a significant lift of his brows, he said, "Believe me, any curse you put on me would be pale compared to what my Grandma Rosa would do to me."

Obviously satisfied with his statement and with what she saw in his eyes, Jenna turned to leave. At the door, she said, "Call me later, Beth. I want details. Lots and lots of details."

The moment she opened the door, the room came alive with the faint purl of a dozen different wind chimes. She cast one more long look over her shoulder without saying a word. With a rustle of skirts and the rattle of the door, she was gone, and he and Bethany were alone.

Glancing from Beth to the airy scarves draped over a pole covered with climbing ivy, he said, "Interesting place. Is your friend really a Gypsy?"

That won him her first smile of the evening, which in turn sent a shock of attraction chugging through his bloodstream all over again. This was crazy. The fact that he was here was crazy. He didn't believe in Romany curses, and he couldn't believe an honest-to-goodness nurse did, either. So it wasn't a hex or a magical spell that drew him closer. It was intrigue, and quite possibly the strongest flare of desire he'd experienced in his entire life.

"How did you find me?" she asked.

Tony tossed the suit jacket he'd been carrying over his arm onto a velvet chair. He'd loosened his tie hours ago, and would have loved to remove it entirely. Afraid she might misconstrue his intentions, he settled for raking his fingers through his hair. "Let's just say that Jenna Maria Brigante was less formidable than the super in your building."

"So you've met Mr. Willoughby."

"Oh, I've met him, all right. But I have to tell you that it was easier to convince a first-time mother that she could deliver a nine-pound baby than it was to convince Mr. Willoughby that I'm not Jack the Ripper."

She looked up at him, her eyes searching his face, for what, he didn't know. He'd seen her in her nursing uniform at the hospital, and he'd imagined her wearing nothing at all in his fantasies, but this was the first time he'd seen her exactly like this. She was wearing red jeans and a black tank top, her dark auburn hair waving past her shoulders. He didn't know how she did it, how she managed to pull off looking sexy and regal at the same time. It was one helluva potent combination.

"What was it?" she asked.

Tony wasn't surprised that he had no idea what she was talking about, not when most of the blood in his brain seemed to be making its way to a place straight south of there. "What was what?" he asked.

"The nine-pound baby you mentioned."

"Oh. It was a girl. If she's half as ambitious as her parents, she'll either be a linebacker for the Broncos or the president of the United States."

His attempt at humor didn't have the effect he'd hoped for. Although Beth's lips lifted into a smile, it didn't quite reach her eyes. "Why did you come here tonight, Doctor?"

There was a question. And the truth was, he wanted to give her an honest answer. He just wasn't exactly sure what the answer would be. Taking his time meeting her eyes, he finally said, "I've received my share of propositions, but I have to say it's been a long time since a woman has come right out and proposed marriage."

Beth was vaguely aware of screechy brakes and smooth-running engines on the street outside, but most of her attention was turned inward at the sensation flickering to life in her chest. It could only be one thing—hope; tiny maybe, and precarious for sure, but it was hope just the same. Not trusting herself to move, she said, "Does this mean you might consider it?"

He stared back at her for a long time. She wished she had Jenna's uncanny knack for reading people's expressions, because for the life of her, she didn't know what was going on behind Tony's dark brown eyes. The way he raked his fingers through his hair could have been fatigue, it could have been unease or it could have been indecision. There wasn't much Bethany wouldn't have done for an inkling as to what she was dealing with. Unfortunately, all she could do was wait.

A dozen images and sensations crowded through Tony's mind. The memory of the pouty expression on his patient's face earlier today when he'd backed from the room, stupefied that the woman thought she could seduce him in his own office. The sound of Noah's voice when he'd mentioned the promotion and the hospital board's position on marriage. The disastrous blind date his younger sister had felt obliged to send him on last week, and his parents' desire that he pass on the family name. As strange as it sounded, the heat that seemed to have taken up permanent residence in the very center of him was stronger than all those other things combined.

But marriage?

The thought brought him up short, another idea close on its heels. Beth Kent was pretty and hard-working, and had a kind of class and sophistication that couldn't be learned. A woman like that could have her pick of men. All she would have to do was say the word and men would line up for her attention.

It suddenly occurred to him that she didn't seem to want suitors. She wanted a husband. The question was why.

He strolled forward, looking at her intently. "I don't honestly know what I'm considering, but I know I'd like to understand. Maybe you could start at the beginning."

For a moment, Beth studied him, measuring, appraising the situation. She supposed he had a right to want to understand. The question was, what should she say? How much should she include? And exactly where was the beginning?

One thing she'd acquired the summer she and her family had spent in England was an appreciation for the tradition of sipping tea. And because brewing tea gave a person something to do with her hands, Beth decided this was the perfect time to prepare a pot.

Without preamble, she strode to the doorway in the back of the room. Lifting the beads aside, she glanced over her shoulder. "Won't you come this way?"

Tony followed her to a tiny kitchenette. Since he doubted

his legs would fit underneath the ornate, glass-topped table in one corner, he leaned against the counter, ankles crossed, one hand in his pocket, watching as Beth filled a kettle with water and removed two tea bags from an airtight jar.

"First of all," she began tentatively, "I want you to know that I don't make a habit of asking men to marry me. Now I know why."

Tony settled back, strangely intrigued by her subtle wit and the way her lower lip was slightly fuller than the top.

"Anyway," she continued, turning on the gas beneath the kettle, "I wouldn't have asked you today, but I'm desperate."

She had the grace to look apologetic at her choice of words. Tony only smiled.

"You see, I overheard Dr. Howell mention that the board of directors would prefer to give the promotion of head of obstetrics to a married man. Now, I'm not pretending that it's fair, but since I was raised in a family that could have written the book on putting on airs, I understand all about maintaining the proper appearances. I had recently come from a meeting, myself, when I overheard your conversation with Dr. Howell, and I'd hoped that perhaps you and I could both gain something from a marriage of convenience, so to speak."

Tony found himself standing up a little straighter, his gaze sharpening with every passing second. "What would you gain, Beth?"

She turned slowly and looked up at him. "A baby. A son."

If Tony lived to be a hundred, he'd never forget the open look of longing in her eyes and her voice during that moment in time. "What do you mean?" he said, more slowly and gently than before.

"Do you remember Christopher Moore? The baby you delivered the night of the blackout? Something happened to me that night. I can't explain it, but I took one look at him and I was lost. Maybe there was magic in the air, or maybe it was all just destiny. I don't know. But I was sure you felt it, just as I was sure Annie Moore felt it, too. She was so brave for a girl so young. Do you remember? She asked me to take care of Christopher for her. At the time, I thought she meant for the moment, but now I wonder if she wanted me to adopt him even then. It's what I want more than anything else in this world. But the social worker said that in order for that to happen, I must be able to provide him with a two-parent home."

By now, Tony had straightened to his full height, his feet spread slightly, his stance ready. For what, he wasn't sure. She continued, everything she said sounding very matter-of-fact, very tidy. It all made perfect sense, and he had to admit, he'd benefit from the arrangement, too.

What was he thinking?

The tea was brewed by the time she'd reached the end of her "sales pitch." Tony could have used a shot of whiskey. He didn't understand what was happening to him, but God help him, he was actually considering her proposition.

She'd mentioned that something had been in the air that night when Christopher had been born. While he didn't doubt that a bond had formed between Beth, Annie Moore and the tiny baby he'd helped bring into this world, he remembered another kind of link, this one between him and Beth. It had been a purely sexual experience, although they hadn't even touched. He'd been feeling strangely on edge ever since. As a doctor and a man, he knew of only one way to relieve his pent-up need.

Tony happened to believe that free sex was worth about as much as dandelion wine. It went down with about as much grace, and left the same bad feeling in the pit of a man's stomach. Blah. Give him a bottle of hard whiskey and an honest chase, and he'd give back ten times as much as he asked for. Although he'd never actually admitted it out loud, one-night stands were boring. A man could get *that* much gratification by himself. That, however, wasn't the kind of gratification he wanted or needed.

"Well?" she asked. "What do you think?"

Tony didn't know what to think. Inching closer, he said, "Before I can answer that, there's something else I have to know."

She turned those violet eyes of hers to his, and damn, he couldn't have formed a coherent thought if his life depended upon it. Letting his instincts guide him, he did the only thing he could do. In one fast move, he covered her mouth with his.

Her surprise whooshed out of her, but she didn't pull away. His instinctive response to her was powerful, but nothing could compare to the sensations surging through him at the joining of their mouths. He deepened the kiss, fitting her closer to his body, moving his mouth over hers, his hands spreading wide across her back, inching up and down, kneading. Needing.

She opened her mouth beneath his, sending desire pounding through him even faster. He slanted his lips over hers, clinging, devouring her softness. The kiss went on for a long time, but it wasn't enough. He wanted, needed, more.

Beth couldn't think, and she certainly couldn't step away. Tony had moved fast, but she still should have seen this coming. His hands warmed her through her tank top, his kiss heating her from the inside out. It had been a long time since she'd felt warm in exactly this way. She hated to admit how much she'd missed it.

The kiss finally broke on a need for oxygen, if nothing else. Beth took a shuddering breath and tried to get her thoughts under control. No wonder the rumors circulating through the hospital about Tony's sexual prowess had always run rampant. According to one of the nurses who worked with him, ninety-nine percent of his patients fell a little in love with him in the delivery room. Dr. Petrocelli obviously had a very good bedside manner. Now she was beginning to believe the stories about his in-bed manner, as well. Thankful that he couldn't read her mind, she turned her back on him and tried to keep a blush from climbing to her cheeks.

"We'll tell our families tomorrow."

Her head came up and around with a start. "What?"

"Our families. They're going to have to be told."

"You mean you'll marry me?"

Tony had a feeling he would always refer to this as the day he lost his senses, but, with desire still thick inside him, it didn't feel that way right now. Fighting an uncharacteristic urge to toss his head back and laugh, he decided to forget about potential problems and concentrate on this instinctive need he had to make Bethany Kent his.

Looking at her with smug delight, he said, "I can hardly believe it, but yes, that is what I mean."

"When?" she asked.

"As soon as possible."

The huskiness in his voice threw her for a moment. Recovering, she said, "Yes, I think it would be best if we were married before Christopher is released from the hospital."

"For that reason, too."

His dark eyes held a sheen of purpose she simply couldn't ignore. Wishing she knew where to put her hands, she said, "All right, then. I guess that's that."

Tony made a sound only men could manage. "You won't know the meaning of the term *that's that* until after you've met my family tomorrow."

Beth hadn't considered meeting his family. Actually, other than Christopher, there were a lot of things she hadn't considered. "Are they going to be terribly upset?" she asked.

The shake of his head was too slow and too sure to be anything but genuine. "Are you kidding? They've been

trying to marry me off for years. Believe me, they're going
to be thrilled with you and with Christopher. What about
your family? How will they take the news?''

Beth considered her family's reactions one by one. Her
mother's eyes would widen, and her father would get a little
stuffy, and her sister and brother-in-law would share a long,
meaningful look, but none of them would actually *say* anything outright. They had far too much social breeding for
any real show of emotion.

"Actually," she said, "I think I'll wait until after the
fact to tell my family."

Tony shook his head. "My grandmother would never
forgive me if I didn't let all of them in on the news. I'll
call them first and give them a little time to get used to the
idea of not only a wedding but another grandchild, too.
They're going to want to meet you, of course. And they'll
insist upon feeding you. They always close the grocery
store at five-thirty on Saturdays. I'll pick you up at six."

Beth felt as if she were caught up in a whirlwind. Placing
a hand to her temple to try to still the dizziness, she said,
"It seems as if we should shake on it or something."

One second later his mouth was on hers all over again.
She didn't gasp, but she very nearly swooned.

Raising his head, he said, "There, that was better than
any handshake. I'll see you tomorrow. Good night, Beth."

The next thing she knew, he strode through the beads in
the doorway and scooped his suit jacket off the chair on
his way to the front door. Pulling her gaze from his retreat-
ing form wasn't easy. Tony Petrocelli had a smooth gait
and a strong masculine physique that was impossible to
ignore. She half expected him to glance over his shoulder
as if he knew it. The fact that he didn't made her heart feel
strangely tender.

Just who was Tony Petrocelli? He was no whipping boy,
and he certainly wasn't a shrinking violet. People at the
hospital said he was a complex man, one who wasn't easy

to know intimately. Beth was beginning to realize that there
was a lot more to him than rumors and tall tales.

She stood in the doorway, staring through the colorful
beads for a long time after he left, feeling as if she were
viewing the world through rose-colored glasses. Oh, what
a difference a day could make. In the span of twelve hours
she'd experienced nearly every emotion there was. Sadness,
despair, embarrassment, desire and relief. Her head was
spinning as a result.

Jenna would have said, "All's well that ends well."

Bethany supposed it was true enough. After all, according to Mrs. Donahue, she would be able to begin adoption
proceedings as soon as she was married. She already loved
Christopher as her own. Now she would be able to raise
him as her own, as well. She smiled at the thought, her
arms aching to hold the child that would soon be hers.

Soon. That was when Tony said he wanted to get married.

Good heavens, she was getting married, when she'd
promised herself she'd never get married again. Touching
the tips of her fingers to her lips, she only hoped she knew
what she was doing.

Beth slid from the seat and rounded the front of Tony's
Lexus. Her feet stopped at the foot of the porch steps, her
eyes trained on the welcome sign fastened above the front
door.

"Ready?" Tony asked, reaching for her hand.

No. As a matter of fact, she wasn't ready. Oh, the house
looked inviting enough. It was located in what her mother
referred to as the working-class district. These houses were
old but well kept. They were far less ornate than the huge
Victorian mansions that had been built by businessmen and
prospectors who'd struck it rich in the silver mines a hundred years ago, and far less pretentious than the new struc-
tures built by present-day businessmen and the social elite.

The houses in this neighborhood had painted porches and bare spots in the lawns where children played and dogs snoozed in the shade. The exterior didn't concern Beth in the least. It was the people waiting for her inside that had her nerves standing on edge.

During the ride from her apartment, Tony had hit most of the high spots concerning his family. She now knew that his Grandpa Mario had fought and died in the *big* war, and that the Petrocellis were the kind of people who still referred to wall-to-wall carpeting as a rug, and who ate dinner at noon, and supper as soon as they closed the Italian grocery store that had been in the family for more than forty years. Other than a love for gossip, they sounded like kind, good-hearted men and women. So why were her feet frozen to the sidewalk?

"Come on," Tony said softly. "You're going to be fine."

She took a deep breath and went up to the first step. Mentally preparing herself for what was to come, she stared straight ahead. "All right. Let's go in. I only hope I don't drop my spaghetti in my lap."

Tony was still laughing when he opened the front door and ushered her inside. Every person in the room turned to look at them, more than a dozen pairs of brown eyes narrowing with a critical squint. Accepting the squeeze Tony gave her hand for moral support, Beth did her best to hold her head high and refrain from fidgeting. But honestly, a germ under a microscope had never received a more intense scrutiny.

"Everyone," Tony began, "I'd like you to meet Bethany Kent. My future bride."

Only one person in the entire room moved. A small woman with white hair leaned heavily on her cane as she ambled closer.

"This is my Grandma Rosa," Tony said quietly.

Rosa Petrocelli was eighty-five years old if she was a

day, and obviously accepted her position as head of the family as her just due. Her gaze started at Beth's feet and trailed upward, ending at her face. She finished her perusal, pausing for a moment for effect. When she was good and ready, she said, "You're very thin."

Beth looked past the thinning white hair and the wrinkles lining a face that had lived through a lot of years, and into the other woman's sharply assessing eyes. "Maybe. But not too thin."

Rosa Petrocelli's eyebrows went up. Tapping her cane on the floor to still the gasps behind her, she said, "You also have a strong will, yes? This is good. You're goin'ta need it to hold your own with our Antonio."

A chuckle started in one corner of the room, circled around and back again, picking up volume along the way. Rosa muttered a prayer in Italian, and in no time at all, chaos and confusion erupted. Beth was introduced to Tony's parents and his sisters, and so many other family members she had a difficult time keeping everyone straight. She thought she tallied up eleven children, but she might have counted one adorable little boy who looked to be about four years old twice.

She managed to make it through dinner, or supper, as the Petrocellis called it, without spilling her spaghetti in her lap, although it was surprising that she could eat at all considering all the questions she answered. She glanced up several times and found Tony watching her, and at least one of his sisters nodding in approval.

The dishes were whisked away to the kitchen, Beth's offer to help with the cleanup quickly denied. The Petrocelli women were very formidable, giving their men strict orders to watch the children and keep Beth duly entertained. It didn't take long for Tony's father and brothers-in-law to draw him into a discussion about baseball, oblivious to their children's noisy play and the woman they'd been instructed to amuse. Seizing a moment of solitude,

Beth strolled through an arched doorway and into another room.

The room was small and appeared to be used as some sort of den. An overstuffed sofa took up one wall, and a cozy armchair was placed at a comfortable angle nearby with doily-topped end tables on either side. There was an old television in one corner, and everywhere, on every available surface, sat framed photographs in all shapes and sizes. Beth studied them, intrigued.

There was a black-and-white snapshot of a man in uniform, another of a solemn-faced wedding couple, and color photos of everything from first communions to weddings to smiling babies. Tony's sisters looked so much alike it was difficult to tell who was who. But Tony was easy to spot. She'd noticed the way his mother, grandmother and four sisters all doted on him, making it obvious that he was the family favorite—because he was the only boy, or because he kept himself slightly aloof, she couldn't be sure.

"Are you hiding or wandering?"

Beth spun around, flushing guiltily. Tony was leaning in the doorway, one hand in his pocket, a lazy light in his eyes. Wondering what had happened to her air of calm and self-confidence, she said, "A little of both, I suppose."

He pushed himself from the doorway and ambled farther into the room. "They can be overwhelming at times. Believe me, I know."

Beth found herself smiling. Although she *had* wandered into this room to catch her breath and grab a moment of solitude, she certainly couldn't fault the Petrocellis for the way they'd welcomed her tonight. Shrugging, she said, "Your family is wonderful. I'm just not used to all the touching and embracing and, well, all the noise."

Tony stopped a few feet away, his gaze trailing over photographs he'd seen a thousand times. "You learn to tune it out. Your family isn't noisy?"

"Hardly. I only have one sister. We're very different."

Something about her tone of voice drew his gaze. "Different, how?" he asked.

She shrugged one shoulder. "Janet is beautiful, poised and gracious. She's two years older than I am, and she has always made all the right choices. She married a handsome, intelligent man and has three beautiful, intelligent children."

Tony thought they all sounded extremely politically correct, and wondered why it irked him. Before he was able to come up with an answer, Beth began clicking off names on her fingers. "Let me see if I've gotten your family straight. Your father's name is Vince, your mother is Elena. Carmelina is married to Nick Santini. Gina's husband's name is Teddy Bulgarelli. There's Andreanna and Rocky Grazanti, and Maria and...what's Maria's husband's name again?"

"Frank Giovanni." His answer had been automatic. Why wouldn't it be? He'd known Frankie all his life.

With a rustle of silk that kicked his heartbeat into overdrive, she bent down to study another photograph. "Is there anyone in your family who hasn't married a fellow Italian, Tony?"

He caught a whiff of decadently expensive French perfume, and suddenly, he didn't want to talk about his family. He waited for his silence to draw her attention, letting his gaze travel over her soft, elegant blouse and long, straight skirt.

"There's me," he whispered.

Beth straightened slowly. Had she moved closer, or had he? In the tight space so near him, she couldn't think of a single thing to say or do. Tony seemed to have no such problem. His breath felt warm on her cheek. A moment later, his lips touched hers. This was the first time he'd kissed her today. She suspected he'd been on his best behavior, but there was no disguising the passion running through him right now.

There was a ruckus in the next room, but it was Elena Petrocelli's voice coming from the doorway that drew Tony and Beth apart. Calling for attention with a loud clap of her hands, she said, "It's nice to see that my son takes after his father, but there will be plenty of time for that later. Now, come. Quickly. We have wedding plans to make."

Beth and Tony ended up in the next room, surrounded by Petrocellis who were all talking at once.

"Bethany," Elena said, "will your mother be helping you with the wedding plans?"

Beth barely had time to shake her head before Tony's mother rushed on. "Uh! No problem. I've planned four weddings already, and would love to help with yours and my Anthony's. I know the two of you will be busy with adoption proceedings—I can hardly wait to meet my new grandson. You just leave the wedding plans to me."

"We'll have to see about a hall."

"And food, Mama. We'll need plenty of food."

"Tony, were you thinking of an autumn wedding? Or winter?"

Beth cast a look at all the people who were talking and gesturing a mile a minute, then slowly turned her gaze to Tony's. He leaned closer and said, "I told you they were overwhelming."

She smiled. She hardly knew this man, yet she had an unsinkable feeling that everything was going to be all right. Tony obviously had strong family ties, and would undoubtedly be a good father to Christopher. Although arranged marriages weren't common in this day and age, they'd certainly been effective in other eras. She'd married Barry for love. And look how that had turned out. Perhaps a marriage based on mutual respect and the love of an innocent child would fare better.

Tony raised his voice above all the noise. "Sorry to disappoint all of you, but Beth and I aren't going to have time for a big wedding. We're going to be married as soon as possible.''

"As soon as possible!" Rosa exclaimed.

"That won't give Aunt Pasqualina much time to make her famous wedding cake," Elena sputtered.

"The nice thing about Aunt Pasqualina's cakes," one brother-in-law, Beth thought it was Frank, said, "is that you don't actually eat them."

"That's right," Nick Santini agreed. "We're still using the cake from our wedding to prop open the back door."

After giving her husband a sharp jab in the ribs, Carmelina asked, "What do you mean by as soon as possible?"

Tony glanced at Beth. "A week at the latest."

A gasp went through the room. "A week!" Elena said. "But, Anthony, we've been waiting all our lives to hear you say 'I do' in a proper wedding ceremony."

Beth didn't like the guilt that flooded her. Trying to soften the family's disappointment, she said, "In order to adopt Christopher, we must be married as soon as possible."

Mention of the baby changed everything. The Petrocellis took turns nodding and shaking their heads. "A week!" Rosa said. "That don'a leave us much time."

"That's all right, Grandma," Tony said. "We're planning to be married by a judge."

A little girl whined over a bumped knee, and a baby started to cry. The adults took the news even worse. Mouths dropped open, then snapped shut, and chaos erupted all over again. Grandma Rosa muttered in Italian, and Vince and Elena sputtered between themselves. Turning suddenly, Elena said, "Anthony, this is a wedding, not a traffic violation. If you must be married within a week, so be it, but at least do it in front of God and Father Carlos."

"But, Mama," Gina insisted, "Father Carlos insists upon a six-month waiting period."

Elena, whose black hair was streaked with gray, turned to Tony and Beth. Raising her chin at a haughty angle, she said, "You two see to the baby, the license and the blood tests, and leave Father Carlos to me."

Tony and Beth exchanged a look, then slowly nodded. It seemed there wasn't much more to say. Tony made noises about leaving soon after. Pulling Beth along behind him, he shouldered a path to the door.

"Antonio, wait!"

The crowd parted to make room for Tony's grandmother to pass. Rosa peered up at her grandson for a long time, then moved on to the woman at his side. Age might have shrunk her frame, but it hadn't dulled her intelligence or softened her temperament. A flicker of apprehension shot through Bethany. *She knows,* she thought to herself. *Tony's grandmother knows that this marriage is all because of Christopher. Only because of Christopher.*

"Is there something you wanted to say, Grandma?" Tony asked.

When Rosa nodded, Beth tried to prepare for what was to come.

"I just want to welcome you into our family, Bethany. I've seen the way you watched all the little ones here tonight, and I believe you're goin'ta be a fine mother to the child you and my Antonio plan to adopt, and a fine mother to the babies you'll birth yourself, too. Even if you are a little thin by Italian standards."

A lump rose to Beth's throat, making speech impossible. Carmelina flashed her a wink that spoke volumes and a smile that said even more. "Don't mind Grandma Rosa. She's always trying to fatten us up. Honestly, my Nicholas was a thin man when I married him."

"What do you mean, 'was'?" Nicholas protested.

Ignoring her brother-in-law, Maria said, "That's right. When Grandma Rosa tells us we're just right, we always know it's time to go on a diet."

"Yes," Andreanna quipped. "She and Mama are firm believers in feeding a cold *and* a fever. Besides, you'll probably put on a little baby fat when you're pregnant."

"All these women think about is making babies," one of the brothers-in-law admonished.

He dodged the jab from his wife and laughed along with the other men. Tony and Beth left seconds later amid a chorus of "goodbyes."

Beth only wished it was easier to smile.

Three

"Is everything all right, Beth?"

She glanced at Tony, relieved to see that he was too busy watching for his family's arrival to take his eyes from the end of the corridor. It was the third time he'd asked that question in as many days, and the third time she didn't know what to say. The first time, he'd voiced his concern before pulling out of his parents' driveway three nights ago. She hadn't been able to explain the niggling doubt hovering in the back of her mind then, and she couldn't explain it now. What she needed was a few hours alone to get her thoughts in order, but with the wedding a mere four days away, she hadn't had two minutes to think, much less a few hours.

The hospital was abuzz with the news of the great Dr. Petrocelli's imminent fall from bachelorhood. He and Beth had taken their blood tests, applied for the marriage license and spoken with Elena every day. Beth wasn't sure how the other woman had managed it, but the wedding was set for this coming Saturday at two o'clock.

Although everything else they'd done had been necessary, as far as Beth was concerned, the most important order of business was the appointment they'd kept with the social worker yesterday. Florence Donahue, the caseworker who'd been assigned to Christopher, was fifty-five years old, and since she'd turned forty she had accumulated an extra pound with every passing year. She wore the pinched expression of a woman who was squeezed between the de-

sire to help and the bureaucracy of an imperfect system. If
Tony had noticed, he hadn't let on, charming her right
down to the roots of her overpermed brown hair. Beth still
smiled every time she thought about the phone call she'd
received a few hours ago. According to Mrs. Donahue, the
proper forms had been filled out, and barring any new de-
velopments, the system was going to place Christopher in
Beth and Tony's care upon his release from the hospital.

The Petrocellis, too eager to wait until then to meet the
newest addition to their family, were due to arrive at the
hospital, where they could at least see him through the nursery window. Tony was pacing back and forth, as nervous
as any expectant father she'd ever seen. He would be wonderful to Christopher, she knew he would, and Christopher
would have the added stability and love of a huge extended
family.

Telling herself that the misgivings that had been scraping
the edges of her mind these past three days were just
nerves, she leaned over the baby's incubator. "Hello, sweet
pea. Remember when I told you how much I want to be
your mommy? Lo and behold, it looks as if I'm going to
get my wish. Do you remember that man over there? He
helped bring you into this world, and he's going to be your
daddy."

Tony stopped pacing and slowly turned around. He took
his time looking at Beth, his eyes traveling over every inch
of her. She was leaning over the plastic crib, seemingly
oblivious to everything except the baby. Her hair was loose
around her shoulders, one side fastened high on her head
with a black clasp. She was wearing a thin, airy-looking
skirt and matching top. Although the color was an understated slate blue, the material clung to her hips and legs in
the most enticing way. She probably had no idea how sensuous her voice sounded. No wonder the baby was gazing
up at her, mesmerized. She was having a similar effect on

him. Tony didn't know what was happening to him. He only knew he liked it.

"Beth?" he said, catching a movement out of the corner of his eye.

"Hmm?"

"They're here."

She came to with a start, her eyes going wide as she looked beyond him at the men and women and children hurrying toward them en masse. With a tilt of her head and the lift of one shoulder, she said, "Yes, they certainly are. Would you like to carry Christopher to the window so they can see him?"

"No," he said, ignoring the taps on the pane behind him. "I think you should do the honors. You're a natural with him."

The smile she gave him nearly buckled his knees, rendering him immobile. That night, more than two-and-a-half months ago, like now, he'd felt it—warmed by her smile, flushed with heat, excited by something as simple as a look.

Beth wrapped Christopher in a white blanket and scooped him into her arms, Tony's words playing through her mind. *You're a natural with him.* She swallowed the lump in her throat, certain she'd never received a higher compliment.

She stood next to Tony in front of the window and held up the baby for all to see. Christopher, with his dark tuft of hair and serious gray eyes, stared unblinking at all the people who were making complete fools of themselves on the other side of the window.

Children were held up for a better look, chubby little fingers pointing, questions asked and answered with ease. Tony's mother and sisters all wiped tears from their eyes, his father and brothers-in-law grinning and nodding for all they were worth. When everyone had looked their fill, Beth returned Christopher to his bed, and together, she and Tony joined the rest of the family in the hall.

"I can't believe how much hair he has."

"He's an angel."

"He's beautiful."

"He's a boy. He can't be beautiful."

"He can so. And he is."

"And smart. He knows us already."

"Oh, but he's so small. I swear our Dominic was twice that size at birth!"

"Yes, but Dominic was born half grown."

Tony almost smiled. Although he'd delivered hundreds of babies, they were usually red-faced and squalling and mad as blazes to find themselves beneath the glare of lights in the big, cold world. Staring at Christopher, who was silently studying a stuffed bear Beth had placed in his bed in the first days of his life, a sense of pride came out of nowhere, and he had to admit that the baby was an exceptionally handsome child.

"I can see the pride in the set of your shoulders, son."

Tony's eyes took their time meeting his father's. When their gazes locked, they both nodded. Tony was the first to smile.

Vincent Petrocelli was a couple of inches shorter than Tony and had thinning gray hair and a face and hands that bore the lines and calluses of a man who worked hard for a living. He didn't speak loud or often, but when he talked, people sat up and listened. They'd been the only two men adrift in a turbulent sea of talkative, demonstrative women. Despite it or because of it, their relationship was based on companionable silences. Tony could count on one hand the times he and his father had had heart-to-heart talks. He'd always known what his family had given up to help him through medical school, just as he'd always known what was expected of him in return.

He wasn't sure why he chose that instant to turn his head slightly, but once his gaze settled on Beth, he couldn't look away. At five foot eight, she was at least three inches taller than the women in his family. From here, her hair looked more red-gold than auburn, her skin pale, her lips tinted a soft pink. She was talking to two of his sisters—listening was more like it. She nodded politely at something Carmelina said, then casually glanced his way. For a moment, she seemed to stare, unseeing, past them all. Slowly, her eyes focused on him, and she smiled. Desire roused inside Tony all over again.

From a dozen feet away, Beth saw the invitation in the depths of Tony's eyes. She couldn't remember any man ever looking at her in exactly that way, and she could hardly believe what such a look could do to a woman.

See? she told herself. *Everything is going to be fine. There's no need for self-doubts.*

"I think it's a good thing the wedding is only four days away, don't you, Maria?" Carmelina asked.

"From the look of that brother of ours, I don't think he'd be able to wait much longer," Maria agreed.

Beth glanced at Tony's sisters, one older than him, the other younger. Heaven help her, but she was at a complete and utter loss for something to say.

Maria laughed, and Carmelina said, "Don't look so stricken. I always knew he had it in him. Our mother and father have been waiting a long time for this. Tell me, Beth, how long do you and Tony plan to wait to have another child?"

Unease crawled down Beth's spine, a disturbing thought close on its heels. Suddenly, she was face-to-face with the doubts she'd been having these past three days.

She didn't remember how she responded to Carmelina's question, but whatever she said must have satisfied both of Tony's sisters. The entire family left soon after. If they noticed that Beth's smile looked strangely out of place on her own face, they didn't comment.

Tony stood to one side, arms crossed, waiting for Beth to unlock her door. She knew she'd been more quiet than usual since leaving the hospital, but she just hadn't felt up to making small talk.

The door opened on silent hinges, the carpet muting her footsteps as she led the way into her quiet apartment. Other than the rasp of Tony's deeply drawn breath, the only sound she heard was the door closing behind her. Choosing her words very carefully, she turned to face him. "Your family seems very excited about the idea of future Petrocellis."

He studied her thoughtfully for so long she wondered if he was going to answer. "They're very old-fashioned in that respect. Does that bother you?"

Bother? It terrified her, but not for the obvious reasons. Hoping against hope that she was reading more into this than was necessary, she took a deep breath to calm her nerves. What she really needed was something to do with her hands. Clasping them in front of her, she said, "Everything has happened so fast, we really haven't had much of a chance to get to know each other. Do you have time to talk? Because if you do, I could brew a pot of tea."

Tony took a step toward her. Brewing tea was *not* what he would have preferred to spend the next several minutes doing. Or even the next several hours. "I have all the time in the world, Beth. For talking. Or whatever."

Either she didn't hear the double entendre in his voice, or she chose to ignore it. Extending her hand in a sweeping gesture toward the living room, she said, "Would you like to wait in here?"

Tony Petrocelli enjoyed a lot of things but cooling his heels in the living room wasn't one of them. Instead, he followed Beth into the next room. While she filled a copper teakettle with tap water, he leaned against the counter in her small kitchen, quietly watching.

"Did Carmelina say something to upset you, Beth?"

The mugs in her hands clanked together as she swung around to face him. Turning back much more slowly, she shook her head.

"Then, what was it you wanted to talk about?" He was vaguely aware that she'd pulled her lower lip between her teeth, but before he could make more than a sweeping assumption that she was nervous about something, he caught a whiff of her perfume, and all but the haziest of impressions were lost on him.

"If you could have anything," she said quietly, "anything you wished for, what would it be?"

Staring at the smooth skin below her cheekbone and the fine line of her profile, he drew a blank.

She turned her head to look at him. "Don't tell me you have everything you want, Tony. There must be something you'd like. And I don't mean peace on earth and no more hungry children. I mean what do *you* want for yourself and nobody else."

In that instant, he only wanted one thing. Her. In bed, under him, all over him. He wanted her. Since he doubted that was what she'd meant, he said, "I'll have to think about it and let you know. What about you, Beth? What do you want?"

Her answer was as direct as her gaze. "That's easy. I want Christopher."

He turned slightly, the movement bringing his chest within a few inches of her shoulder. "Then, you're going to get your wish. Christopher will be leaving the hospital in a week or two. And he'll be coming home with us. Isn't there anything else you want?"

She looked up at him, her blue eyes wide open and brimming with tenderness and emotion. The Sicilians had a word for what was happening to him. Translated, it meant *thunderstruck.* Only a person who'd felt it would truly understand the enormity of the sensation.

The teakettle whistled, startling them both and saving her from having to answer. She turned off the burner with one hand, reaching for the kettle with the other. Pouring the steaming water into a small, round teapot, she cleared her throat and finally said, "Your family seemed very taken with Christopher."

She'd said something similar before, but he answered her, anyway. "They love kids. Always have."

"I've heard more than one of them comment on their excitement over the prospect of meeting future Petrocellis."

Without a clue as to where the conversation was headed, he crossed his ankles and settled himself more comfortably along the edge of the counter. "I come from what very well could be the last completely functional family in the United States. Oh, we had our normal fights and tussles growing up—Gina had a screech that could make your ears ring for two days, and Andreanna could pinch hard enough to draw blood—I tell everybody that I became a doctor out of self-defense. But when push comes to shove, we're always here for one another. We're working-class people, and we're proud of it. My sisters gave up a lot to help me through medical school, but no one gave up more than my mother and father. All they've ever wanted or expected in return is that I carry on the family name."

Beth watched the tea seep into the clear, steaming water, her tension seeping out of her in a similar fashion. *There,* she told herself. *See? There's nothing to worry about. By adopting Christopher, Tony will be doing as his family wishes. In his new son, the Petrocelli name will continue.*

His shirt rustled as he uncrossed his arms, his voice dropping in volume as he said, "Oh, and of course they want me to pass on the family genes."

She felt as if a hand were closing around her throat, cutting off her oxygen. They both jumped again when his beeper went off, but Beth was secretly thankful for the momentary reprieve. While he went to the phone to call the hospital, she tried to draw a deep breath.

"I have to go," he said, hanging up the telephone a few minutes later.

"Another mother in labor?" she asked.

He started to nod, then seemed to change his mind, drawing his eyebrows down, instead. "Are you sure you're all right?"

She nodded, but she wasn't sure about anything, except that all the pleasure of the past few days had drained out of her.

Beth had thought her shift would never end, but it was over now, and was on her way to the nursery. She could hear the babies crying all the way down the hall. She'd certainly spent enough time in the nursery these past two-and-a-half months to know exactly how it happened. It only took one baby's tiny wail to set off another, and another, until there was a chorus of healthy cries and flailing fists, and one or two frantic nurses trying to calm them all.

Glancing in the window on her way by, she smiled in spite of herself. There was just something in a newborn's cry that warmed her heart every time she heard it. She strode to the next window, her smile growing. Of the three preemies in the special nursery, two had taken up the call. Christopher was one of them.

Donning a gown, she scrubbed her hands and went to pick up the child she loved more than she thought possible. Christopher was angry, his face red, his movements jerky and stiff. Scooping him into her arms, she crooned into his ear, "There, there, what's all the fuss about?"

A quick glance at his chart told her that he'd already been fed. That meant he either had to burp, or he just wanted to be held. She patted his back, crooning unintelligible words of comfort, her lips nuzzling his tiny head, his cheek, his adorable little ear. His cries lost their vehemence, gradually trailing away completely on a shuddering breath. Snuggling closer, he curled into her warmth.

Ah, yes, this was what he needed. It was what she needed, too.

She'd meandered from one end of her apartment to the other last night after Tony had left, thinking, praying, wishing. Her home wasn't fancy, but it was all she needed. Although Barry had done his best to take the biggest share of their assets, she'd hired an attorney who'd made sure she held on to those that were rightfully hers. After the lawyer had taken his cut, she'd invested her *winnings*. As a nurse, she earned enough money to live on, and had planned to use her savings to put Christopher through college. Of course, Tony would probably insist upon helping choose the right school.

If he married her, that is.

"Of course he'll marry me," she whispered in Christopher's ear. "He's already committed to as much."

But he doesn't know, a voice whispered inside her head. *You have to tell him.*

No!

Covering Christopher's back with the flat of her hand, she lifted her face and closed her eyes. *Please. I love Christopher. Let me have him. I'll do anything. Please.*

Please.

The cry of babies was her only answer.

She continued to walk with Christopher, occasionally laying a hand on another infant who seemed to need nothing more than a human touch. Christopher didn't seem to mind sharing her. It was as if he knew she loved him more than anybody else.

It felt right that he was secure in her love. It was one of the reasons she'd come here every day since the night he was born. There had been times when she'd been sure that her will alone had kept him alive. Oh, she loved him so. In her heart he was hers already. Was it so wrong to want him to be hers in the eyes of the law?

She deserved to be his mother.

Didn't she?

Beth closed her eyes for a minute, because she knew better than anybody that life wasn't always fair. Happiness had nothing to do with justice, or merit, or divine rights. Everything came down to doing one's best. And the best thing she could do, the only thing she could do, was tell Tony the truth.

Beth had been pacing back and forth in Tony's small office for five minutes, rehearsing what she was going to say word-for-word. The instant she heard the door open, she stopped, her eyes trained on his framed medical license on the wall.

"Connie said you wanted to see me?"

With her heart in her throat, she turned around. Tony closed the door behind him, slowly running his hand down the length of his silk tie, waiting for her to tell him why she'd come.

Her eyes had been burning from lack of sleep all day, her conscience burning with the need to tell the truth. Suddenly, she didn't know where to begin. Clasping her hands behind her back, she raised her chin and quietly said, "There's something I have to tell you."

He took a step closer and held up one hand. "If you're about to tell me that you used to be a man, you can stop right there, because I'd never believe you. My instincts couldn't be that far off."

His attempt at humor sent a small smile to her lips and a tiny ray of hope to her heart. He really was a good man. Perhaps what she had to say to him wouldn't alter his decision to marry her.

"You're right about that," she said quietly. "But there are other things you don't know about me."

He walked farther into the room, casually settling his hands on his hips. "I'm listening."

She thought she detected a flicker of longing in his dark

eyes. It added to the tiny ray of hope that had started to glow inside her. "Do you remember when you asked me what I'd wish for if I could have anything in the world?"

He nodded. "You told me you want Christopher."

"Yes. But five years ago, one year ago, even six months ago, I would have said I wanted to have a child of my own."

She paused, studying him. His expression changed, becoming serious. Taking a deep breath for courage, she surged on. "Acceptance came slowly, Tony. One day at a time over the past seven years, to be exact."

"What are you saying?"

"I'm not saying anything very well, but what I'm trying to tell you is that I can't have children."

He took a step back, his head coming up with the shock of discovery. Beth released the breath she'd been holding, her last ray of hope extinguished by the surprise, and then the realization, that crossed his face. As one moment stretched to ten, she lowered her gaze to the grip she had on the back of his leather office chair. She'd recognized the expression deep in Tony's eyes. Barry had worn the same look more than a year ago when the doctor had given them the results of all the tests, all the surgeries and attempts that had failed.

"Are you sure?"

Pulling her gaze from her white knuckles, she said, "I'm sure. I have a severe case of endometriosis. Believe me, I've tried everything, every way there is."

A knock sounded on the door, breaking the silence that stretched tight between them. "What is it?" Tony said, his voice a low growl.

The receptionist poked her head into the office. Obviously aware of the tension in the room, her gaze swung from Tony to Beth and back again. "I'm sorry to bother you, Doctor, but there's an urgent message for Bethany."

She turned her attention to Beth before continuing. "You're to go to the employee lounge immediately."

Slowly coming to her senses, Beth nodded, although the message didn't make sense. Her shift was over. Why would she be needed in the lounge? "Thanks, Connie," she said. "Tell them I'll be right there."

Casting one last glance at the clear-cut lines of Tony's profile, she said, "Let's talk later!" Taking careful note of his slight nod, she followed the other woman from the room.

If Beth had been thinking clearly, she would have known something was wrong. The corridor was unusually quiet, the door leading to the employee lounge closed tight, the blinds drawn. Feeling strangely disoriented, she turned the knob.

The sudden roar was deafening, the burst of lights blinding. Nearly everyone she worked with on a daily basis was huddled together in the small room, laughing expectantly.

"Surprise!"

"We gotcha!"

"You didn't think we'd let you get married without throwing you a surprise shower, did you?" Kitty Garcia, the nurse who worked in the nursery, exclaimed in a thick Spanish accent and friendly brown eyes.

"She's surprised, all right," someone else declared. "Just look at her."

Beth did her best to smile. They were right. Her surprise was completely genuine. If they knew the half of it, the joke would be on them.

Karen Sloane, one of the most loved resident doctors at Vanderbilt Memorial, looped her arm through Beth's and said, "We didn't know whether to throw you a baby shower or a wedding shower. Then we remembered *who* you were going to marry, and we knew exactly what kind of shower we had to have for you."

Beth didn't know what to say. She wasn't even sure the wedding was still on now that Tony knew about her infertility. She bit her lip, shuddering inwardly at the thought.

"Come on, Beth," Karen insisted with an understanding smile. "These people aren't going to give up until you've opened every last gift."

Beth had known Karen Sloane for years. They were alike in many ways, so alike, in fact, that they both tended to keep their problems to themselves. When Karen's eight-year-old daughter had been trapped in a cave during the mud slide, the two women had found strength in their similarities. A friendship had formed in the days following the blackout, and although Victoria had been found, unharmed, there were still shadows in Karen's gray eyes.

Kitty Garcia grasped both women's hands and drew them into the center of the room. Winking mischievously at Beth, she said, "I can't wait to see your face when you open the gift from me. You will be happy. *Sí?*"

Beth didn't fully understand the reason for all the elbow jabbing and jovial laughter, but she said a silent prayer of thanks for the poise she'd learned as a child. Accepting the plate of food being pushed into one hand and the gift being pressed into the other, she pasted a smile on her face and pretended that everything was right with the world.

Tony's chair creaked as he leaned back in it and tried to relax, but it was nothing compared to the sound it made when he jumped to his feet a second later. At this rate, he was going to wear the blasted thing out, which was exactly what he would do to the new carpet if he didn't stop pacing.

His last patient of the day had canceled. It was a good thing. His concentration had been nil ever since Beth had told him that she couldn't have children.

Good God. Beth couldn't have children.

He still couldn't believe it. But at least a few things about Bethany Kent were beginning to make sense. He remembered thinking it was strange when she'd brought up the subject of marriage. Strange, hell. It had left him speechless.

Face it, Petrocelli. The woman has been leaving you speechless since the night of the blackout.

That was true enough, but those other bouts of raw surprise had been sexual in nature. In comparison, her disclosure concerning her inability to have children had felt like a kick in the chest.

Tony strode to the window, but for once in his life, the view of the mountains rising in the west failed to reach him. A dozen images of Beth played through his mind. He could practically see the lone tear that had trailed down her cheek that night when Christopher had been born. He could practically hear the depth of emotion in her voice each time she mentioned the baby's name. She loved that child. There was no doubt about it. She deserved to have him, too. There was no doubt about that, either. But she couldn't have children. And if he married her, he couldn't, either.

He paced to the other side of the room. Running a hand through his hair, he turned and repeated the process.

Beth didn't have to tell him about her infertility. That fact had left him in awe of her strength of character. But dammit, it also filled him with doubts and questions. All jokes about his Don Juan image aside, he took his commitment to his family very seriously. He'd always assumed he'd meet the right woman and settle down to raise a family like each and every one of his sisters had done. It was the Petrocelli way. How could he even consider marrying a woman who couldn't give him children, or his parents grandchildren?

He didn't know why he left his office, and he sure as hell didn't know what he hoped to gain from standing outside the nursery, watching Christopher sleep. The baby's hand jerked, then slowly relaxed, his little mouth suckling

an invisible bottle. Tony knew it was a reflex action. But
then, so was the clenching in his own gut.

Laughter and raised voices carried to his ears from someplace down the hall. Of their own volition, his feet followed
the sound. He came to a stop a few feet from the employee
lounge. Holding very still, he stood in the doorway, silently
watching. Balloons bobbed from a centerpiece on one of
the tables, voices rose and laughter trailed from one side
of the room to the other. Beth stood in the midst of it all,
looking regal and poised in her hospital whites. He wondered if he was the only one who saw the stiffness in her
shoulders or the forced brightness in her smile.

"Open mine next," Kitty Garcia insisted, thrusting a
brightly colored package into Beth's hands.

There was a lot of speculation as Beth slid her finger
beneath a piece of tape and lifted the paper away. "Hold
it up!" someone yelled. "This I've gotta see."

Using both hands, Beth pulled a see-through scrap of
lace and red satin from the box. A blush tinged her cheeks,
but she played along, holding the skimpy teddy to her body,
smoothing her hand down its length. She chose that moment to look his way, her gaze meeting his from the other
side of the room. Karen Sloane nudged her, and a heartbeat
later, the other woman waved. Beth's lips lifted in a semblance of a smile, and Tony felt as if the wind had been
knocked out of him all over again. He returned Karen's
wave and did his best to return Beth's smile, but it wasn't
easy. Hell, breathing wasn't easy.

"Come on in, Tony," somebody yelled.

Others took up the cry, but Tony only stood there, holding Beth's gaze. She lowered her hands, the teddy dangling
from two fingers. Something intense flared through him. He
didn't know what it was, but he knew he'd never felt anything quite like it in his life. This wasn't just a simple case
of him wanting a woman. There was nothing simple about
it.

"Come on, Doctor! Have a piece of cake."

Tony hesitated, casting a cursory glance at the people in the room. He knew that if he took that next step, there would be no turning back. Glancing back at Beth, a jolt went through him, a thought close on its heels. Tony Petrocelli had been raised to trust two things: his Grandma Rosa's homemade pasta sauce, and his gut instinct. And his gut instinct told him he wanted Bethany Kent.

That want was complicated, not to mention confusing. But he'd been confused before, and truth be told, he liked complications, at least the kind that left him feeling strong and masculine and more alive than he'd felt in a long, long time.

With his eyes trained on Beth, he walked into the room.

Four

"Goodbye, Beth, see you tomorrow!"

"Yeah, bye, Bethany. Bye, Dr. Petrocelli!"

"Goodbye! Thanks for everything," Beth called from the doorway, waving as the last two guests left the party. Suddenly, the employee lounge seemed awfully quiet.

"Would you close the door?" Tony asked from a few feet behind her.

Although she would have preferred to postpone their conversation, she closed the door and slowly turned around. She hadn't known what to make of the sight of him standing in the doorway half an hour ago, and she certainly didn't know what to make of the sight of him standing an arm's length away right now, but fear and hope were fighting over the butterflies in her stomach. And fear was winning.

Tony was wearing his ordinary doctor attire—dress slacks, shirt and tie. There was, however, nothing ordinary about the barely there smile pulling at the corners of his mouth. Rather than take the risk of reading too much into his expression, she waited for him to begin.

Eyeing the lingerie and other gifts lying on a nearby table, he finally said, "Now that I know what goes on at bridal showers, I understand why my sisters like them so much. Add a stripper and a keg of beer, and they're not much different from bachelor parties, are they?"

From now on, Beth told herself, she was going to expect him to say the last thing she expected. Shaking her head slightly, she said, "Not all bridal showers are like this one. I had several prior to my first marriage, and believe me, they were all extremely prim and proper."

"No wonder the marriage failed."

He'd done it again. Surprised every coherent thought right out of her head. Luckily, her answer was automatic. "I think you and I both know why my marriage failed, Tony."

She had his undivided attention now. Lowering her voice slightly, she said, "I ran into Barry and his new wife last week. She was very beautiful, and very pregnant."

Tony didn't say anything, and she surged ahead. "Barry couldn't deal with my endometriosis. He couldn't even bring himself to say it."

Tony's eyebrows rose slightly at the medical term. As a doctor, he knew it well. In mild to moderate cases, it made menstruation painful and conception difficult. In severe cases it made one excruciating and the other impossible. "What has your doctor done about your condition?" he asked levelly.

"For now, I'm on medication. Eventually, I'll need a hysterectomy. It's pretty much textbook, isn't it?"

Outwardly, Tony didn't move, but inside, his thoughts were surging in every direction. He knew firsthand how devastating a diagnosis of endometriosis can be. He'd broken the news to a number of his patients over the years. Suddenly, he wished he could have been there for her, to hold her hand, or offer her his understanding, because he had a feeling her ex-husband hadn't been concerned about *her* needs.

Beth stared up at Tony. He'd been quiet for a long time, obviously absorbing the information. He brushed a strand of hair off her face, his fingertips moving to her cheekbone as if he'd been wanting to touch her all day. She stared up at him, afraid of what he might do. Afraid of what he might not do.

Calling on her last vestige of courage, she said, "I'm thirty-five years old. Adopting Christopher could very well be my only chance at motherhood. I don't blame you for having doubts, but this arrangement doesn't have to be permanent. I'll sign a prenuptial agreement, and I'll give you a divorce anytime you want. Of course, I won't blame you if you've changed your mind completely."

Tony let his fingers glide through the wisps of hair in front of Beth's ear, trail down the smooth column of her neck and brush the delicate ridge of her collarbone. He could hear her breath catch in her throat, could see the slight quiver in her proud chin. He couldn't name all the emotions crashing through him, but he knew damn well a woman like her shouldn't have to beg.

Moving closer, he said, "Are you having second thoughts, Beth?"

If the situation hadn't been so serious, he would have smiled at her double take.

"Do you mean...?"

He nodded.

"But I thought..."

He shrugged.

"Then, you're not...?"

He shook his head.

Beth had never much cared for sounding like an idiot. But she couldn't help it. She could hardly believe her eyes or her ears. Tony hadn't changed his mind about marrying her. Or if he had, he'd changed it back again. He still intended to marry her. What kind of a man would do that, knowing what he knew? Just who was Tony Petrocelli?

The shadow of a five o'clock beard gave him a rugged look, but it was the smile tugging at the corners of his mouth that sent her thoughts into a tailspin all over again. His eyes darkened with amusement and a kind of fire she'd never seen before. He wanted her. He was making no effort to disguise it, or hide it, or deny it.

He wanted her. It was that simple.

An unwelcome tension settled over her, because there had been nothing simple about the look that had crossed his face when she'd first told him about her inability to have children. Doing everything in her power to hold on to her composure for a few more minutes, she squared her shoulders and took a backward step. Tony only followed. She took another, and so did he. Holding up her hand in a halting motion, she said, "Tony, we have to talk about this."

"*Are* you having second thoughts, Beth?" he asked again.

His voice was too low, too husky, too *Italian* for her peace of mind. "No, but..."

"Good, because I'd hate for my mother to have to try to explain things to Father Carlos, wouldn't you?"

Actually, Beth would have liked to hear Elena trying to explain things to Father Carlos. When the other woman was finished, perhaps she could explain what went on in the deepest recesses of her only son's mind.

Holding her ground, Beth said, "I don't want you to look back ten years from now and view this as your biggest mistake. I love Christopher, and I know I can be a good mother. I wouldn't even consider this if I didn't believe you'd be a good father, too. I just don't want you to do anything you'll regret."

"Give me an update here, Beth. Are you trying to convince me to marry you? Or to *not* marry you?"

She wouldn't have been surprised to see a smile lurking around the edges of his mouth. The fact that there wasn't made his questions even more pointed, and her answer more important. "I want you to do this for the right reasons."

He reached for her hand, easily drawing her closer. "I know what I'm doing," he said, his lips brushing hers.

In that moment before he kissed her, everything felt

right, and oh, so true. She and Tony were going to be married. And they were going to adopt Christopher. It was as if everything she'd ever done, every heartache she'd ever experienced and endured, had led her to this point in time. It was almost as if it was all meant to be.

"Annie!"

The glance over her shoulder was a reflex action, as was her slide into an alley at the first glimpse of the police car on the next block. Annie knew without looking that whoever had called out hadn't been talking to her. How could they be? She didn't know a soul in Grand Springs except for Todd, and he'd left town months ago. And no one knew her. And really, she had no reason to fear a police officer. She'd done nothing wrong. Unless she counted running away from home more than a year ago when she was sixteen. The memory of the way her mother's latest boyfriend had looked at her made her skin crawl even now. Running away had been necessary, and quite possibly the first smart thing she'd ever done. But it wouldn't be the last. She had someone else to think about now. She had her baby. Her son.

She hadn't intended to leave the hospital without a word shortly after Christopher's birth, but she'd panicked. She'd had a lot of time to think since then. A lot of time to plan. She hadn't seen Christopher in almost two weeks. She didn't have a car, and hitchhiking was risky. She didn't want to take any more risks than she had to. For once in her life, Annie Moore was going to do things right. That meant she had to take her time, she had to plan, and she had to prepare.

Air brakes hissed as a semi stopped at the corner, the diesel fumes mingling with the greasy smells coming from the fast food restaurants on the corner behind her. Her stomach rumbled with hunger, but a glance at her watch told her that visiting hours were under way at the hospital.

The halls would be congested with people, which meant that it would be easier for her to blend in. And it would be easier for her to see her baby without anyone noticing her presence. The last time she'd been to the hospital, the nurse on duty kept watching her, suspicion written all over her face. Annie didn't understand it. It wasn't as if there was a law against making sure her own baby was all right. She ached to hold him, but knew she'd have to wait a little while longer. For now, she would have to be content just to see him through the glass.

"Oh, Christopher," she whispered. "I'm coming."

Ignoring the emptiness in the pit of her stomach, she tucked her hair underneath a baseball cap and stepped out of the alley.

"How do I look?" Beth asked, gliding her hands over the pale blue fabric of her dress.

"You look beautiful, and very nervous, which serves you right for allowing the groom to see you before the wedding. Have I taught you nothing about omens and bad luck?"

The soft jingle-jangle of Jenna's bracelets was comforting, even if her words were clipped and her black eyes were flashing imperiously. Beth tucked her lower lip between her teeth and did her best to hide her smile from her best friend. "I'm not superstitious, remember?"

Jenna Maria Brigante swung around, the hem of her dark green skirt flouncing just above her ankles. Planting her hands on her hips, she sputtered in Romany. Beth crossed her arms and waited for Jenna to finish her tirade. Although she didn't understand the words themselves, their meaning was universal.

They were in a small room at the top of the stairs in Vince and Elena Petrocelli's house, waiting for the music to begin downstairs. Chairs were set up in the living room; white bows and fresh-cut flowers had been placed on end tables and shelves in every room on the first floor. Father

Carlos had arrived a few minutes ago, which meant that the wedding would begin right on time.

Beth checked her reflection again, wondering if she should have worn her hair up, after all. No, she'd had a traditional wedding once. That time she'd done everything according to custom, wearing her mother's lace, her grandmother's pearls, even a penny in her shoe. This wedding would be as simple and true as the reason for its occurrence. For Christopher.

"Here," Jenna said, pressing a tube of lipstick into Beth's hand. "For someone who knows exactly what you're doing and the exact reasons why you're doing it, you've chewed off an awful lot of your lipstick."

Leaning closer to the mirror, Beth reapplied the pink gloss. Jenna was right. She was nervous, but whether Jenna believed her or not, it had nothing to do with superstition. She'd been this way ever since Kitty Garcia had reported someone lurking around the nursery a few days ago. Beth had read articles about babies who had been stolen from hospitals, and it stood to reason that a baby who'd been abandoned would be a prime target. The thought of someone taking Christopher tore at her insides. Hospital security had been stepped up, but she wouldn't rest easy until he was safe in her arms once and for all.

The beginning strains of music filtered up the stairs. "That's our cue," Jenna said. "Are you ready?"

Before Beth had finished nodding, Jenna tossed her long black hair over her shoulder and spun around. "All right, then. Let's go. But watch your step. You might not believe in bad omens, but I'm superstitious enough for both of us."

Beth took the single pink rose Jenna handed to her and slowly followed her friend. Whether it was luck or poise, she didn't trip on the way down the stairs or falter as she placed her hand in the crook of her future husband's elbow. She might have held her breath at the width of Tony's shoulders beneath his dark suit and at the expression in his

eyes. She ached just a little because she no longer believed
in living happily ever after, but she could hardly blame that
on luck, good or bad.

They strode to the front of the room, where Father Carlos
was waiting. Side by side, she and Tony listened as the old
priest began to read from his frayed book. She answered
the questions with the appropriate responses, telling herself
there was no reason for her heart to feel too large for her
own chest. She *was* prepared to marry Anthony Joseph
Petrocelli. She *wasn't,* however, prepared to fall in love
with him. Their marriage wasn't going to last forever, anyway. Why, then, did she cross her fingers for luck moments
before Father Carlos declared them husband and wife?

Raising her face for Tony's kiss, she realized that she
might have been the tiniest bit superstitious, after all.

Tony ran his finger between his neck and his shirt collar,
even though it wasn't really his collar that felt too tight.
His eyes were trained on the newest member of the Petrocelli family. Beth was standing on the other side of the
room, cornered by three of his four sisters. Her dress was
a pale shade of blue and bespoke of a woman with good
manners and exquisite taste. It fit her to perfection, stopping
several inches above her cream-colored shoes. All in all,
her entire outfit looked elegant. Her hair was another matter, waving past her shoulders, unruly and just enough out
of control to entice a man to want to touch it, to harbor
thoughts of taming it. He flexed his fingers at his side,
wondering how much longer he had to wait before he and
Beth could leave.

The wedding had come off without a hitch, unless he
counted his mother's and grandmother's tears, the squabble
between two of his brothers-in-law, a little spilled punch
and the sour notes Gina had hit on the piano while Beth
was descending the stairs before the ceremony began. It
was strange, but the instant Beth's eyes had met his, ev-

erything else had receded, until there was only her, and
him, and the rousing jolt that went through him as he'd
waited for her to place her hand in his.

"She's beautiful, isn't she?"

Pulling his gaze from Beth, Tony reeled in his thoughts
and glanced at the raven-haired woman standing next to
him, watching him with eagle eyes. Oh, boy. Jenna Maria
Brigante was all he needed.

She peered up at him, chin raised, hands on her hips, her
gaze unwavering. A lot of people thought Tony was un-
observant, but he wasn't. He'd always kept to himself,
that's all—his feelings, his thoughts, especially his emotions. He was a private person, and he wasn't comfortable
with people traipsing through his thought processes, especially when the woman doing the wandering claimed she
was a bona fide Gypsy.

Holding her gaze with a firm look of his own, he said,
"Are you having a good time?"

She shrugged. "You know what they say. Always a
bridesmaid, never a bride."

"Do you want me to try to set you up with one of my
associates at the hospital?"

Coal black eyebrows rose slightly as she said, "I think
you and I both know that wouldn't be a very good idea."

The image of a black-widow spider eating her mate
flashed through Tony's mind. He didn't know why he
smiled, but in all honesty, he didn't dislike Beth's friend.
She'd done a wonderful job as Beth's maid of honor. A
light had been dancing in her dark eyes all afternoon. Now
her gaze was strangely direct.

"I did want to talk to you about something, Tony. I'm
just not sure this is the right place."

Glancing down as two of his nephews streaked by, he
said, "If you were thinking about giving me my sex talk,
don't. I'm still waiting for my father to do the honors."

Apparently, she didn't feel like dignifying his remark

with a comment of her own. She simply stared at him, her expression so serious that Tony felt inclined to say, "This is a wedding reception, Jenna. Not a funeral."

Glancing away, Jenna said, "Yes, I know. Beth's happy today. I'd like to keep it that way."

"And you don't believe that's possible?" he prodded.

"She has her heart set on adopting Christopher. I don't know what she'd do if something went wrong."

Tony followed the course of her gaze to the other side of the room. Beth chose that moment to look up, a smile stealing across her lips. He wondered if she had any idea what that smile of hers was doing to him. He was well schooled in what to do and what to think about to keep his desire from becoming obvious, but today it required all his concentration to accomplish such a feat. A need had been building in him for months, and there was only one way to satisfy it.

Without taking his eyes off Beth, he said, "If you're trying to tell me not to hurt her, don't bother. I intend to do my best to make her happy. Besides, what could possibly go wrong?"

Jenna sputtered something he couldn't understand, then finished her tirade in English. "There's nothing more frightening than a nonbeliever begging for trouble."

"I'll keep that in mind," he said sardonically, "while I try not to step on any cracks in the sidewalk or break any mirrors. Now, if you'll excuse me, I believe it's time to take my wife home."

"The wedding was lovely, wasn't it?"

Tony's answer was a deep, mellow hum, just as it had been the first two times he'd answered the same question. If Beth had been alone, she would have pressed both hands to her face. But then, if she'd been alone, she wouldn't have been repeating herself in a frantic effort to hold her nerves at bay.

This wasn't the first time she'd taken the winding street that led to Tony's house. It was, however, the first time she'd taken the route as Mrs. Anthony Petrocelli. Therein lay the problem.

Although today was the sixth of September, the day was still summer warm. People everywhere were sitting on porch swings and lawn chairs, lazily passing a pleasant afternoon. In contrast, Beth's nerves were scrambling. When she and Tony had first left his parents' house, she'd concentrated on taking one slow, easy breath, and then another. When that had failed to calm her, she'd tried to fill the quiet with inconsequential talk of everything from the weather to a bumper sticker that read Don't Blame Me. I Voted Republican.

She'd turned her head at Tony's throaty chuckle, the look deep in his eyes draining the laughter out of her chest. She knew what the look in his eyes meant. She'd been married before, after all.

Struggling for something, anything, to say, she peered straight ahead. "Do you see that road winding up the mountain?" she asked. "That leads to Jenna's cabin."

"How far up the mountain does she live?"

Thankful to have finally hit upon a safe topic, she said, "It's a ten-minute jaunt the way the crow flies, but like they say here in the Rockies—"

"You can't get there from here." Their voices came in unison, his deep and husky, hers throaty and soft. There was something about the combination that replaced the nerves in her stomach with a warmth that seemed to have a life of its own.

Her emotions whirled; her thoughts spun. Staring at the sharp lines of his profile, she said, "Jenna claims that every time two people speak in unison, a wish is about to come true."

He took his eyes from the street long enough to look

directly at her. "Sometime I'd love to hear the story of how you and Jenna met."

"Sometime?" she asked quietly.

He nodded.

"But not now?"

He shook his head slowly. "Now I'd rather concentrate on making that wish you mentioned come true."

She swallowed hard as Tony pulled his car to a stop in front of a Victorian-style house that had probably been built almost a hundred years ago by some prospector who'd struck it rich in a nearby mine.

"Here we are," he said, opening his door.

Struggling with uncertainties, she peered at the house that was about to become her home. Suddenly, she wanted to back up, to start over at the beginning. Everything had happened so fast. She and Tony were about to stride into his house as husband and wife, and they hadn't even discussed the most fundamental elements of their marriage. Rather than wait for him to come around to her side of the car, she got out and met him on the sidewalk that led to the side door. "Tony, I think we should talk."

She let out a little yelp when he swung her into his arms and shouldered his way through the door. Inside, he asked, "What did you want to talk about?"

Beth felt weightless in his arms, and strangely shy. Eyeing the threshold behind them, she whispered, "Are you superstitious, Tony?"

He kicked the door shut and lowered her to her feet an inch at a time. "Let's just say that after your friend's pep talk, I'm not taking any chances."

If need had a sound it was the rasp of his breath in her ear. If it had a texture, it was velvet over steel. She closed her eyes as he moved against her and covered her mouth with his, letting her know without words that there was a time for talking. And it wasn't now.

The nerves in Beth's stomach turned into warmth, and

then into need. Opening her mouth, she returned his kiss, answering with a need of her own.

His hands were everywhere, molding her closer, gliding up her back, his palms skimming over the smooth material of her dress. She didn't remember sliding her hands around his back, but she'd never forget the contour of muscle beneath her fingertips. His touch was gentle and sure, his fingers slipping into her hair, only to glide down the sides of her neck, kneading her shoulders until she felt like a willow switch, slender and pliant and strong.

She'd been in this house yesterday when she'd moved some of her things, but today, she had only a hazy impression of her surroundings. She stepped out of her shoes in the hall, her stocking feet practically floating over the hardwood floor. Little by little, she and Tony made their way to an open staircase that reached invitingly toward the second story.

Their kiss continued as they mounted the first step. She might have been able to catch her breath somewhere near the fourth stair, but he lowered her zipper so slowly, so smoothly, that she wasn't sure she'd ever be able to catch her breath again.

This was a new experience for her, this spontaneity that was melting her from the inside. Barry had been arduous and thorough, and in the early years of their marriage, at least, he'd been loving. But Tony's passion was explosive. It obliterated all thought, allowing instinct to guide her. And her instincts were turning her into a creature she barely recognized, one who was wanton and sensuous and sure of what she wanted.

She slid his tie from his collar and deftly tossed it over her shoulder. It landed on the railing with a quiet swish. She felt him swallow as she unfastened the top button of his shirt. Feeling bold and ever so brazen, she reached up on tiptoe and kissed the strong column of his neck, slowly moving to his chin, and finally his mouth, where she captured his groan, deftly unfastening buttons all the while.

His jacket and shirt came off together, inside out, landing on the top step. Her dress came next, falling to the floor in a pool of blue.

He kissed her chin, her neck. His lips nuzzling the straps of her slip aside, his fingers slowly pushing them from her shoulders. She was vaguely aware of the carpet at her feet, of walls painted a cool white, the color blending into nothingness as her eyes drifted closed. His hands brushed the outer swells of her breasts, her head tipping back when he cupped them, one in each hand, through the satiny material of her slip and bra. Hazy images floated through her mind, playing across her senses, glimmering with the shards of daylight filtering through her eyelids.

The ring of a telephone must have come from far away, because there were no telephones in the place Tony was taking her. He seemed as reluctant to be distracted as she was, turning his head away from the sound.

"Do you think you should answer that?" she whispered.

He pulled her hard against him, letting her know without words exactly what he wanted to do. "I couldn't get an entire week off for a proper honeymoon, Beth," he said while the telephone rang on. "But I'm not on duty tonight. Tonight is all we have. So no, I definitely do not want to answer that."

His lips were wet from her kisses, his hair disheveled from her hands, his breathing as ragged as hers was shallow. In the background the answering machine clicked on. Ten feet away, he lowered his face to hers for another kiss.

"This is Florence Donahue at Social Services. I'm sorry to bother you, but this is urgent. I must speak to one of you immediately. Please return my call as soon as possible."

Their eyes opened, their gazes locked, silence growing tight with tension. "Christopher," Beth said, breaking out of his embrace. "Oh, my God! What if something's happened to Christopher?"

Tony knew he should do something, but his mind was still foggy with desire. Slowly coming to his senses, he said, "We have to call Mrs. Donahue right away."

Beth was already dialing the phone.

Five

"All right, Mrs. Donahue...yes. Yes, of course."

Tony could practically see the tension drain out of Beth's shoulders as she spoke into the telephone. There was excitement in her voice. It wasn't exactly the kind of excitement she'd turned loose in his arms moments ago, but it was excitement just the same.

Powerful relief washed over him. Christopher was obviously okay. When Beth replaced the phone and turned around, grinning, his relief gave way to desire all over again. He hadn't appreciated the interruption, but he was thoroughly enjoying the anticipation of picking up where they'd left off.

"That was Mrs. Donahue."

"Yes," he answered, taking one slow, easy step toward her, "I figured."

She had the grace to shake her head at his drollery, the movement drawing his attention to the hair waving around her face and shoulders in total disarray.

"It wasn't bad news, after all."

He nodded and took another step closer. "I figured that, too. Has anyone ever told you that you have a very expressive face?"

The startled look of surprise that crossed her features had his pulses pounding in a rhythm as erratic as a mountain storm. But it wasn't thunder rumbling in the very center of him. It was instinct, and it was telling him to take her to bed. As soon as possible.

He'd based his decision to marry her on instinct, and he knew better than anyone that it seldom let him down. After all, his instincts had saved patients' lives on more than one occasion. The hospital board was pleased with his decision to marry, his mother and father were happy with his choice, and although he was still in a state of shock over Beth's inability to have children, he couldn't deny the fact that there was something different about the desire he felt for her. She was his wife in Father Carlos's eyes, and in the eyes of the State of Colorado. If he didn't make her his wife in the conjugal sense real, real soon, he would surely explode.

"Mrs. Donahue said that Christopher is being released from the hospital earlier than planned."

He spent an inordinate amount of time staring at her lips. So much time, in fact, that he was having a difficult time comprehending what she was saying.

"Tony? Did you hear me?"

He nodded, his gaze gliding down the smooth column of her throat, straying to the bodice of her slip where her taut nipples were clearly visible through the thin fabric.

She darted past him so suddenly his pant leg stirred in her wake. By the time he turned around, she was bending down, scooping up her dress.

"Beth, what are you doing?"

"I'm getting dressed."

She glanced at him, her eyebrows arching slightly, a blush climbing to her cheeks. Tony didn't have to glance down to know what had caused it.

Averting her gaze, she said, "You'd better get dressed, too, don't you think?"

He looked at her, disoriented. "What do you mean?"

"The hospital is ready to release Christopher."

"Now?"

She lowered her voice as if to counter the raised volume of his. "Yes. That's why Mrs. Donahue called. Someone was seen lurking around the nursery again. So, for security reasons, not to mention insurance purposes, they decided to release Christopher as soon as he reached five pounds.''

Realization dawned. He didn't understand why someone had started lurking around the nursery, but he was familiar with hospital policy and insurance practices. Christopher had been in the hospital for nearly three months. Any costs not absorbed by Vanderbilt Memorial would be picked up by the State of Colorado. These days, patients weren't allowed to remain in hospitals a day longer than was absolutely necessary. It was hospital policy to send premature babies home when they hit the five-pound mark, providing they were healthy, of course. And Christopher had hit the mark today of all days.

''Just think,'' Beth said, slipping into her dress. ''He's coming home the day before his three-month birthday. Isn't that a coincidence?''

Staring at the wisp of her slip that was steadily disappearing as she raised her dress's zipper, Tony thought it was a coincidence, all right. A coincidence of catastrophic proportions.

She started down the stairs. With one hand on the banister, she turned to look at him. ''Are you coming?''

Tony practically snorted. *Apparently not.* Grimacing, he refastened his belt. ''I'll be right there.''

He strode to his bedroom for a clean shirt, thinking that someday he'd probably see the irony in the situation. Hell, someday he might even see the humor. But right now he found nothing funny about it. In fact, if he had to choose between laughing and crying, crying would win by a mile.

Crying. The entire house had been echoing with it for hours. It was 2:00 a.m., and although Tony had heard of new parents crying from sheer exhaustion and desperation, he wasn't the one raising the roof tonight. Christopher was responsible for that. The baby had been extremely even-

tempered throughout the entire ordeal of being released
from the hospital. Mrs. Donahue had been there, papers had
been signed, and everybody who'd gotten attached to the
little tyke during his stay in the nursery had held him and
kissed him and told him goodbye. Cameras had flashed,
hands had waved. Chris had started fussing about an hour
after they'd brought him home, and he hadn't let up for
more than five minutes at a time since.

Beth had remained surprisingly calm. Fifteen minutes
ago, she'd decided to try to rock him to sleep in the room
they'd quickly converted into a nursery. Evidently, it hadn't
worked, because Tony could still hear the baby's cries.
Glancing up, he saw Beth coming down the stairs, the
squalling infant in her arms. Christopher's red face was in
stark contrast to her pale pink robe; the worry and fatigue
in her eyes was very different from the sensuality he'd seen
in their place hours ago.

"I don't understand it," she said, moving the baby to
her shoulder. "He was never this fretful in the hospital."

Tony tried to recall some of the advice he'd given expectant parents over the years. Shrugging, he said, "I'm
sure he isn't the only baby who's cried his first night
home."

"You're probably right, but I envisioned his first night
with us a lot differently."

Tony had to agree with Beth on that one. He'd envisioned tonight a lot differently, too. He only hoped his expression looked less pained than he felt.

It took a moment for him to realize that Christopher had
begun to quiet down. He and Beth took a collective deep
breath and shared a hopeful look. The baby seemed to have
relaxed, his eyes closing as if he was exhausted. Tony
didn't move, not even to breathe. It was only a little after
two. Maybe the night could be salvaged, after all.

The baby started to squirm. Within seconds, he was crying his little eyes out all over again. Tony nearly dropped

his head into his hands. "Maybe he's hungry," he said helplessly.

"I tried feeding him a little while ago. Maybe he has a bubble." She patted his tiny back, to no avail.

Tony ran a hand through his hair, then glanced at his watch. He had to be at the hospital in less than five hours. It wouldn't be the first time he'd functioned on very little sleep. Hell, he hadn't planned to get any sleep at all tonight, but for an entirely different reason.

Beth's voice rose over the noise the baby was making, somehow managing to sound contrite despite its volume. "I'm awfully sorry about this, Tony."

Studying her intently, he shifted his weight to one foot and calmly said, "I need an update here. Exactly what part of this is your fault?"

She swayed to and fro, the motion having little effect on Christopher. "I guess none of it, but I'm still sorry. Since you have to be up early for work and since I'm taking the equivalent of a maternity leave, I have the day off. Why don't you go on up to bed?"

Tony had been waiting to go to bed all day. He just hadn't planned to go alone. Eyeing the squalling baby, he faced the fact that consummating his marriage was going to have to wait. "Maybe I will try to get a little sleep. If you're sure you're up to handling him on your own."

"I'm sure."

Reluctantly, he headed for the stairs.

"Tony?"

He was halfway to the stairway when he turned around. She made quite a picture standing in the doorway, the hem of her satin robe skimming her ankles, her dark auburn hair catching the rich hues of soft lamplight, her eyes steady and serene despite the fretful baby in her arms.

"Thanks," she said, so quietly he had to strain to hear.

"For what?"

"For everything. But mostly for giving me the opportunity to have Christopher. And for being so patient."

"What makes you think I'm patient?"

Her smile was subtle and sleepy, and nearly buckled his knees. Desire, slower now, but no less intense, reared inside him. Cocking his head slightly, he said, "This wouldn't have been my first choice of ways to spend my wedding night, but you're right, Beth. I am a patient man. I can wait. As long as I don't have to wait too long."

He retraced his steps and kissed her soundly on the lips, the crying baby between them. "Good night, Beth. You, too," he said, capturing the baby's flailing hand in his own. And then, without another word, he turned on his heel and quickly made his way to the stairs.

Watching him go, everything inside Beth went strangely still. There had been nothing lust-arousing in his parting words. Although his kiss had come as a surprise, it had been delivered amid Christopher's wails. And yet, watching Tony disappear up the stairs, soft-touched thoughts shaped her smile.

A light went on upstairs, and a door was closed at the end of the hall. Coming to her senses, she began to walk with Christopher, hoping the swaying motion would lull him to sleep. As she strolled through the unfamiliar, dimly lit rooms, she thought about the man she'd married. Tony Petrocelli had a masculine charm and a potent sensuality that was impossible to ignore. He was sexy when he wanted to be and concise when it suited him. Underneath it all, he was a very patient man.

"Oh, Christopher," she whispered, "your new father would be awfully easy to love."

That thought brought her up short. She admitted that she had strong feelings for Tony, but what she felt was awe, and gratitude, and quite possibly the strongest remains of unspent desire she'd ever experienced. It had nothing to do with love. Nothing whatsoever.

Staring down at the baby in her arms, she thought about the emotional roller coaster she'd been on with Barry these past several years. If he'd been able to break her heart a little at a time, she could only imagine what a man like Tony could do. Bethany had survived it once, but she had no desire and no intention of allowing it to happen again.

Since she had no idea how she was going to make sure her heart didn't end up broken again, she kissed Christopher's forehead and said, "What do you say you and I go into the kitchen and see if we can't figure out some way to calm you down so we can both get a little sleep?"

If he hadn't been crying so loudly, and if he could have actually understood her words and not just her tone, she had a feeling he would have agreed that *that* was a very good idea, indeed.

Beth came awake with a start. Unsure where she was, she peered into the darkness, trying to get her bearings. For a moment she thought she must have been dreaming, because her body felt heavy, her brain groggy. As her mind cleared, she remembered that she'd crawled into the spare bed for a couple of reasons, one of them being that she hadn't wanted to wake Tony. At first, the unfamiliar surroundings had seemed odd, but gradually, the sounds of the old house settling around her had lulled her to sleep.

She glanced at the clock radio on the bedside table, then snuggled into her pillow. Christopher had finally settled down shortly after three. She didn't know whether it was the warm water bottle she'd placed on his tummy, or the fact that he'd simply worn himself out, but he'd been sleeping peacefully in his crib for almost two hours.

Beth rarely awoke for no reason. Wrapped in warmth and darkness, she wondered what had roused her from sleep tonight. A branch scraped the side of the house ever so softly, and somewhere, a shutter rattled in the wind. Acknowledging the sounds, she knew she should try to get

some sleep. After all, there was no telling how much rest
she would get once Christopher woke up again. Telling
herself she had absolutely no reason to worry, she swung
her feet over the side of the bed. Necessary or not, it
wouldn't hurt to check on her baby one more time.

Her bare feet thudded softly as she padded into the hall,
her long robe fluttering behind her. Following the faint yellow glow of a duck-shaped night-light, she strolled into the
nursery, stopping in front of the crib. Christopher sighed in
his sleep, one tiny fist curled close to his ear, the other
resting on his chest. Feeling as if everything was right with
the world, she retraced her steps to the hall, then descended
the stairs to get something to drink.

Since she'd walked the floors so many times with Christopher, she had the floor plan memorized and didn't bother
to turn on a light. Letting moonlight guide her to the
kitchen, she deftly stepped around a box of belongings she
hadn't had a chance to unpack, then reached for the handle
on the refrigerator door.

A doorknob rattled behind her. Beth's eyes darted in that
direction, but the rest of her froze in place.

There was a long, brittle silence as she strained to hear
another sound. Another came. From the short hall that led
to the back door.

The image of the faceless person who'd been seen lurking around the hospital nursery leapt into Beth's mind.
Bringing her hands to her throat, she wanted to scream for
Tony, but the doorknob rattled again, and she couldn't
make a sound.

She heard a scrape, as if someone was dragging something, and then a series of thuds. Beth glanced longingly
toward the stairway, wishing Tony would wake up. Pressing her back against the refrigerator, she knew that with or
without his help, she would fight to keep Christopher safe.

She drew in a shallow breath, then moved to the adjacent
wall where she'd be out of sight. With blood pounding in

her ears, she positioned herself the way she'd once learned in a self-defense class. And waited.

The door opened on silent hinges, and the shadowy shape of a man moved slowly into the room. Letting loose a bloodcurdling scream, Beth jumped into the intruder's path.

She was all set to kick him where it counted when she heard an oath and a deep yelp of surprise. Cardboard tore and dishes clattered as the intruder fell over backward. With her heart in her throat, she flipped on the light. And froze all over again.

A huge man with blond hair and bulging biceps was half sitting, half lying on the floor, a mortified expression on his face. His ankle, which was ensconced in a white cast, was twisted at a painful-looking angle.

"Who are you?" Beth cried.

"Who the hell are you?" the man said at the same time.

"Gib, what are you doing here?"

They both jumped all over again as Tony walked into the room with Christopher, who was awake and wiggling, held stiffly in his arms. Beth's mouth dropped open, but she couldn't help it. Now that her heart had slid down a notch in her throat and she could actually breathe, she cried, "You know this man?"

Tony had grown accustomed to being awakened in the middle of a deep sleep, but he had to admit he'd never walked into the middle of a scene such as this one. Beth's scream had surely taken years off his life, but the sight of his best friend sprawled on the floor was one of the most comical things he'd ever seen.

"Beth," he said, trying not to grin, "I'd like you to meet Gibson Malone. Gib, this is my wife, Bethany."

Gib released a low whistle. The two men went back a long way, so long, in fact, that Tony recognized every nuance in his best friend's expression. Of course, it didn't take a genius to figure out what was going through Gib's mind right now. He was staring at Beth, and as far as Tony could tell, his gaze had yet to make it all the way to her face. Another time, Tony might not have minded. After all, Beth made quite a picture straddling Gib's cane, one sleeve of her robe draping off her shoulder, the lush contours of her breasts visible through the thin fabric of her pale pink gown.

Gib's hair looked lighter than it had the last time he'd seen him, undoubtedly the result of being bleached under the sun of some foreign country. Gibson Malone had acquired medals of honor for things he couldn't even talk about, but if he didn't stop ogling Beth, Tony was going to flatten his nose.

Gib glanced at Tony, a grin busting out all across his face. "Lucy," he said, wiggling his pale eyebrows expressively, "you've got some 'splaining to do."

Tony shook his head, thinking the man was about as subtle as the Ebola virus. Some things never changed, that was for sure. Gib had been doing a horrible Ricky Ricardo impersonation for as long as he could remember. "Malone," he said, offering his friend his hand, "I thought you were out of the country."

Steadying himself with his cane, Gib placed his hand in Tony's and slowly rose to his feet. "I was."

"Did you do that jumping out of a plane?" Tony asked, pointing to the cast.

Gib shook his head. "The jump was routine. But the landing was a doozy. They call this a walking cast, but that's a damn sight easier said than done." Balancing on his good leg, he glanced at the baby and then at Beth before finally meeting Tony's gaze once again. "I've been gone for six weeks, but the stories I could tell would probably sound tame compared to what's been happening in your life. You've obviously been a very busy man, Antonio."

Beth moved as if she'd suddenly come to her senses. She pulled at the front of her robe and quickly tied the sash, then reached for Christopher, who was making those squeaking noises he made when he was getting ready to yell for his bottle. Tony liked the way her fingers smoothed over his chest as she took the baby in her arms. He liked the way she smelled, like morning and woman, and he liked the way she looked, sleep tousled and sexy. But mostly he liked the way she smiled up at him. If they'd been alone, he would have shown her just how much.

Beth, always poised and good-mannered, cast Gib an apologetic look. "I'm sorry I made you fall, Mr. Malone. I thought you were an intruder."

"No harm done," Gib said, shrugging one massive shoulder. "Except to my pride." Leaning closer to Bethany, he lowered his voice and patted his derriere. "And maybe to my ego. Perhaps a kiss would make everything better."

Tony stepped neatly between them. Flattening one hand in the middle of Gib's chest, he said, "The day she kisses your...*ego* is the day I'll kick it to the far side of the Rockies."

Gib grinned at Beth and made a clicking sound with his tongue. "He's so territorial. At least call me Gib."

"All right, Gib," she said, glancing down at Christopher, who was starting to cry. "Now, if I don't warm a bottle for this little guy in short order, he's going to pitch a fit that could wipe out your hearing for the rest of the day."

"The kid sounds like his old man."

Gib Malone didn't understand the look that passed between Beth and Tony, but he understood all too well what was behind the way Tony watched her every move. Anthony Petrocelli had a hungry look in his eyes, all right. Not necessarily for food.

Gib released a pent-up breath. He usually bunked down at Tony's place when he found himself between assignments. From the look of things here, his timing was way off. "I should probably be going," he said to Tony.

"What? Oh, yeah, I'll walk you to your car."

Gib felt his brows draw down in an affronted frown. "Gee, Tony. You might as well come right out and tell me there's no hurry but here's my hat."

Something about the tone of Gib's voice drew Tony's attention. He took a frank look at his friend and wasn't entirely comfortable with what he saw. "Gib, are you all right?"

Gib kneaded the back of his neck. "I guess I'm more tired than I thought."

Tony didn't think he'd ever heard that particular tone in his friend's voice. Following him out the door, he said, "I didn't mean that the way it sounded in there, you know. You're welcome to stay here as long as you want."

The sun was an hour away from poking up over the mountains in the east. It would be longer before it took the chill out of the early morning air. Tony felt the cold on his bare chest, but it didn't cause him to hurry, and it didn't diminish the sincerity in his invitation.

Gib glanced at the house. "I know, and I appreciate the offer. But I think it would be best if I bunked down at J.J.'s place. How long have you and Beth been married, anyway?"

It was Tony's turn to glance over his shoulder at his own lighted windows. "Since yesterday."

Gib let out a whoop that probably woke up the neighbors. "No wonder you're so anxious to get rid of me this morning."

Tony shook his head. "You don't know the half of it."

"Yeah? Well, when you get a few minutes, you'll have to fill me in. And while you're at it, you can tell me how you came to be a married man *and* a father in the span of six short weeks."

Following Gib to his Jeep, Tony said, "Six weeks? Ha! This has all happened in just over one week. It'll probably take that long to explain."

Gib opened his Jeep's door and stashed his cane in the back. "That baby didn't happen in a little over a week."

"Like I said, it's a long story."

"I'm looking forward to hearing it."

Tony nodded. "When I'm through, you can tell me why you really came home."

"I told you. I fell."

"You know what they say," Tony countered. "The bigger they are, the harder they fall."

"I was thinking the same thing about you."

The two men exchanged a long, meaningful look. Like opposite mirror images, one dark, the other fair, their mouths slowly lifted into grins. Tony was the first to speak. "It *is* good to see you, Malone. We have a lot to catch up on. Give me a call as soon as you get settled. And that's an order."

"Aye-aye, sir," Gib answered. "Now, get your bony butt back in that house and give your wife a kiss for me."

"That," Tony said to himself, watching Gib back out of the driveway, "is going to be a pleasure. A pleasure, indeed."

He ambled back inside and found Beth in the living room, sitting in the old wood rocking chair he'd gotten from his Grandma Rosa. She looked up at him when he entered the room, and continued to pat Christopher's back.

Tony wondered if she had any idea how she looked at that moment, all sleepy and rosy and warm. Christopher burped loudly, the sound bringing out Beth's smile. Tony swallowed, then returned her grin.

"Did Gib leave?" she asked.

He nodded.

"And you think *I* have a strange best friend?"

Tony had the grace to shrug. "He takes a little getting used to, but believe me, he's the best. He feels really bad about scaring you, though," he said, walking farther into the room.

"I thought it might have been the person Kitty saw hanging around the nursery."

He nodded again, his estimation of Beth rising another notch. The woman was incredible. Not only was she beautiful and intelligent, but she was brave, too. "Did you get any sleep at all last night?" he asked.

"A couple of hours."

Tony's eyebrows drew down in consternation. He was certain her side of the bed hadn't been slept in. As if she read his mind, she said, "I crawled into the bed in the spare room. I didn't want to disturb you."

Could she really not know how much he *wanted* her to *disturb* him? "Believe me, Beth, I wouldn't have minded. How long before Christopher finishes that bottle?"

She shrugged. "He's a slow eater."

Beth held her breath as she waited for Tony's reaction. She knew what he was thinking, and why he was eager for Christopher to finish eating. He didn't appear to be impatient, but he didn't appear to be trying to disguise his desire, either.

The sky beyond the windows had gone from black to gray as morning prepared to break on a new day. Their wedding night had been a long one. Beth was almost glad it was nearly over.

Tony rotated a kink from his neck and shoulders, the action drawing her gaze to the muscles in his arms and chest, and to the washboard ridges that disappeared into the low-slung waistband of his slacks. If he'd been Greek, he could have been Apollo, himself. He obviously didn't have a self-conscious bone in his body. A man like that would be incredible in bed.

That thought had her mind scrambling like leaves in an autumn wind. She'd done a lot of thinking after he went to bed last night. She knew she would always feel enormously indebted to him for helping her adopt Christopher, but she had to find a way to make sure her feelings stopped there.

In order to accomplish that, she had to slow things down. That wasn't easy to do with him standing, shirtless and sexy, less than a dozen feet away.

The events of the past week played through her mind in fast-forward. She realized that there were a lot of issues she and Tony hadn't considered, let alone discussed. The sexual aspect of their marriage was one of them. The length they expected the marriage to last was another. She'd gone into her marriage to Barry believing it would last forever. With him, sex had become a means to an end: pregnancy—something she'd failed miserably. Beth had heard all the rumors about Tony's sexual prowess, and frankly, she didn't want to fail again. She definitely didn't want to end up with a broken heart.

"I could start a pot of coffee while you finish feeding Christopher."

Tony's voice drew her from her thoughts. She panicked for a moment, then seized the first excuse she could think of. "You go ahead. I don't want the caffeine to keep me awake."

She saw the surprise cross his face. Bless his heart, she saw the understanding, too. It was no wonder so many of his patients fell in love with him. She wasn't entirely certain how she was going to keep it from happening to her.

"Are you going to try to get some sleep?" he asked.

She nodded. "If that's all right with you."

Reeling in his thoughts, Tony took a frank look at Beth. This time, he noticed the dark smudges beneath her eyes and the fatigue in the set of her shoulders. She'd been awake most of the night. Of course she was exhausted. *Damn.*

"Of course it's all right with me," he answered.

"What time are you due at the hospital?"

Tony took a calming breath, then said, "Rounds usually start at seven, but since it's Sunday, I'm due whenever I get there. I don't have office hours, but after rounds I have some paperwork to catch up on. I should be home shortly after one.''

Now that he thought about it, it would probably be better for both of them if he spent the morning at the hospital. He could clear up his schedule for the rest of the day, and Beth could get a little much-needed sleep. He didn't want their first time to be hurried, anyway. This would give him time to make it right. He practically snorted. Right, hell. He intended to make it better than that. If he had his way, it would be darned close to perfect.

They talked for a few more minutes, then Tony went upstairs to take a shower and get ready for work. He came down twenty minutes later, whistling. Christopher was sleeping in Beth's arms when he kissed her goodbye.

Reading the question in her eyes, he said, ''That was from Gib.''

Without warning, he slanted his mouth over hers again, this time much more thoroughly, much more sensuously. ''That,'' he whispered, ''was from me.''

Beth smiled dazedly. Watching him leave, she thought about all the things she had to think about, all the decisions she had to make, and all the things she had to do. Tony would be back shortly after one. That didn't leave her much time.

Six

Tony pulled his Lexus into his driveway and cut the engine in front of the garage. With a slow smile of anticipation, he took a bouquet of flowers in one hand and a bottle of fine wine in the other, and headed for his own back door.

The entire hospital staff had been in typical form today, dishing out tongue-in-cheek comments and basically ribbing him mercilessly. With a knowing sort of smile, Noah Howell had insisted that Tony had a jaunty walk. One of the nurses claimed it was buoyant. Even Abigail Horton, the most difficult nurse in the entire hospital and quite possibly the most difficult woman on the planet, had commented on the grin that kept finding its way to his mouth. He hadn't had it in him to mind.

He'd told Beth he'd be back shortly after one. He'd finished early, and he knew why. He was anxious to get home. Anxious, hell, he was as excited as a kid at Christmas. Only he wasn't a kid. He was a grown man. And he'd never been more excited about anything in his entire life.

Classical music was playing from a radio in the kitchen. Tony didn't know whether it was Beethoven or Bach, but he knew Beth must have been busy, because the box Gib had tripped over earlier was sitting along the far wall, empty.

Her touches were everywhere, in whatever was baking in the oven, in the salt-and-pepper shakers on the stove, the yellow towel hanging from the bar near the sink, the rugs on the floor. Tony wondered if every newly married man felt this sudden burst of anticipation and appreciation for the feminine changes in his life. Of course, that wasn't the only reason for the enthusiasm racing through him right now, not by a long shot.

He listened for some indication as to Beth's whereabouts, half expecting to hear a baby's cry. Instead, he heard the clink of silver and the clatter of dishes. He found her in the dining room, setting the table. She didn't look up, which allowed him the opportunity to watch her, unseen.

She'd fastened her hair on top of her head, the style calling attention to her cheekbones and her long, slender neck. She was wearing a cream-colored pantsuit with gold buttons and trim. The woman certainly had class, but she probably knew that. He wondered if she also knew how sensuous the outfit made her look, the V-neckline dipping just low enough to be interesting, the material just soft enough to follow the contours of her body the way he wanted to.

She chose that moment to glance his way. For an instant, she seemed flustered, but the look faded, only to be replaced by a warm smile. "You're early."

"I know."

His movement toward her was automatic, the shift of his weight to one foot while he handed her the flowers very debonair, his reach for her instinctive. He'd never know how she managed to take the flowers and spin away so quickly that his hand came away with nothing but thin air. His mind obviously hadn't caught up with his body. But that was all right. He was thoroughly enjoying what was happening there.

"I'll just put these in water," she called on her way out of the room.

She looked over her shoulder when he followed her into the kitchen, a friendly smile on her face. "What kind of wine did you bring?"

"Chardonnay."

"It's one of my favorites."

Tony knew he had no business feeling so jubilant simply because he'd guessed correctly about the wine, but jubilant was exactly how he felt.

"How was your morning?" she asked, placing the flowers in a crystal vase.

"Fine. How was yours?" Tony answered, grinning inanely. It was strange, but he remembered his parents having this kind of conversation almost every night when he was a kid.

"Oh," she said, peeking into the oven. "It was wonderful. Christopher and I went to the store. He was an angel. I think last night was a fluke."

Tony hoped so, although it was highly possible that they weren't talking about the same thing. "Where's Chris now?"

"Sleeping."

"Has he been sleeping long?"

"I just laid him down."

Good, Tony thought to himself. Everything was working out perfectly. He strode a little closer, lowering his voice at the same time. "Is that lasagna I smell?"

"I hope you like it."

He was aware of the invisible pattern she drew on the counter, but he was more interested in the scent of her shampoo and the swish of satin against her skin. "You've obviously been extremely busy. Did you get any rest at all?"

"No, but I feel amazingly energetic. Honestly, I think I'm running on pure adrenaline."

Boy, oh boy, oh boy, did Tony know the feeling. Heart hammering, he brought his hand up with the intention of brushing a stray lock of hair out of her eyes. When she spun away this time, a furrow creased his forehead.

"I'm afraid the lasagna isn't quite ready. I didn't think you'd be home so soon." She peeked into the oven again, making him wonder if she was running on nervous energy, and not pure adrenaline.

"Why don't you turn the oven down," he said quietly. And then, with a lingering huskiness, he added, "Way down."

Her head jerked around, her gaze meeting his, only to slide away almost immediately. "All right," she said quietly. "I suppose dinner can wait."

She wet her lips, the flick of her pink tongue stoking the gently growing fire within him. "There's no need to be nervous, Beth," he said, his voice sounding low and husky in his own ears. "We're married, remember?"

Her gaze shot to his. "That's what I want to talk to you about."

It took a moment for her words to filter past the blood pounding through his ears. Talking was the last thing he wanted to do right now. "Beth, is something wrong?"

She spun around again, turning to face him only after she'd placed herself on the other side of the narrow table across the room. "No, no, nothing's wrong. Of course nothing's wrong. It's just that everything's happened so fast. I mean, two weeks ago we didn't even know each other, and here we are, married."

Tony felt his eyes narrow as he said, "I thought that was what you wanted."

"It is. I mean, I'm thrilled. It's just that things got a little out of control last night. And I don't want it to happen again."

An ominous sense of foreboding crawled down Tony's spine. "What are you saying?"

Her lips parted as if she couldn't breathe. She clamped her mouth shut, visibly trying to pull herself together. "Look," she said, finally finding her voice. "I know I'm not saying this properly. I'm afraid my sister got all the poise in the family. Maybe the fact that Christopher's fussiness kept us from...sleeping together...was meant to be. I know it forced me to take a long, hard look at what we're doing."

Beth chanced a glance at Tony and very nearly cringed. He was making that low, growling sound men everywhere made when their tempers were about to go through the ceiling. Barry had done it every time she'd failed a pregnancy test.

"What we're doing," Tony said, his temper barely controlled, "is making a life together. I thought that's why we got married."

Thoughts of Barry reinforced her resolve and gave her the courage to continue. Holding her head high, her gaze direct, she said, "I was under the impression that you married me to satisfy the board of directors, not to mention to carry on the Petrocelli name."

Tony tried not to swear a blue streak, but it wasn't easy. His blood was doing a slow boil, and so was his temper. He should have known how to handle himself when squaring off opposite a presupposing, potentially perturbing, impossible female. He'd grown up with four of them. But dammit, he had no words to convey his frustration. And he sure as hell didn't know what to say to change Beth's mind.

"Let me get this straight," he finally rasped. "You're telling me you don't want to go to bed with me."

She cringed, but Tony simply couldn't muster up much remorse. He was having his own problems, and Beth headed the list.

Biting her lip, she said, "It sounds harsh when you put it that way."

"How would you put it?"

She took a deep breath, probably to gather her wits. After a moment of tense silence, she said, "I know I have no right to expect you to be celibate. And I don't."

Sirens went off inside Tony's head. "You don't."

"No. I mean, I've heard the rumors about your sexual prowess, and I can't expect you to remain faithful to an arranged marriage. Although I'd appreciate it if you'd be discreet.''

"You're giving me your permission to take a mistress?"

At her nod, his voice dipped ominously, menacingly low. "As long as I'm discreet?''

When she nodded again, Tony let loose the first of the long string of expletives running through his head. Now that he'd singed the hairs in both their ears, he did the only thing a man in his predicament could do. He cast her a withering scowl, turned on his heel and stormed out of the house, slamming the door so hard the windows rattled.

He'd gone four blocks before he calmed down enough to recognize his first rational thought. How was it that he'd gone from buying flowers and wine to storming out of his own house in a matter of minutes? He didn't know, but smack dab in the middle of it all was Beth.

A dog stood up in the front yard of one of the houses he passed. The sign on the doghouse read Bowser. Fur and hackles raised, Bowser looked ready and willing to take a good-size bite out of Tony's hide. Tony glared at him and kept on walking. Other than a low growl followed up with a mean bark, the animal stayed exactly where he was. *Smart dog,* Tony thought to himself. Old Bowser obviously recognized a hopeless situation when he saw one. Tony couldn't help wondering if the dog was smarter than he was.

Was the situation with Beth hopeless?

He lengthened his stride and increased his pace. It was going to take a lot more walking to figure that one out. Glancing at the mountains in the distance, he wondered if he could make it to Crystal Pass by sunset. Maybe by then he'd have his new wife figured out. But then again, maybe not.

The house was strangely quiet when Tony arrived home. The radio had been turned off, but the oven was still on low. He wasn't sure what he was going to say to Beth, but he figured that since she'd gone to the trouble to make lasagna, he might as well eat it. Taking a fork and plate in one hand and the pan in the other, he sat down at the small table in the kitchen.

The lasagna had probably been delicious three hours ago. Now it was overbaked and bone dry. Since it was his own fault, he ate it, anyway. He'd eaten worse. Hell, he was pretty sure he was about to eat crow.

He'd walked for a long time, but he hadn't quite made it all the way to Crystal Pass. He'd tried to understand exactly what was behind the things Beth had said. A person would think that growing up with four sisters ought to give a man a little insight into those seemingly bottomless vagaries that made up a woman's mind. Tony didn't have a clue. He had come to one conclusion, though, and that was that Abigail Horton, the orneriest nurse at the hospital, could take lessons from Beth in ways to exasperate an ordinary man. Still, he wished he hadn't raised his voice and stormed off without a word of explanation.

He finished his meal in silence, then placed his dishes in the dishwasher. He didn't know what to do with the leftover lasagna. His first choice would have been to throw it out, but since he didn't want to hurt Beth's feelings, he left it on the counter.

Footsteps sounded behind him. Tony turned around as Beth walked into the room, Christopher in her arms. The look in her eyes reminded him of a stray cat, hungry, battle weary, yet leery of a helping hand. It made him feel like a heel.

Nodding toward the baby, he said, "Is he hungry again?"

She inclined her head, hurrying to the refrigerator for the prepackaged, prepared bottles of formula the hospital sent home with them. "He wants to eat every two hours."

"He has a lot of catching up to do."

She nodded again, then went about warming Christopher's bottle. Wishing he knew where to begin, Tony said, "I'm sorry I stormed out on you, Beth. What have you been doing while I was gone?"

She switched the baby to her shoulder and tested the formula on her wrist so slowly Tony assumed she was testing her answer, as well. When she finally spoke, it was in a voice carefully schooled in neutral tones. "I did a lot of thinking, and I put some of my things away in the spare room."

"The spare room?" Tony clamped his mouth shut because he knew he shouldn't have asked, but hadn't been able to stop himself.

Keeping her eyes on the baby, she said, "That bothers you."

Bother? He'd passed bothered hours ago. Actually, he'd gone all the way to full-scale frustration. "Why would that bother me?"

Beth didn't know what to say. She heard the heavy note of sarcasm in Tony's voice but saw no point in bringing it to his attention. She began to feed Christopher, who calmed down the instant she placed the bottle to his lips. Lord, she was tired. She felt the lack of sleep in every muscle. The strain between her and Tony was even worse.

She glanced at him and found him watching Christopher, his expression changing with his changing thoughts. She hadn't appreciated his earlier anger, but she liked the wariness and frustration in his eyes right now a lot less.

What had she done?

She'd asked herself that question a hundred times. What if Tony had changed his mind about the marriage? She'd been married to an attorney for seven years. Among other things, she'd gained enough understanding of the law to know that a marriage could be annulled if it was never consummated. Why hadn't she just gone to bed with Tony? So what if she ended up falling in love. She'd been terrified to let that happen, thinking she couldn't live through another broken heart. But could she live through losing Christopher? The very idea sent ice-cold panic all the way through her.

Shoring up her courage, she said, "I'll move my clothes to the closet in your room if that's what you want."

Tony's head came up with a start. After a long moment of silence, he shook his head. "No, Beth."

Although his eyes were little more than two slits in his face, there had been no anger in his voice. Beth didn't know what to say, but she found herself wishing for his anger. At least she'd know how to deal with that. The air of calm surrounding him felt more like impending doom with every passing second.

"I've been thinking," she began. "And I realize I overreacted."

"Maybe. But my answer is still no."

His simple words brought her up short, made her stammer. "But, I mean, I thought you wanted…"

He held up a hand, and her voice trailed away.

"I don't want charity, Beth, and I sure as hell don't want a virgin sacrifice. No, we'll do this your way. Or no way."

Beth's mind floundered, her thoughts scrambling. "My way?" she whispered.

He placed his hands on his hips and quietly said, "We'll get to know each other before we consummate the marriage."

"We will?"

"Believe me. We will."

Beth doubted that they were talking about the same thing, but Tony looked very sure of himself. Wasn't it just like a man to have a one-track mind? She was too relieved to care. He wasn't going to annul the marriage. Suddenly, she felt weak in the knees.

From the doorway, he said, "By the way, I ran into

Martin Smith while I was walking. I asked him to help me move the rest of your things over here tomorrow night.''

''Martin Smith? Isn't he the amnesia patient who wandered into the hospital the night Christopher was born?''

Tony nodded, and Beth thought about the man who'd stopped to talk to her a few times since his accident. Martin Smith—that was the name the nurses had given him—was six foot three, at least, and had blond hair and intense blue eyes. He had no idea where he came from, and no idea where he was going. Beth couldn't imagine losing her memory as he had. It reminded her that everyone had problems, many of them far worse than hers.

Tony began to speak, his voice drawing her from her thoughts. ''Martin's having a tough time coming to terms with his amnesia. He's been making his living doing odd jobs—painting houses and mowing lawns. Although he's a hard man to read, there's something about him I trust. I'm pretty sure he'll keep the fact that you're sleeping in the guest room to himself.''

For the first time, Beth thought about what it would do to Tony's ego if that piece of information was made common knowledge. ''All right,'' she said. ''I'll take Christopher over to my apartment tomorrow and get all my belongings boxed up.''

Tony nodded and started to walk away. He stopped suddenly and turned around. If she lived to be a hundred, she doubted she'd ever see a more serious expression on another man's face. Finally, he said, ''There's something I want to make clear. I didn't marry you for the sole purpose of obtaining a higher position at the hospital. If I get the promotion, fine. If not, so be it. You aren't the only one who's adopting that baby. He'll have my name, and he'll be my son as well as yours.''

Moisture gathered in Beth's eyes, a sudden quaking buzzing to her fingertips before heading for her knees.

''And for your information,'' he said more vehemently

than before, "I have no intention of seeing other women, discreetly or otherwise. So when you're ready, I guess you're going to have to let me know."

When he walked away this time, he didn't look back. Beth was left standing in the kitchen, her heart beating an erratic rhythm, her throat thick with tears, thinking that even angry and difficult, Tony Petrocelli was an incredible man.

"Where do you want these chairs?"

Beth glanced from Tony to all the clutter in his living room. Turning in a complete circle, she eyed the wicker chairs he and Martin Smith each held. Her gaze strayed to a sliding glass door facing the back of the house. Pointing, she said, "How about putting them on the patio for now?"

Settling Christopher in the crook of one arm, she slid the door open for the two men, but her eyes remained on Tony. He nodded politely, then carried the chair out to the patio, only to hurry out to the truck for another load of her things. She told herself she had no right to feel disappointed.

"Goodness," she said to Chris after Martin and Tony disappeared around the side of the house. "Moving is hard work. But you were a very good boy today, weren't you? I've never heard Mr. Willoughby speak baby talk before. The super in my building was obviously very impressed with you. I don't suppose you were surprised."

The baby looked up at her as if he was hanging on her every word. The strangest thing happened each time he did that. Her chest swelled up and her heart pumped softly, a smile of wonder finding its way to her lips.

Lowering himself into one of her own chairs on the patio, Beth continued to talk to Christopher. A lot of what she said was nonsensical gibberish, but he didn't seem to mind, gazing at her as if he understood every word. He'd only been with them a matter of days, but Beth was already becoming familiar with what he wanted from the sound, pitch and vigor of his cries. He ate often, slept between feedings and was literally growing before her very eyes. This was one happy, healthy baby, if she did say so herself. In fact, the only time he was the least bit fussy was in the evenings.

Tony's voice had been clipped, his words direct and precise every time he'd addressed her since yesterday. It seemed that neither of them knew how to break the barrier she'd erected when she'd informed him of her decision to sleep in the spare room.

"Your daddy and I need to talk," she murmured. "Or he's going to 'please' and 'thank you' himself right into a heart attack. Are you going to be like that when you grow up? Keeping everything bottled up inside until you're ready to explode? If you ever need to talk about something, I want you to know that you can always come to me and I'll always listen."

Tony hoisted the wicker settee higher into his arms. Since he couldn't see where he was going, he followed the sound of Beth's voice. It was incredible, crisp and clear as a mountain stream one minute, smooth and sultry the next, inviting always. This was their third day as husband and wife, and although they weren't exactly experiencing wedded bliss, they were both cordial and polite, which was still one helluva long way from what he wanted. What they needed was an icebreaker, or, better yet, a long, hard night of lovemaking. Yeah, that would definitely break the ice once and for all.

"It looks like this is the last of it," Martin said, placing a glass-and-wrought-iron table between the two chairs.

Tony came to with a start. Dragging his gaze from Beth, he reached for his wallet. "I appreciate all your help, Martin."

"We both do," Beth said, looking up from the baby in her arms.

Tony understood the softening in Martin's eyes. After

all, Bethany had that effect on a lot of people. The other man accepted the bills and quietly said, "No problem. I've got to keep busy or I'll go crazy. A man can't just sit around and wait for his memory to return."

Tony didn't nod or shrug, because he couldn't pretend to understand the kind of panic and fear and isolation a person with no memory would feel. Tony was more than six feet tall, but he still had to raise his chin slightly to look the other man in the eye. Martin Smith knew nothing about himself, but there was innate intelligence in those eyes.

He'd seen Martin's eyes narrow shrewdly when Tony had instructed him to put Beth's things in the spare room, but the other man hadn't said a word. Sensing an unspoken alliance, Tony said, "Do you have time for a beer before you leave?"

Beth rose to her feet lithely and disappeared inside to get the drinks before Martin had had a chance to respond. If Tony had been looking, he would have noticed the subtle lift of Martin's eyebrows. But Tony was too busy watching Beth's retreat to pay attention to anything else. He'd never seen a more graceful woman, and he sure as hell had never wanted one more.

By the time he turned his attention back to Martin, the other man was staring at the backyard, his shoulders rigid. Tony tensed, automatically following the course of Martin's gaze.

His property was on the outskirts of town, in the city limits but as large as a country lot. There were houses next door and across the street, but behind his yard there was only a meadow and a stand of pines, and beyond that, the mountains rose in the west. He'd purchased the property because it was on the edge of both worlds, having the convenience of the city and the view of the country. He saw nothing amiss in that view right now, but there was something about the look in Martin's eyes that made him wonder where he'd been headed when he'd gotten in the way of that mud slide and ended up losing his past.

"What's wrong?" Tony asked, instinctively lowering his voice.

Martin stared at the trees lining the meadow for a long time before answering. "I thought I saw a movement out of the corner of my eye."

Tony stood perfectly still. "A movement?"

"I suppose it could have been a bird, or some other animal. But I think it was human. Does anyone live back there?"

"No, the land's vacant." Peering out over his property and beyond, Tony was reminded of the person several different witnesses had seen lurking around the hospital nursery. Unfortunately, no two descriptions were the same. Nobody could even say for sure that it was a man or a woman they'd seen. Still, the very idea that someone could be watching from behind scrub trees and bushes near his own house had his nerve endings standing on end.

"Where are you going?"

Tony answered without taking his eyes from the trees in the distance. "Maybe what you saw was a bird or an animal. Maybe not. I'm going to find out."

Without a word, Martin was at his side. Stealthily making his way over the grass, Tony said, "Can you describe what you saw?"

Martin shrugged his massive shoulders, his eyes still trained on the landscape, his gait predatory, his voice low. "I don't know. It was more a feeling than an actual sighting."

There was something secretive about this man, and it wasn't just his amnesia. Tony couldn't help wondering just who Martin Smith really was, and what he'd done for a living before he lost his memory. Right now, Tony was glad the man was on his side.

It was dusk; shadows stretched across the ground and

sounds hung in the still air. The dry grass crinkled beneath their feet, an occasional twig snapping against their pant legs.

At the property line, Tony stepped over a fallen log. He veered to the right of a dying birch tree, Martin turned to the left. In the blink of an eye, something reared up beside Tony, sending him wheeling and stumbling backward. A huge owl took flight on a whoosh of air Tony could feel, the flap of wings rivaling the rush of blood pounding through his head.

Both men released the same expletive. Both raked their hands through their hair. Both slowly shook their heads.

Martin scowled, his expression full of self-reproach. "That was probably what I saw out of the corner of my eye. Sorry if I alarmed you. I seem to be jumping at my own shadow these days."

Tony glanced all around him, trying to imagine how strange it would feel to know nothing about his past. Hell, he'd be skittish, too. Seeing nothing out of the ordinary, he said, "No problem. I'd rather be safe than sorry any day. Come back to the house. Beth will be bringing that beer any second."

Martin raked his fingers through his hair one more time, his chest visibly expanding with the deep breath he took. "I appreciate the offer, but if it's all the same to you, I think I'll just head for home."

Tony shot the other man a quizzical look he didn't stick around long enough to see. "Don't you want a ride back to your place?" Tony called to Martin's back.

The other man turned around but didn't stop walking. "The hike will be good for me. Besides, it looks as if you could use a little time alone with your wife."

Tony stared at Martin's back for a full five seconds before starting off toward his own house. What very well could have been Tony's first smile of the day tugged at his mouth. Martin Smith may not have known who he was, but he was incredibly astute. He was also right. Tony did need to spend a little time alone with Beth. She'd said she wanted to get to know him before inviting him into her bed. He happened to believe a bed was the perfect place to get to know each other, but this was her call. He wanted her, but he had to let her play it out her way. Still, a little icebreaker couldn't hurt. Unfortunately, he was fresh out of ideas.

He barely noticed the first few drops of water that soaked into his slacks, but when others began pelting his shirt and face, he stopped in his tracks. Within seconds he was surrounded by a cool spray of water and a chi-chi-chi, chi-chi-chi sound coming from ground level. It was eight-thirty. His sprinkler system had burst on, right on schedule.

"Tony, you're getting soaked to the skin. How do I turn it off?"

He'd been about to make a mad dash for dry ground, but the sight of Beth standing on the patio changed his mind. She was wearing pale yellow cotton slacks and a matching shirt. Two long-necked bottles were balanced on a tray in her hand. Even though her clothes were wrinkled and disheveled from her unpacking, she managed to look elegant. Then she tipped her head to one side and he knew her elegance came from the inside.

Concentrating on taking a deep breath, and then another, he said, "I don't want you to turn it off."

"Are you crazy?" she called.

"Maybe."

The smile on her lips found its way to her voice as she said, "I see. Are you going to stand beneath that spray all night?"

Tony thought about telling her that this was hardly the first cold shower he'd taken in the past two days, but his gaze took in the infant seat on the table behind her, and he had a better idea. It looked as if Christopher was napping.

Evidently the sprinkler system *and* his new son both had perfect timing.

"Actually," he said, taking a few steps toward Beth, "I was thinking that you might want to join me."

Outwardly, Beth didn't move, but inside she felt something shift and slowly give way. She thought of the short, polite conversations she'd had with Tony since yesterday. Now she realized that he'd probably been on his best behavior. She had no word for the way he was acting right now, although she didn't believe for a second that it was an act.

His features were always striking and strong, but never more than at this moment. His black hair was shiny and wet; beads of water clung to his cheeks and ran down his neck. The spray plastered his white shirt to his body, making the material appear to disappear, and the skin on his chest and abdomen was clearly visible through the translucent layer.

She liked Tony this way, wet and playful and inviting, and very nearly took him up on his offer. The side of her that wanted to join him had always appalled her parents, and while she couldn't quite bring herself to take that first step, she found herself wishing she could. "Why do you want me to join you underneath the sprinklers?"

He took another step, but only one. "It occurred to me that we don't really know each other very well."

She'd told him the same thing only yesterday, word for word. Holding back a smile, she said, "Is that a fact?"

He nodded. "Oh, I know we're practically an old married couple...." He let his voice trail away for emphasis. "But you probably have a million questions, so go ahead, I'm yours for the asking."

Beth stared wordlessly at him. She'd come across a lot of men in her day, but she'd never met anyone quite like Tony. She knew darn well what he was saying. She had, after all, been raised in a family where words said one thing, and the tone of voice something else entirely.

"What?" he prodded. "Cat got your tongue? All right, I'll go first."

"No," she said, interrupting him. "It just so happens that there is something I want to ask you."

"Yes?"

His question was as transparent as his shirt. Arching her eyebrows, she said, "That water must be freezing."

He took a few more steps but made no move to walk completely out of the spray. "Do I *look* cold, Beth?"

Beth swallowed and slowly shook her head, thinking the man knew exactly how he looked.

"What was your question?" he asked, his voice dipping ever lower.

The second shake of her head was barely discernible, her voice barely more than a whisper. "Did you mean it when you said you would wait for my invitation?"

A familiar heat pulsed through Tony. Relying on instinct alone, he strode out of the soft spray of water, stopping just outside the sprinkler's reach. "Yes, I did, Beth." Sensing that it was important to let Beth set the pace, he held her gaze and added, "Although I have to say it hasn't been easy. Did *you* mean it when you said you wanted to get to know me better?"

He stared at her. She stared at him and slowly nodded.

"You know what we're doing, don't you?" she asked.

Tony knew what *he* was doing.

"We're using the classic *pause, ponder and parley* tactic."

He couldn't help himself. He had to ask. "The pause, ponder and parley tactic?"

"Yes. We're very likely doing it for the same reason."

"You think so?"

"Mmm-hmm," she replied. "But from very different vantage points, with very different outcomes in mind."

Tony didn't bother telling her how smart she was. He was too busy concentrating on the sensation, the need, taking hold deep in his body. Not even the cold water could stop it. Unfortunately, he'd just agreed, again, to wait for her to invite him into her bed. For the first time in his life, he wished he would have been born into a less honorable family. If he had, he'd walk over to her, swing her into his arms and carry her straight to his bed.

"Oh, I don't know," he said, imagining what he'd like to do with her there. "I think we both have the same *outcome* in the back of our minds right now, don't you?"

He watched her wet her lips, his gaze trained on her mouth as she said, "I *do* want to get to know you better, Tony."

He took another step closer. "I'd love to hear how you propose to do that."

"The first thing we need to do…"

"Yes?"

Beth shook her head once to let him know that he couldn't rattle her. "As I was saying, the first thing we need to do is rearrange our work schedules."

"Our work schedules?"

She nearly laughed out loud at his obvious bafflement. "I've spoken with Mrs. Donahue about this, and it's very important that you or I be with Christopher most of the time. I'd like to scale back my workload to every other weekend. Does that sound all right with you?"

"I see no problem with that."

"Good. I'll speak with someone in personnel at the hospital tomorrow. Also, Mrs. Donahue wants to get started with the home study, the next step in the adoption procedure, as soon as possible."

"Anything else?" he asked.

"I still have to tell my family about you and Christopher, but I have a feeling that once we begin the home study, everything else will fall into its rightful place."

"And do you see the physical aspect of our marriage falling into its rightful place, too, Beth?"

She hesitated a moment, watching his expression. This was it. The moment when she said "Yes, I'd like to go to bed with you" or "No, I'm sorry, but I'm not ready." This was definitely it. Do or die. Beth knew what she wanted, and it had nothing to do with dying.

After allowing herself a long look at the width of his shoulders and the breadth of his chest visible through his wet shirt, she placed the tray on the patio table. And nodded. She hadn't planned to. In fact, she'd planned to wait, to guard herself against getting hurt. But part of her didn't want to wait, had never wanted to wait. She wanted a real marriage, and she wanted it to begin right now.

"Yes, Tony. I see the physical aspect of our marriage falling into place, too."

He seemed to be holding perfectly still, his eyes on her. "Do you see it happening anytime soon?"

She nodded again. "I was thinking along the lines of right now."

"I'm not going to ask you if you're sure."

Watching him take the last step separating them, she believed him.

"Aren't you going to ask me why?" he asked.

When she shook her head, he said, "Good, because I'm sure enough for both of us."

She didn't know what she'd expected, but it wasn't the slow descent of his mouth and his soft kiss on her cheek. Holding perfectly still, she closed her eyes. There was something incredible about the brush of a man's lips on a woman's cheek. In her experience, it was something few men bothered with. She waited to see what he would do next, half expecting him to cover her lips with his. Instead, he pressed a kiss close to her ear and whispered, "Let's take Christopher inside."

He strode to the table and reached for the baby, infant seat and all.

"Do you want me to get you a towel?" she asked.

He paused near the doorway, the baby seat held a few inches away from his body. "It's only water. Don't worry, I won't get Chris wet."

Laying a hand on his arm, she said, "I think Christopher is in very capable hands, soaking wet or not."

Tony felt at once humble and ten feet tall. He wasn't entirely sure why. He only knew that he'd just been paid an incredibly high compliment. He watched the course Beth's gaze took as it rested upon Christopher and slowly climbed to his face.

"He'll probably sleep for another hour or so," she said quietly. "That should give us enough time, don't you think?"

Outwardly, Tony didn't move, but inside his heart lurched and desire uncurled like the smoke of a raging forest fire. "Oh," he said, his voice a low vibration in his own ears, "I think the next hour is going to go by awfully fast."

She smiled softly and slid open the screen door. Ever careful of the baby in his arms, Tony turned to follow.

A shadow flickered across the dry grass in the meadow. It stopped suddenly, blending with the larger shadows thrown by the trunk of a dying birch tree not far from where the owl had been roosting. If Tony's senses hadn't been so filled with the scent of Beth's perfume and the promise in her smile, he might have glanced over his shoulder. If he had, he might have been able to make out the brim of a baseball cap, and the tumble of dark, wavy hair.

Seven

Beth stepped to the side as soon as she walked through the door, allowing Tony enough room to follow. He slipped out of his soggy shoes, then shouldered his way past the lamp and bookcase he and Martin had moved from her place. Standing barefoot and dripping wet, he looked at her, the need in his brown eyes warming her despite the cool evening breeze.

Christopher made a mewling sound in his sleep, drawing both their gazes. As if the sight and sound of the baby reminded them that he wouldn't sleep forever, they both strode farther into the room. Moving around a box containing some of her things, Beth bent down to turn on a low lamp; Tony leaned over a sturdy table, ready to place the baby seat in the center.

"Wait," Beth said quietly. "Let's take him upstairs to his room."

"You don't think we'll hear him if he wakes?" Tony asked.

"Are you kidding? The next time I talk to Jenna, I'm going to ask her if she can hear him all the way from her cabin in the mountains. I'd just feel better knowing he's upstairs with us."

Cradling the infant seat in his arms, Tony said, "All right, lead the way."

Beth felt his eyes on her and doubted that it was an accident that he stayed three steps behind her all the way up the stairs. She wasn't accustomed to leading, or setting

the pace, or making the first move. The fact that Tony
didn't seem to think twice about allowing her to do all those
things cast a spell over her, making her feel winsome and
beautiful and strong.

She switched on the night-light in Christopher's room,
then watched from the doorway as Tony placed the baby,
infant seat and all, in the center of his maple crib. Brightly
colored animals danced from the end of the strings of the
mobile. When Tony turned around to face her, her nerve
endings danced in a similar fashion.

She felt heat spread to her throat and a fluttering sensation in the pit of her stomach. Tony pulled his shirttails free
on his first step toward her, unfastening the top button on
the second. By the time all the buttons were undone, he
was standing directly in front of her, and the butterflies in
her stomach had been replaced by the most amazing sensation.

Before her stood a man who obviously had but one thing
on his mind. She'd always thought of him as aggressively
male, and yet he'd waited for a sign from her. The enormity
of what he'd done for her filled her with a quiet urgency
she'd never known before. She and Tony had become husband and wife in name two days ago. Tonight, she wanted
them to become husband and wife in every way.

Tony followed Beth to the next doorway down the hall.
He'd been waiting for this moment for weeks, and had
imagined it dozens of times. In his fantasies, he'd been as
strong and passionate as the rumors about him. Every time
he'd thought about this since that night three months ago,
he'd taken his time and had made it last a long, long time.
The desire kicking through him right now wasn't going to
be easy to slow down.

He strode to the head of the bed and turned the lamp to
its lowest setting. Peeling the shirt off his back, he turned
around, the soggy garment landing on a chair at the same
time he drew in a quick breath at the sight of Beth standing

less than two feet away. He hadn't heard her come closer, but he swore he'd never seen more open longing in another woman's eyes. He wanted to allow her to set the pace, but if she didn't touch him soon, he was going to explode.

He smoothed a strand of her hair away from her face, taking the touch he needed. She went perfectly still for a moment, then swayed the tiniest bit toward him. It was all the invitation he needed. His arms shot around her, clasping her to him, molding her to the hard planes of his body. Still, she wasn't close enough.

He felt along the back of her blouse for buttons, and then in the front. It wasn't until she'd worked the button at her shoulder and then those down the side of her blouse free that he understood the reason behind the indulgent, knowing smile on her face. He almost told her that that was the damnedest place for buttons he'd ever seen, but she dropped her arms, the yellow fabric slid from her body, and he forgot everything except the need pulsing through him.

Her bra was beige lace and was probably very beautiful, but he was more taken with the ease with which the front clasp gave way. He sucked in a quick breath at his first sight of her breasts. And then conscious thinking ceased. He pulled her to him in one motion, breast to chest, skin to skin, man to woman. Still, they weren't close enough.

Beth felt Tony's hands move along her back. They encircled her waist, searching for the side closure on her slacks. She'd half expected the first time they made love to be awkward. After all, they didn't know each other, weren't familiar with all the little secrets their bodies held. But there was nothing awkward in the sensations quaking through her right now. And there was certainly nothing awkward in the strong hands effortlessly doing away with her clothes.

Her palms smoothed over his slacks, the fabric wet and cold. She heard the clink of a belt buckle and the rasp of a zipper. Her eyes fluttered closed, her hands brashly gliding over flesh that was amazingly warm.

She'd never be sure how they ended up in bed. One minute she was standing, the next minute her back was being pressed into a soft quilt, and her legs were tangling with his. He kissed her mouth, her breasts, her stomach, the curve of her hip and the length of her smooth thigh, in that order, and in every other order, until she lost track of exactly where his mouth ended and her skin began. She writhed, and moved, and returned his kisses, caress for caress, pleasure for pleasure.

His skin dried in the late summer air, but his hair remained damp and cool beneath her fingers. He smelled of pine and man and something infinitely elusive. His touch was strong and sure one moment; gentle and inquisitive the next; arousing, always.

In the early years of marriage to Barry, sex had been a pleasurable, mutually satisfying act. But in the last few years when she'd been trying so desperately to conceive, she'd always been aware of exactly what they were hoping to accomplish. And she'd failed him every time.

Tony barely gave her a moment to think, let alone worry about failure. He brought her to the brink of completion, sending hot, heavy desire rolling through her. In her desire-laden state, she was vaguely aware of the scrape of a drawer, and a sudden coldness on her body where he had been. She went up on one elbow as he had done.

Moving close to him, she wrapped her arms around his waist, pressing herself into his back. What she did after that brought a moan from a place so deep in his throat she felt its vibration in the kiss she placed between his shoulder blades. As if he couldn't stand another moment of her ministrations, he turned in her arms, pressing her into the mattress and parting her legs all in one motion. She gasped, her hips finding that age-old rhythm.

His face was hard and beautiful and intense in the dim light. His mouth covered hers, then broke away at the last second, but it didn't matter, because he joined her on another level, in another place, in a world where only lovers could go.

Sometime later, they caught their breath, floating back to reality just as Christopher's first cry carried to their ears. Tony rolled to his side and smoothed his hand along her thigh. "That baby has perfect timing."

Beth heard the smile in his deep voice. Feeling sated and sure of herself, she smiled back. "That isn't what you said on our wedding night."

She sucked in a breath as his hand inched up her ribs, his fingers spreading wide over her breast, then slowly closing, kneading, caressing. There was smug satisfaction in his voice as he rasped, "Believe me, you were worth the wait."

The mattress moved beneath his weight, bouncing slightly when he stood. "Where are you going?" she asked, her eyes following the play of muscles stretching and bunching with every step he took.

"I thought I'd go get Chris," he said, pulling on a pair of sweats. "I want to thank him for sleeping so soundly this past hour."

Beth watched him go, thinking he didn't have a self-conscious bone in his body. She pushed the tangled hair out of her eyes, then sat up, gingerly smoothing her hand across the bedspread. Her fingers bumped against a small object. She scooped the sealed foil package into her hand, turning it over in her palm, her thoughts turning over at the same time.

His reach for a condom had probably been automatic. At the time, she'd been too lost in sensation to question it. Now she wondered what thoughts had gone through his mind in that moment when he'd realized that protection wasn't necessary. Pregnancy was impossible.

She could hear Tony's voice as he tried to talk Christopher out of crying. Slipping off the bed, she hurried into the next room, where she quickly donned a robe.

The sight of Tony bent over Christopher, who was working his way to a red-faced wail, sent her hopes soaring and doubts to the back of her mind. So what if he'd thought of protection. So what if he'd realized he couldn't make her pregnant. As a lover he'd been incredible. Reminding herself that she'd always spent too much time on self-doubts, she strode to her husband's side and reached for the baby who was fast becoming their son.

"Would you say everything has been going okay since you brought Christopher home?" Florence Donahue asked, scribbling something on a yellow legal pad.

Beth began rattling on about how well Christopher was doing, how much he was eating at each feeding, and how sweet his disposition was. Now that Tony thought about it, that probably *was* what the social worker had meant, although the answer that had popped into *his* head was slightly different. As far as he was concerned, everything was a helluva lot better than okay. He and Beth had moved all her things into his room last night. They'd made love after they'd gotten Christopher fed and changed and back to sleep, and again this morning before the alarm had gone off. Yes, everything was definitely going very well, indeed.

"All the paperwork seems to be in order," Florence Donahue said, placing several forms in a ragged leather case.

Beth unclasped her hands in her lap and took a deep breath. This was by no means the first time she'd met with the adoption worker. In fact, she knew more about the Colorado social service system than she'd ever dreamed she'd know. Terms such as *voluntary* and *involuntary abandonment, the termination of parental rights* and *supplemental petitions* had become nearly as common to her as IV tubes and bandages.

"I'm aware that someone was seen lurking around the hospital nursery and that there is much speculation as to

this person's identity,'' Mrs. Donahue said. "I'm a bit surprised and enormously relieved that the press hasn't
chomped down on this story and exploited it for everything
it's worth. In recent years, adoption cases have been big
news. In those instances, tragic mistakes were made. I want
you both to know that I'm going by the book on this one.
I've filed the proper petition, amended it at the proper time.
It's been more than ninety days since the birth mother abandoned Christopher. We'll publish on her this week. If she
still hasn't come forward by the end of September, there's
nothing she can do in a court of law, nothing she can say,
no way she can regain the parental rights she forfeited when
she turned her back on her child.''

"You make Annie sound callous."

Tony glanced at Beth. Although she'd spoken the words
quietly, there was no disguising the strength behind them.

Florence Donahue looked at her over the top of her reading glasses, then slowly removed them from their precarious perch on the end of her nose. "That wasn't my intention.''

"Of course it wasn't,'' Beth answered, as if she truly
understood how being placed in the position of having to
decide the fate of children, some of whom were beaten and
abused by the very people they loved, could taint a person's
view of the world. "Because Annie isn't bad, Florence.
She's a girl who was all alone, a girl who gave birth to a
baby she was too young to have, a girl who was scared to
death of having her baby two-and-a-half months early in
the middle of a power failure.''

Mrs. Donahue's pinched expression slowly gave way to
a stiff pull at her lips that very well could have been her
first smile of the day. Turning shrewd eyes to Tony, she
said, "I believe I've been duly chastised. It's obvious that
your wife has an incredible capacity to love and to forgive.
How about you, Tony? How do you feel about Christopher
Moore?''

"He's a fighter. But his name is going to be Christopher *Petrocelli*."

The speed with which Tony corrected the social worker raised Mrs. Donahue's penciled-on eyebrows and gave Beth pause. As if realizing how defensive he sounded, he lowered his voice before continuing. "He'll be christened Christopher Vincent Petrocelli."

Slowly turning a pencil over from lead to eraser and back again, Mrs. Donahue said, "I understand you come from a large Italian family."

Tony shrugged. "Two parents, one grandmother, four sisters, eleven nieces and nephews and a partridge in a pear tree."

"*Eleven* nieces and nephews. Family gatherings must be very noisy and terribly messy."

Tony crossed his arms on the table and cast Mrs. Donahue the kind of grin that so many of his patients fell in love with, his shrug undoubtedly as natural as his masculine smugness. "That's what Petrocelli kids do. Make noise and messes."

"All children make noises and messes, Dr. Petrocelli."

The slight change in inflection in Florence's voice didn't escape either of them. Tony narrowed his eyes and said, "Of course they do."

Beth watched Florence scribble something on her legal pad, wondering where the other woman was headed with this particular vein of conversation. In a seemingly casual tone, she said, "I understand that Beth is unable to have biological children."

Beth had never heard a more pregnant pause. Even the clock on the mantel seemed to stop ticking, waiting for Tony's reply.

"Yes," he finally said. "She told me before we were married."

"And how do you feel about that?" Mrs. Donahue asked.

Suddenly, Beth remembered the foil package she'd found on the bed after the first time they'd made love. He hadn't reached for a condom again, and she hadn't given it much thought. Until now. She looked at Tony, schooling her expression to appear casual and unconcerned about his answer.

He stared into her eyes for a long moment, then turned back to the other woman. "I think it's a shame. You should see her with Christopher. Beth is one of those women who could easily handle a house full of kids."

Beth appreciated his insight, but Florence Donahue wasn't as easily appeased. "It only takes one child to make a family, Doctor."

The fact that Tony didn't seem to know how to reply brought a whole new set of worries to mind. Coming to his rescue, Beth said, "For Tony and I, that child is Christopher."

Mrs. Donahue raised her penciled eyebrows again. Beth braced herself for whatever she was about to say. Instead of stating facts or voicing her opinion, the heavy-set woman said, "I think we've covered enough for today."

She set a time for the next appointment, gathered her things and left.

Tony was quiet, seeming to pay an inordinate amount of attention to shrugging into his suit jacket. Since Beth couldn't very well just stand there staring, she began tidying up the table.

"Remind me to tell Gib about Florence Donahue."

She turned suddenly, pencils in one hand, a notebook in the other, "what" undoubtedly written all over her face.

Tony smoothed his hand down his tie and cast her one of his most appealing half smiles. "Gib spent his formative years in combat in the marines and the past ten years working for a private agency that deals with covert action. He's been trained by the best, but he could still take a tip or two from Mrs. Donahue concerning tactical maneuvers and pointed interrogations.''

She was sure Tony expected her to smile, and she did, eventually, although she really wanted to ask him about the expression behind his eyes. Even though the sexual aspect of their marriage had advanced considerably—she nearly blushed at that understatement—she still didn't know him well enough to decipher his moods.

"You're quite a woman, Mrs. Petrocelli."

Bethany was at a complete and utter loss for words. Tony was having no such problem. "If I didn't have to be back at the office in fifteen minutes, I'd show you what I mean."

Her smile was real now. So was the slight shake of her head. "Is that a fact?"

He nodded, his hands settling on his hips. "I have a feeling Mrs. Donahue will think twice before she uses that particular tone while referring to a birth mother, don't you?"

He kissed her goodbye quickly, telling her not to overdo, and walked out the door. Beth was left standing in the doorway, her fingers pressed to her lips, wondering how he did it, how he made her want him with just a look and a masculine half smile and a kiss that was barely a kiss at all.

Turning around, she realized that he'd done something else, too. He'd evaded an issue that was going to have to be raised one of these days.

He *had* reached for a condom two nights ago, and he *had* sounded defensive with Mrs. Donahue today. Beth suspected that he hadn't come to terms with her infertility. She couldn't blame him, really. He'd only known about it for a matter of days. It had taken her seven years to accept. Barry never had.

Tony isn't Barry.

She squeezed her eyes shut and whispered it out loud. Barry had hurt her in nearly every emotional way, making her feel guilty for something that wasn't her fault, then casually throwing her away. But she was right. Tony wasn't Barry. Barry never would have married her if he'd known she couldn't give him children. And he certainly wouldn't have told her she was special because she'd defended Annie Moore. But then, Barry hadn't been there the night Christopher had been born. She and Tony had both seen how brave Annie was that night. Until her dying day, Beth would always remember the expression on Annie's thin face when she'd asked Beth to take care of Christopher.

She could only imagine what that young girl had been through in her short life. Hugging her arms close to her body, Beth turned around. Remembering the tears that had streaked the girl's face and the pain that had racked her thin body, Beth prayed that Annie Moore was safe, wherever she was.

It was late morning by the time Annie found the house she was looking for. A customer who'd come into the truck stop had called this part of town the Downs. For good reason. Most of the houses were close together and run-down, but the one she was looking at was worse than the rest. Paint peeled from the wood siding and the roof had a sag that made the whole place look tired. The yard wasn't much better, but the cats stretched out in the patches of sun didn't seem to mind.

A woman wearing men's trousers and a straw hat was cutting flowers near a rotting porch. Taking a few tentative steps on the dirt driveway, Annie called, "Are you the lady with the room to rent?"

The woman turned stiffly and studied her through the oldest-looking eyes Annie had ever seen. "Will be in a coupla weeks. You lookin' to rent a room?"

"If the price is right."

"What's your name?"

"Annie Moore."

"Where are you stayin' now?"

Annie hesitated, measuring her answer. "With...with a friend."

The woman's beady stare made her nervous, but Annie set her chin, clamped her lips together and looked her right in the eye, anyway. When she turned eighteen she was never going to lie again. Then she'd be safe, and nobody could send her back to that town or that life ever again.

A breeze picked its way around overgrown bushes, ruffling her T-shirt and hair. She took a deep breath and barely stopped herself from moaning out loud. The place looked like a junkyard, but it smelled like heaven.

With a considerable amount of effort, the woman rose to her feet. "Folks 'round here call me Crazy Cora. But I prefer Cora if it's all the same to you. Yer welcome to look around, and I'd be more'n happy to show you the room, but I b'lieve my coffee is perked and the biscuits are prob'ly cool enough to eat. You can join me if you wanta."

"I ate before I came." Another lie, but Annie didn't have much except her pride.

Without missing a beat, Cora said, "Never know'd that to stop a young person from eating again. But suit yourself."

Cora led the way to the back of the house, where an addition jutted out from the main structure. It might have been newer than the rest of the house, but it wasn't in any better shape.

Taking a key from the deep pocket in her overalls, Cora unlocked the door. "The guy who was rentin' this room took off without a word a coupla weeks ago. His rent's due and his lease is almost up. It don't look like much right now, but cleaned up, it ain't a bad room."

After following Cora inside, Annie had to wait for her eyes to adjust to the dim interior. A weaker person would have turned around and hightailed it out of there right then, but Annie Moore wasn't weak. She took a few steps farther into the room. A torn shade hung from the only window, a dilapidated sofa crouched nearby. There was a dirty stove and an old-fashioned refrigerator in one corner, a narrow bed in another. A metal table and three vinyl chairs took up most of the middle of the room; papers and ratty clothes were strewn over the floor. There was a closet, and a bathroom that had all the essentials, even if the porcelain was chipped and stained.

"How much you asking for rent?"

Cora eyed her in that way that made Annie nervous. Then, out of the blue, she started to hum. It was a little unnerving, but not a bad tune. She named a price that was cheaper than Annie had expected, making her wonder if the woman might have been a little crazy, after all.

"'Course, with that price, I'd expect you to clean the place up. And you'd hafta give me a reference. You sure you're old enough to be out on your own?"

Annie crossed her thin arms and felt a smile starting somewhere deep inside. Things were going to work out, she just knew they were. Without looking at Cora, she said, "I'm older than I look."

"It's a good thing, because ya look about fourteen."

Imagining what the dismal room would look like with a little spit and polish, Annie absently said, "Sometimes I feel ancient. Thirty-five, at least."

That got a cackle out of Cora. "Ain't that a coincidence. That's exactly how old I feel. Come on. You can write down the name and number of your reference and test my biscuits at the same time."

Annie wasn't sure how it happened, but fifteen minutes later she was sitting at an old wooden table between two cats, munching on homemade biscuits and real honey. Cora was cutting up vegetables for her stew, talking about everything from her cats to the patch of garden she had out back. "I know this place don't look like much, but it's home. Most people only see what's on the outside. They think I'm old and senile." She made the last word sound like two words instead of one, like *sea nile.* "I ain't crazy. And I'm younger'n I look."

Annie thought that was a good thing, because Cora looked older than dirt. Her hands were gnarled, her face wrinkled, her stringy hair the color of dirty steel.

"This your first trip to Colorado?"

"I've been here almost a year."

"Got family in these parts?" Cora asked without looking up from the pot she was stirring on the stove.

"No. I mean yes," Annie said softly. "I have a baby boy."

"I had a little boy once."

Annie stopped chewing and turned her head. "Where is he now?"

Cora was humming again. When it became apparent that either she hadn't heard Annie's question or just plain didn't feel like answering, Annie stood and headed for the door. The quavering old voice behind her stopped her in her tracks.

"You don't hafta go. This here stew will be done in an hour. You can stay and have some with me if you want. Ya can stay longer than that if you need ta."

Annie eyed the room's rustic interior and swiped at her eyes. Must have been a delayed reaction to the onions Cora had put in the stew. Suddenly, Annie felt bone tired. It reminded her of how she'd felt a few nights ago sitting in a meadow on the other side of Grand Springs, watching as lights came on in Dr. Petrocelli's house. A yearning so powerful she'd barely been able to fight it had nearly sent her crawling to Beth's door and asking—begging—her to take care of her the way she was taking care of Christopher.

Shaking her head to clear it, Annie said, "Thanks, Cora, but I can't. I've gotta work this afternoon. I'm saving my money so I can give my baby a good life."

"Your mama know about him?"

Annie's answer was a snort. Her mother didn't give a damn about her. Never had. All she cared about was her current boyfriend. Her mother didn't know about the boy Annie had met after she ran away, and she never would. Annie wasn't going back there. She'd escaped with her virtue, what there was of it, intact. She shivered at the thought of the greasy, hairy-chested man with a week's worth of whiskers and a leer that made her skin crawl even now.

"What's your baby's name?"

"What?" she asked, coming to with a start. "Oh. I named him Christopher. After my sister, Christie."

"My boy's name was Willie. Sweetest li'l boy in the Rockies, and smart, my he was smart."

"What happened to him, Cora?"

For a minute, Annie thought Cora was going to start humming again instead of answering. In a way, she did both, her answer coming to Annie's ears on what sounded like a song. "He went to live with the angels the winter he turned five."

Annie couldn't think of anything to say to that.

As if Cora understood all too well, she said, "You take good care of that baby of yours, you hear? Because a baby needs his mama more'n he needs anyone else in this here world."

Annie swallowed the lump in her throat and called good-bye. She didn't expect an answer, and she didn't receive one. Cora stirred her stew and hummed a tuneless song, lost in whatever world she'd created in her head. It wasn't surprising that other folks called the woman crazy. Maybe she was. But she was right about one thing. Babies did need their mothers. And Annie Moore was going to be the best mother she could be.

Things hadn't gone right from the beginning. Hell, for her and Christie, things had never gone right. But with Christopher, it was going to be different. From the moment she'd faced the fact that she was pregnant, she'd vowed to do everything right for him. It would have worked, too, if Todd hadn't forced her to get out and gone into labor two-and-a-half months early.

But that nurse, Bethany Kent, had been there that night, and everything had felt better somehow. Beth had promised to take care of Christopher, and every time Annie had checked up on him, he'd looked better, healthier, stronger than before.

She'd gone tearing into the bathroom in a panic that time when she'd crept up to the nursery and found him gone, but when she'd overheard two nurses talking about how Beth and Dr. Petrocelli had gotten married, she'd known where to find her baby.

The house had been easy to locate, the meadow nearby the perfect place to watch from undetected. She'd had to clamp her hand over her mouth to keep from screaming at the top of her lungs when the doctor and another man almost stumbled upon her. They probably would have found her, too, if that owl hadn't distracted them. But they hadn't seen her, and she'd been able to watch her baby from afar, sight unseen.

She thought about the way Dr. Petrocelli had picked him up, thought about how safe he'd looked in those strong arms. Mostly, she thought about the way Beth had talked to Christopher. The love and sunshine in that voice had carried all the way to Annie's ears.

Her heart ached a little bit when she imagined how sad Beth would be when Christopher was gone. But he wasn't Beth's kid. He was hers. She'd born the censure of carrying him and the pain of having him. She loved him. Beth and the good doctor were newlyweds. They'd probably have kids of their own someday, but right now they had each other. Hell, they probably had families who got together at Thanksgiving and Christmas and had picnics on the Fourth of July. Christopher was all she had.

Casting one last look behind her at Cora's dilapidated house, Annie tucked her hair underneath her baseball cap and headed for the highway where she could hitch a ride back to the truck stop where she worked. She had a job and soon she would have a place to stay. All she needed was a little more money, and a little more time, and she would be ready to bring her baby home.

GET FREE BOOKS AND A WONDERFUL FREE GIFT!

TRY YOUR LUCK AT OUR CASINO, WHERE ALL THE GAMES ARE ON THE HOUSE!

PLAY **Roulette!**

PLAY **TWENTY-ONE**

Turn the page and deal yourself in!

Welcome to the casino!
Try your luck at the roulette wheel ...
Play a hand of Twenty-One!

HOW TO PLAY:

1. Play the Roulette and Twenty-One scratch-off games, as instructed on the opposite page, to see if you are eligible for FREE BOOKS and a FREE GIFT!

2. Send back the card and you'll receive TWO brand-new Silhouette Intimate Moments® novels. These books have a cover price of $4.25 each, but they are yours to keep absolutely free.

3. There's no catch. You're under no obligation to buy anything. We charge nothing — ZERO — for your first shipment. And you don't have to make any minimum number of purchases — not even one!

4. The fact is, thousands of readers enjoy receiving books by mail from the Silhouette Reader Service™ before they're available in stores. They like the convenience of home delivery, and they love our discount prices!

5. We hope that after receiving your free books you'll want to remain a subscriber. But the choice is yours — to continue or cancel, any time at all! So why not take us up on our invitation, with no risk of any kind. You'll be glad you did!

PLAY TWENTY-ONE FOR THIS EXQUISITE FREE GIFT!

THIS SURPRISE MYSTERY GIFT COULD BE YOURS FREE WHEN YOU PLAY

TWENTY-ONE!

It's fun, and we're giving away FREE GIFTS to all players!

PLAY Roulette!

Scratch the silver to see where the ball has landed—7 RED or 11 BLACK makes you eligible for TWO FREE romance novels!

PLAY TWENTY-ONE!

Scratch the silver to reveal a winning hand! Congratulations, you have Twenty-One. Return this card promptly and you'll receive a fabulous free mystery gift, along with your free books!

YES!

Please send me all the free Silhouette Intimate Moments® books and the gift for which I qualify! I understand that I am under no obligation to purchase any books, as explained on the back of this card.

Name (please print clearly)

Address   Apt.#

City   State   Zip

Offer limited to one per household and not valid to current Silhouette Intimate Moments® subscribers. All orders subject to approval.

PRINTED IN U.S.A.

(U-SIL-36-02/98)   245 SDL CE6U

The Silhouette Reader Service™ — Here's how it works:

Accepting free books places you under no obligation to buy anything. You may keep the books and gift and return the shipping statement marked "cancel." If you do not cancel, about a month later we'll send you 6 additional novels and bill you just $3.57 each plus 25¢ delivery per book and applicable sales tax, if any.* That's the complete price — and compared to cover prices of $4.25 each — quite a bargain indeed! You may cancel at any time, but if you choose to continue, every month we'll send you 6 more books, which you may either purchase at the discount price...or return to us and cancel your subscription.

*Terms and prices subject to change without notice. Sales tax applicable in N.Y.

If offer card is missing write to: Silhouette Reader Service, 3010 Walden Ave., P.O. Box 1867, Buffalo, NY 14240-9952

BUSINESS REPLY MAIL
FIRST-CLASS MAIL · PERMIT NO 717 · BUFFALO NY

POSTAGE WILL BE PAID BY ADDRESSEE

SILHOUETTE READER SERVICE
3010 WALDEN AVE
PO BOX 1867
BUFFALO NY 14240-9952

NO POSTAGE
NECESSARY
IF MAILED
IN THE
UNITED STATES

Eight

"Bethany tells me you're being considered for a promotion of significant prestige."

Tony found himself removing his hand from his pocket and standing up straighter before he nodded at the petite, middle-aged woman wearing a pastel-colored dress and a single strand of pearls. "I'm not so sure about the prestige, Mrs. Bower, but I am being considered for a promotion to head of obstetrics."

"Every time you call me Mrs. Bower," Beth's mother admonished, placing a perfectly manicured hand on his arm, "you remind me of Winston's mother, whom I called Mrs. Bower for the first five years of our acquaintance. Please, call me Katherine."

Tony did a double take at her wink, then released a deep chuckle. The sound drew several family members' gazes, as if they weren't accustomed to sudden bursts of laughter during their family parties. Within seconds, Beth's sister drew Katherine into conversation, and Beth's father, Winston Bower III, and her brother-in-law, MacKenzie Nelson, returned to their lawyer talk on the other side of the room.

Beth had warned him that her family was a little stuffy. Stuffy, hell. They were bona fide snobs. And *Katherine* ranked at the top of the genteel heap. But she had a sense of humor, dry though it might be, and a haughtiness he wouldn't have minded pitting against the queen of England, not to mention a smile that reminded him of Beth.

Beth entered the room, a sterling silver tray containing

fancy little sandwiches in her hands. She graciously offered one to Winston and Mac, smiling at something her father said. It was strange, but Tony sensed love between these family members, just not closeness.

They were a far cry from the Petrocellis, that was for sure. His family hadn't been able to wait to meet Christopher. The Bowers had yet to see him. Beth had offered to wake him and bring him down, but Katherine had declined, saying that she couldn't fathom disturbing a sleeping child. The Bowers were polite, well mannered and well-bred. Now that he'd met them, Tony understood where Beth had acquired her class. He also understood the reason she'd been running on nervous energy these past few days, trying to make everything perfect for tonight. As far as he was concerned, she'd nearly outdone herself. She'd served wine in fluted stemware and had stacked cubes of fine cheese and hors d'oeuvres on gleaming silver and sparkling crystal trays. He'd never seen her looking more elegant. Or nervous.

Candles flickered on the mantel, threading her auburn hair with gold and honey. A lamp behind her shone through the hem of her ivory-colored dress, delineating the curve of her knee and the edge of a lacy slip. These past few days, Tony had discovered that his wife had a passion for pretty underclothes. He had a passion for removing them.

She glanced across the room, sending him a tremulous smile. For a moment, her innermost feelings played across her face, making him doubt that he was the only one who had sex on his mind. Desire roused inside him, and suddenly he thought of one way to chase away her nerves. Something told him the Bowers would look askance at him if he swung his new wife into his arms and carried her upstairs. But it would definitely liven things up.

Beth shook her head at Tony, doing her best to school her features into a mask of calm. Still, she felt warmed by the expression in his dark eyes, and flushed with heat that had nothing to do with the mid-September temperatures outside. Her family had been here for nearly two hours, and she was beginning to believe they might all make it through the evening without incident. She wasn't surprised that everyone seemed taken with Tony. After all, he was a doctor, which was a fitting profession in their eyes. He was also an incredibly charming man.

"Beth?"

The absent way she said "Hmm?" earned her a smile from her sister.

"I'm sorry to break into your reverie, and I know Mother doesn't think we should wake a sleeping child, but MacKenzie and I would like to be home before the children go to bed. And I'd really love to see the baby."

Beth started to turn toward the doorway that led to the foyer, but was stopped by Janet's quiet voice. "I know how much work planning an evening such as this requires, and here you've done it with a newborn baby in the house. You must be exhausted. May I bring him down?"

Beth nodded, and Janet walked away, the swish of her skirt as elegant as her demeanor. Janet was two years older than Beth. Their hair was a similar color, but Janet's was smooth and manageable. She was pretty and bright and nice—the perfect Bower sister. In comparison, Beth had always felt second-rate, especially in their parents' eyes. Her grades had never been perfect, her choice of careers a mystery to them, her divorce shameful. She hadn't even been able to get something as simple and basic as motherhood right.

"Look, everyone. Isn't he adorable?" Janet called softly, practically floating toward the center of the room with Christopher in her arms.

Beth smiled just as she did every time she caught a glimpse of that small bundle of joy. Christopher was sucking on his fist. Honestly, she couldn't have felt more pride burgeoning inside her if he had been negotiating world peace. In that instant she realized that there was no wrong way to become a mother. It didn't matter that her baby hadn't grown beneath her heart. This special child had grown within it.

She glanced at her family and was pleased to see them smiling their approval.

"He's a fine-looking boy."

"He seems very alert."

"He's undoubtedly extremely bright."

"Just look at all that dark hair."

Tony wasn't really surprised at the Bowers' reactions to Christopher. If they hadn't been decent people, Beth wouldn't have turned out the way she had. She was standing next to her sister. Side by side, the family resemblance was unmistakable. Both of them had inherited their height and hair color from their father, and their poise and bone structure from their mother.

"Beth," Janet said, "wouldn't it be wonderful if his eyes turned blue like yours?"

"If his eyes are blue, they'll be like Annie's, not mine," Beth said, accepting Christopher from Janet's outstretched arms.

"Who's Annie, my dear?" Winston Bower asked.

"She's the young girl who gave birth to him."

Tony had never heard a more simple statement change the atmosphere in a room so suddenly and completely. The Bowers were far too polite to gasp, but they did share collective deep breaths and furtive glances.

"You've actually met the birth mother?" Katherine asked.

At Beth's nod, her father said, "Do you think that's wise?"

"It would have been difficult to deliver Christopher if Annie hadn't been present, Father."

"You delivered that baby?" Winston asked.

Beth's gaze darted around the room. She didn't like

where the conversation was headed but wasn't certain how to curtail it. "Annie did the hard part," she said quietly. "All Tony and I had to do was…"

Having never had a stomach for even the most innocuous scratches and contusions, Katherine held up a delicate hand and gave her head a firm shake. "Bethany, please, you know how I react to the mere thought of…"

"Hors d'oeuvres, anyone?"

All eyes turned to Janet, who seemed to have appeared out of nowhere holding a silver tray containing little cucumber sandwiches and stuffed mushrooms. "Do try the mushrooms, Mother. Beth made them, and they're delicious."

Katherine and Winston both relaxed, accepting one of each. The topic was changed and the moment was saved. Janet smiled demurely at everyone she passed. Beth smiled in return, thinking there was something to be said for having a sister who was perfect in every way.

"Well?" Beth asked, moving Christopher to her shoulder for a burp. "Were they what you expected?"

"I liked them."

The rocking chair they'd received from Tony's grandmother creaked slightly, and Beth's hand thudded quietly as she patted the baby's narrow back. Christopher had finished his formula and was sleeping soundly, which meant the last burp wasn't going to be easy to draw out. Since she'd learned the hard way what happened if she laid him down before he'd released it, she continued to pat his back.

"No, really," she said to Tony, who was lounging in the doorway on the other side of Christopher's narrow room. "You don't have to spare my feelings."

"I'm not sparing anything. I think they're very pompous but nice in an upper-crust kind of way. They seem to have accepted your marriage and the fact that they weren't invited to the wedding with a certain degree of diplomacy. Now I know where all that poise of yours comes from."

"That," she said quietly, "was one thing I got right."

Christopher released a sound that was bigger than he was, eliciting a smile from both Beth and Tony. Staying where he was in the doorway, Tony said, "Oh, I think you've gotten a lot more right than poise."

The baby sighed in his sleep. Kissing his smooth, soft cheek, Beth was filled with maternal love for the child in her arms, and with longing for the man watching them from the doorway. Tony had removed his tie as soon as everyone left and unbuttoned his shirt some time later. His dress slacks were slung low on his hips, his chest and feet as naked as the longing in his eyes.

Wondering if Christopher could feel her heart rate accelerate, she rose from the chair and slowly lowered him into his crib. "They took the news quite well, considering," she said, referring to her family's reaction to her sudden marriage and decision to adopt Christopher. "And they all seemed to like you. Even my mother."

"What's not to like?"

She rolled her eyes before covering the baby with a lightweight blanket. "Janet told me I'd made a wise choice. Coming from her, that was high praise. Janet is the perfect daughter, you see, and I'm her somewhat-less-than-perfect younger sister."

"Families are complicated. God knows, mine is. I get the feeling your mother would have preferred you to choose some nice, safe career, if you *had* to have a career at all. Her remarks tonight were intended to remind you of your place and social standing, and hold you there. That isn't where you want to be."

Beth straightened and slowly turned. Smiling, she whispered, "Thank you for the recap."

"Anytime."

Tony pushed himself from the door frame and ambled

into the room with the easy grace of a man who knew exactly what he wanted. Beth's eyes closed dreamily, because what he wanted was her, and being wanted by Tony Petrocelli was a very heady sensation.

Yesterday had marked the one-week anniversary of their wedding. They'd gotten off to a slow start, so to speak, but they'd made up for lost time these past few days. Sometimes their lovemaking had been as long and languid as a summer afternoon. Other times they came together like two people sharing an illicit stolen moment. Those times, their lovemaking was frenzied, their desire catching fire like a match on dry tinder. Tonight, the passion in Tony's eyes told her he had plans for the two of them, slow, languorous plans he would share with her as soon as he was good and ready.

"What?" he asked, moving around her in a slow circle, noting the amused look on her face.

Turning only her head, she said, "I was just thinking that you were probably a difficult child."

"This from the daughter who defied her parents at every turn?"

"I only defied my parents at every other turn."

He'd circled behind her and was coming around to her right side. "What did your father and brother-in-law say to you when they cornered you just before they left?"

"Mac and my father?" she asked dazedly. "Oh, they wanted to know if we'd signed a prenuptial agreement."

"I'm not after your family's money, Beth."

"What are you after?"

His gaze dropped below her shoulders and took a long time returning to her eyes. Cocking her head playfully, she smiled. "Allow me to rephrase that question. What *else* are you after?"

Tony groaned softly. "What makes you think I'm after anything else?"

"Do you mean sex is all you expect from this marriage?"

"I'm sorry I brought the subject up."

Something in his tone alerted her to an underlying problem. She'd wanted to talk to him about this before the wedding, to pin him down, to force him to tell her exactly what he wanted from their marriage, and how long he expected it to last. Now that they'd broached the subject, she didn't want to ignore it. "I think we should discuss this, Tony."

"No."

Their gazes met, held.

"Why not?" she asked.

"Come on, Beth. You don't really want to talk right now, do you?"

She swallowed her apprehension and said, "This could be for your own protection."

He was shaking his head before she'd finished. "Protect me from what? Your family has a lot more money than mine. And it's not as if you're going to divorce me and hit me up for child support for a half-dozen kids."

They both went still, the light from Christopher's night-light stretching their shadows all the way into the hall. Beth was the first to find her voice. "You don't need protection because I can't have children, is that it?"

"That's not what I meant."

"Isn't it? Barry left me because I couldn't give him children. You can't tell me it doesn't bother you."

"I married you, anyway, didn't I?"

Beth took a step back as if she'd been slapped, and Tony drew in a loud breath. She remembered when he'd told her he didn't want charity or a virgin sacrifice. Raising her chin in a manner she'd learned from her mother, she quietly said, "Who's offering charity now, Tony?"

Tony started to swear. Realizing they were still standing in the middle of Christopher's room, he clamped his mouth shut and whispered, "Beth, this isn't coming out the way

I intended. You caught me off guard, that's all. What I'm giving you isn't charity, not by a long shot.''

"What do you want in return?" she asked quietly.

Beth didn't know what she saw in his eyes this time, but it was more than attraction and seduction. There was anger, and worry, and maybe a hint of sadness, and something else that scared her more than all the others combined, because it looked a lot like remorse. "I've already suffered one broken heart, Tony, and I'd really prefer not to experience it again.''

"I have no intention of breaking anybody's heart, dammit.''

"But?" she asked.

He didn't say anything. And neither did she. They stood perfectly still, staring at each other. She finally nodded, but nothing had really been settled. Neither of them seemed to know what to do to make things better.

"Look," she whispered, "we're both tired and overwrought.''

"Yes," he said, jumping at the excuse so quickly it heightened her concerns. "We're probably not thinking clearly. Let's get some sleep. Everything will look a lot better in the morning.''

Beth thought about how many times she'd told a patient that very thing, and wondered if they felt as suspicious of it as she did right now.

She and Tony used separate bathrooms, then crawled into the same bed. He kissed her good-night, and then they turned onto their sides, facing opposite directions. Her body relaxed eventually, but her mind was more difficult to put to sleep. She reminded herself that she'd put in a grueling two days preparing the house and food for her family's visit. Maybe Tony was right. Maybe they weren't thinking clearly. Maybe the fact that he couldn't talk about her infertility didn't mean that he'd never accept it. Maybe bringing it up tonight hadn't put an irreparable rift in their fragile relationship.

Maybe everything really would look better in the morning.

Morning didn't bring any magical revelations or miracle cures to their dilemma. Tony woke up to his alarm and groggily got out of bed while Beth went to feed the baby. They came face-to-face in the hall, giving each other a wide berth as if by unspoken, mutual agreement.

Christopher had awakened every two-and-a-half hours throughout the night. Each time she'd fed and changed him, she thought about what would have happened if Tony hadn't agreed to marry her, thereby giving this beautiful little boy a two-parent home, and her the opportunity to be his mother. Lord, how she wished she'd left the skeleton of her infertility in the closet. But each time she'd crawled back into bed, she was more convinced that she and Tony had to talk about this, to make peace with it, so they'd know where to go from here.

She'd believed Tony when he'd said he wanted to be a father to Christopher. He wasn't going to divorce her before the adoption was final. But what about later? Could they build a real marriage on the legality of their union? Or would he always wish things could have been different? With another woman, they could be. Barry had certainly proved that. Her first husband had hurt her in nearly every emotional way, making her feel guilty for something that she had no control over. Barry had once said that it was her body that wasn't functioning properly. It was her body that prohibited conception. And on a subliminal level, in some perverse way that wasn't fair, Barry had believed that *that* made it her fault.

She'd come to terms with her own body's inadequacies, had made peace with her fate. None of it had come without scars, or pain or resolutions. The most important thing was the promise she'd made to herself to be honest about her feelings, and to expect others to be honest in return.

Pipes rumbled overhead as the shower was turned off. She quickly started the coffee, then hurried to the back bathroom where she combed her hair, washed her face and brushed her teeth. By the time she returned to the kitchen, the coffee was done and her resolve was firmly in place.

She turned at the sound of footsteps behind her. "Good morning," she called as cheerily as she could manage.

"Good morning," he replied, eyeing her cautiously.

"Are you ready to talk this morning?"

He lumbered past her on his way to the coffeemaker with a dark look and a mumbled "There's nothing to talk about."

"Come on, Tony," she cajoled. "You must have some idea in your mind of what you'll be doing a year from now, or five, or ten. Am I there with you? Or do you see a faceless woman and more children?"

"This is ridiculous."

"Is it? Can you look me in the eye and honestly tell me that you haven't paused for a moment while we were making love, that you haven't thought about the fact that you couldn't make me pregnant?"

He set his mug down so hard coffee sloshed over the side. "What do you want me to say, Beth?"

"The truth."

"I don't know what I see in my future a year from now, or in five years, or ten. And that's the honest-to-God truth."

Beth closed her eyes for a moment, wishing she were more like Janet, who never rocked the boat, or made waves, or got herself into a situation that had no clear and easy way out.

"Look," he said, running a hand through his damp hair. "This is getting us nowhere. Let's forget about it and just go on the way we were."

"I can't do that."

"Why the hell not?"

"Because," she said, imploring him with her eyes, "I thought I would die of hurt and heartache when Barry left me. But I didn't. As time went on, I realized that my life with him had been a lie. What you and I are doing for Christopher and Annie feels good and honorable and right. It feels like destiny, but I need to keep the truth in front of me, so I know where I'm going, and why."

He heaved a great sigh. "Where does that leave us?"

"Between the proverbial rock and a hard place. I'll move my clothes back into the spare room later this morning."

"What?"

She wanted to explain to him that if she continued to have sex with him, she was going to fall in love with him. And she just didn't think she could live through being thrown away twice for the same reason. But she became tongue-tied and ended up saying, "I think it would be best."

"Best?" he bellowed.

"Less awkward."

"I think I should have some say in this," he declared, his voice rising. "We're married, and we should sleep in the same bed, dammit. If you don't want me to make love to you, I won't. I'm not some rutting teenager, you know. I'm old enough to control my own lust."

When she didn't answer, Tony stalked to the door and slammed it behind him.

He arrived at the hospital with his tie loose and his cuffs unbuttoned, wondering what in the hell had happened last night. One minute he'd been contemplating what he was going to do when he took Beth to bed, and the next thing he knew, they were talking about whether or not he saw her in his future. No wonder her mother didn't understand her. Bethany Kent Petrocelli was one obstinate, contrary woman.

He buttoned his cuffs and reached for his suit jacket,

thinking that wasn't entirely fair or true. Beth was beautiful
and smart and thoughtful. That was the problem. She
thought too much. How was he supposed to know how he
felt about the fact that she couldn't give him kids of his
own? Did she want him to say he was happy about it? He
sure as hell didn't believe it was a good enough reason to
move her clothes back into the spare bedroom. What was
he going to do about that woman?

He locked his car and headed for the hospital's back
entrance. At least he knew what he was doing at the hospital. Delivering babies and doling out prenatal vitamins
and listening to unborn babies' heartbeats was his forte.
Unfortunately, he didn't have a clue what to do about his
marriage. Not a stinking clue.

Later that morning, after she'd fed Christopher and had
given him his bath, Beth called her brother-in-law and
made an appointment to have a post-nuptial agreement
drawn up. Then she walked upstairs to the bedroom she
shared with Tony, staring at the king-size bed, lost in
thought. She thought for most of the day. She came up with
a lot of questions, but no revelations or resolutions.

Tony arrived home shortly after six. They shared dinner
and made polite conversation. When he was called to the
hospital to deliver a baby a few minutes before eight, they
both breathed a secret sigh of relief at the reprieve.

By the time Tony returned home, it was after midnight.
He took the stairs two at a time, pausing in the doorway
of his bedroom, where Beth was sound asleep. She hadn't
moved her things back to the spare bedroom. Being careful
not to make too much noise releasing another pent-up sigh
of relief, he checked on Christopher, then undressed and
crawled into bed.

There was absolutely no reason he shouldn't have fallen
asleep immediately. Beth didn't jostle the bed. And he
couldn't smell her perfume or shampoo, or feel her warmth.

She was too far away. But he knew she was there. And sleep was going to be a long time coming.

Beth opened her eyes and lay staring into the darkness, wondering if Tony would reach for her or whisper good-night. He did neither, tossing and turning on his side of the bed while she lay motionless on hers. The line had been drawn, and neither of them knew how to cross it.

MacKenzie worked her into his schedule on Tuesday, fitting her between a sticky divorce and a property dispute that was turning into a feud that rivaled the Hatfields and the McCoys. She thought her brother-in-law looked tired, but she didn't tell him as much. In return, he asked her questions regarding the document she wanted him to draw up. As was their family's way, he handled himself with a certain understated finesse and didn't delve too deeply into her personal life or emotions.

Tuesday night seemed to take forever, as did Wednesday. Beth and Tony had dinner together both evenings. They talked about the baby, the weather, his work, but there were long stretches of silence when they faced each other, quiet and uncertain. They said good-night after crawling into bed together, but they didn't kiss, and they didn't make love.

Thursday morning, Beth picked up the legal document. After strapping Christopher into his car seat in the car, tears gathered in her eyes. They seemed to come out of nowhere with so much force she couldn't stop them. Christopher stared up at her, his expression so serious she cried harder, promising him that everything would be all right all the while.

When the tears finally stopped, she dried her face and kissed the baby tenderly. And then she went to the Silver Gypsy to see Jenna.

Christopher was fascinated with the faint purl of wind chimes and the brightly colored scarves overhead. "Just look at him," Jenna exclaimed. "He's getting a double chin."

Beth smiled. "He's gained half a pound since we brought him home."

"He looks healthy, all right. You, on the other hand, look like hell."

Pretending to be interested in one of the new necklaces Jenna had designed, Beth shrugged. "In order for Christopher to put on weight, someone has to feed him. Often. I'm running low on sleep these days, that's all."

Jenna made a most unbecoming sound. "What a crock. You're one of those people whose eyes become luminous when you're tired, and you know it. Come on," she said, swishing through the beads in the doorway leading to the tiny back room. "We'll brew a pot of tea and you can tell Auntie Jenna all about what's bothering you."

Jenna was three years younger than Beth and looked about as auntlike as a sheikh's belly dancer. Her long black hair swished when she walked, her strappy sandals showcasing small feet and narrow ankles. She was five three and had once said she'd been built low to the ground for easier maneuverability. Suddenly Beth found herself sitting at the tiny glass table in one corner, sipping strong tea and telling Jenna about her married life with Tony.

"We're both miserable," she said, nearing the end of her account. "We're so fidgety and edgy and polite, I want to scream."

"Of course you're fidgety. You're sleeping with a man who can't touch you."

"Do you think I should move back to the spare bedroom?"

Jenna snorted. "Few marriages work without sex, especially when one of the parties involved is nicknamed the Italian Stallion. I think you should take up where you left off several days ago."

Beth shook her head. "That's interesting advice coming from someone who hasn't had a date in years."

Jenna's brown eyes twinkled like her Gypsy ancestors as she said, "We're not talking about my sex life. We're talking about yours. It's a good thing, because I haven't taken a man home in so long I hardly remember who puts what where. Be a pal and refresh my memory. Details would be good. Lots and lots of details."

Beth threw a linen napkin at her and took another sip of her tea. "I don't think I can go back to the way things were before."

"Why not?"

When Beth didn't answer, Jenna nodded knowingly. "Aaah. I think I'm beginning to understand. You're afraid of getting hurt. But you can't guard your heart against falling in love, Beth, no matter how hard you try. If it happens, it happens. You'll have to accept it, along with the risks that go with it."

Her best friend's advice may have been well intended and sound, but Beth didn't know if she could follow it. Maybe marriages couldn't work without sex, and maybe she couldn't protect herself from being hurt. But now that she'd thrown this up between her and Tony, she didn't know how to get past it.

"I don't know, Jenna. I want my relationship with Tony to be more than just sex between two consenting adults. I want emotion and passion."

Jenna narrowed her eyes and lowered her chin. "Oh, my God. You want the fairy tale. Just remember how uncomfortable glass slippers would get in the long haul."

Shaking her head at Jenna's terminology, Beth said, "I don't know how you've made it this long without meeting a man who can match you wit for wit."

"There are none out there. Believe me, I've looked. Just remember the reason you got married in the first place."

"For Christopher," Beth said quietly.

"For Christopher," Jenna seconded.

Propping her chin in her hand, Beth said, "How is it that you always seem to be able to keep sight of what's important?"

Jenna flicked her hair behind her shoulders and busied herself at the tiny sink. "It's a curse. And that's exactly what I'm going to put on you if you don't get out of here and let me get some work done."

"You're the best, Jenna."

Jenna rattled off something in another language. With a mild shake of her head, Beth settled Christopher in the crook of her left arm and reached into the gigantic purse she carried these days. Fumbling around for a diaper and an extra bottle, she drew her hand out. "Here," she said, pressing a tissue into Jenna's fingers. "You missed a tear in the corner of your eye."

It took a lot to render Jenna Maria Brigante speechless. Beth rather enjoyed it, but since she didn't need a hex added to her list of problems, she and Christopher went home. She spent the rest of the morning wondering what she would do if she actually allowed herself to fall in love only to have Tony decide he couldn't live with the fact that he was never going to bring a child of his own into the world.

It's what Barry had done, she thought, rocking Christopher later that afternoon. The baby turned his face into the crook of her neck and sighed as if he had everything he needed. In that instant she realized that this situation was very different from her situation with Barry. When he'd left her she'd had no one. Now she had Christopher, and as soon as the adoption was final, nobody would ever be able to take him from her. Jenna was right. No matter what happened between her and Tony, Christopher would always be her son.

Nine

Tony entered his house the way he always did, via the back door. Trudging into the kitchen, he dropped his jacket over a chair and glanced around for a sign of Beth. She was nowhere in sight, but the kitchen was immaculate. In fact, the only things out of place were an empty baby bottle and a used teacup by the sink. A legal-looking document on the table caught his eye. With a sense of dread he understood all too well, he strode on over for a closer look. He scanned the top page and scowled. He'd been doing a lot of that this week, so much in fact that the people at the hospital had started steering clear of him. He could handle their furtive glances and obvious sidesteps, but the next person who asked him if he'd been taking ornery lessons from Abigail Horton was going to get a piece of his mind.

As per Florence Donahue's instructions, he'd rearranged his work schedule so he could be here to care for Christopher while Beth worked. Normally she worked on the weekend, but this time she was working the Thursday afternoon shift. A quick glance at his watch told him he'd arrived home with a few minutes to spare. Deciding that Beth was probably still getting ready, he headed for the stairs.

The entire house was quiet, except for the occasional note of a home-sung lullaby filtering down the open staircase. He'd heard her sing to the baby before, but he'd never known a lullaby to be desire-inducing. Man, he had it bad.

Following the sound of that low, sultry voice, he strode

to the doorway of Christopher's room. Beth was waltzing the baby around the room in a dance so slow and graceful it made his lungs feel too large for his chest. Christopher's eyes were open, but Beth's were closed, the expression on her face dreamy and full of maternal love.

She was wearing her nursing uniform. Although a lot of nurses wore pants these days, Beth usually wore a dress. It seemed fitting somehow, considering her upbringing. The material looked soft, as if it had been washed a hundred times, the fabric following the graceful contours of her slender body. A shudder went through him, a direct result of all the days of watching her, of wanting her and not having her.

She placed Christopher on the changing table, completely oblivious to his presence and to the chaotic turn his hormones had taken. "Whoever said there was no such thing as love at first sight?" she crooned, unfastening the baby's tiny pajamas. "I took one look at you, and I was lost, yes I was."

Tony stood motionless, listening to the lull of her voice. Her smile enticed, her eyes danced. He'd never seen so much emotion, had never heard so much tenderness, had never witnessed so much pure pleasure in another woman's features. That tiny baby brought Beth to life as a mother, and in a way Tony had never thought about before, Chris brought her to life as a woman, too.

The desire Tony had been fighting changed subtly, only to be replaced with something he liked a lot less. Jealousy. He ground his teeth together, calling himself every name in the book. What kind of man was jealous of the attention his wife paid to an innocent child? A man who hadn't made love to his wife in almost a week, that's who. If that didn't change soon, he was going to go out of his mind.

Beth must have noticed the glide of his hand into his pocket, because she looked up, her smile nearly buckling his knees. "Are you ready to tackle your first night alone with your son?" she asked.

That wasn't all Tony was ready for.

He almost snorted. "What's the matter? Don't you think I can handle it?"

Beth's chin came up like a whiplash, her eyes searching Tony's face. He looked a tad ornery. He'd been looking like that a lot lately. Swallowing, she glanced at Christopher, and suddenly she felt unsure. "Maybe I should call in sick."

"I deliver babies for a living, Beth. I think I'm qualified to handle Chris for one evening, for crying out loud."

Of course, she thought to herself. Tony was extremely qualified to care for Christopher on his own. She was being paranoid. It was just that in the almost two weeks they'd had him, Christopher had never been out of her care, and these last few days, Tony had been as grouchy as a bear with a sore paw.

"I know you're qualified," she said, instilling her voice with as much calmness as she could muster.

"At least we agree on something."

She didn't allow herself to stare, mouth gaping, at the man she'd married. Instead, she went back to the task of diapering Christopher, snapping his sleeper as if she'd been doing it all her life.

"Tony," she said, finishing the task, "I know you're perfectly able to handle Christopher tonight, but if you're too tired or if you run into problems or simply want some company, your mother and two of your sisters offered to baby-sit."

Tony shook his head slowly, feeling like a kid who'd just had a temper tantrum in a public place. Strolling farther into the room, he said, "I know. I'll keep them in mind for backup, but like Mrs. Donahue said, this will be good bonding time for Chris and me."

She seemed to study his expression for a long time. Either she didn't realize that his face had been so prone to frowns all week that the smile he was trying to give her hurt, or she was too prudent to comment, because she smiled in return and placed Christopher in his arms.

"He just finished eating, so he should be ready for a nap soon. If he needs a clean sleeper, they're in this drawer. The extra blankets are here."

"Beth."

She stopped talking and turned to look at him.

"We'll be fine. I'll feed one end and diaper the other. I promise to take good care of him. Now, go. You're going to be late."

Christopher let out a little squawk as if to accent Tony's statement. Beth looked from one to the other, evidently realizing that the baby was in good hands. She strode toward them, lithely leaning down to whisper a kiss on Christopher's forehead. Tony held his breath, wondering if she was going to do the same to him. When she turned, calling goodbye over her shoulder, he told himself he wasn't disappointed.

From the doorway, she said, "Do you have any questions?"

He shook his head. "How about you?"

Her gaze slid from his, then slowly climbed back to his face. "There is one thing."

"Yes?"

"I was just wondering if you've been spending time with Abigail Horton."

She didn't wait around for his comment. That was okay. He didn't know what he would have said, anyway.

The scent of her expensive perfume lingered in the room after she left, the expression on her face lingering in his mind even longer. He wondered if she'd been aware of the smile that had stolen across her face at her stab at wry humor. He wondered if she'd had any idea what that smile of hers had done to him.

Tony thought about scowling, but he looked down at Christopher, who was staring up at him, and he smiled, instead. He hadn't taken lessons from Abigail Horton, no matter what anybody said. But old Abigail could have taken a tip or two from him this past week.

"Bye, you two," Beth called up the stairs. "See you shortly after eleven."

"We'll be here," Tony answered.

By the time he walked to the top of the stairs, the foyer was empty. Moments later he heard the back door close. "Well, kid," he said to Christopher. "It looks like it's just you and me. Bethany said she'll be back around eleven. We should be able to handle things for the next eight hours without too much trouble, right?"

The baby stared up at him silently.

"That's okay. You don't have to answer. I know what you're thinking. This should be a piece of cake."

A piece of cake, hell, Tony thought, stiffly switching Christopher to his other shoulder. The baby cried when he jiggled him. The baby cried when he patted him. He cried when he laid him down and picked him up. He'd been crying for the better part of the past three hours. And Tony was at the end of his rope.

Chris wouldn't eat. He wouldn't sleep. He wouldn't burp.

It was like his and Beth's wedding night all over again. Tony racked his brain trying to remember what Beth had done that night and every night since. She'd made it all look so easy.

"Easy, my eye," he murmured in Christopher's ear.

Christopher seemed to listen. Was it possible that his cries were beginning to wind down as he drew in a shuddering breath? Was his little body relaxing, his knees straightening slightly, his muscles softening just a little? Tony was almost afraid to hope.

"That's better," he murmured, to himself or Chris, he wasn't sure.

The baby turned his head toward the sound of the masculine voice. He stared up at Tony's face. Tony held his breath. Before his very eyes, Christopher's lower lip jutted out in a little pout and his chin started to quiver. And then holy hell broke loose all over again. Tears squeezed out of his eyes and a high-pitched cry worse than fingernails on a chalkboard bellowed from his throat.

"What are you doing to that poor kid?" Gib yelled from the doorway.

Tony jumped, which startled Christopher, making him cry all the harder. Tony swore under his breath. "What does it look like I'm doing to him?"

"Can't you make him stop?"

Tony shot his best friend a penetrating look. Gib, who had grown used to Tony's moody side years ago, limped into the room. "Maybe a pin's poking him."

Tony snorted. A lot of help Gib was going to be. He may have been an expert in tactical maneuvers, but he didn't even know that babies rarely wore diapers with pins anymore.

Tony knew he could have called his mother or any one of his sisters for help. But they'd surely recognize the strain in him, and he simply wasn't willing to discuss his sex life, or his lack of a sex life, with the females in his family. So, he'd called Gib. At the time, it had seemed like a logical course of action. Now he wasn't so sure.

All six foot two, two hundred and twenty pounds of Gibson Malone was looking bewildered and extremely unhelpful. "Maybe he's hungry."

"Of course he's hungry," Tony answered. "He hasn't eaten in more than three hours."

"Then, why don't you feed him, for crying out loud?"

Gee, Tony thought to himself. Why hadn't he thought of that?

Realizing that they weren't going to solve anything by shouting at each other over the top of Chris's dark head, Tony took a deep, calming breath and lowered his voice. "He won't eat for me. He wants Beth. He's not the only one."

Gib leaned heavily on his cane, his eyebrows the only part of him moving. Not much got past Gib Malone. Tony had a feeling he was going to pay for that little slip of the tongue. But right now, with Christopher screaming his mad little head off, Tony didn't care. Right now, he had a baby to take care of. It shouldn't have been so difficult. He'd handled hundreds of babies. Now that he thought about it, most of those had been screaming, too. Great. He brought babies into the world screaming, and he seemed to have the same effect on his new son.

"Here," Gib muttered. "Let me try. Maybe the hair on your chest is tickling him. Where's your shirt, anyway?"

Tony didn't see much sense in explaining that he'd evidently left Chris uncovered too long when he'd been changing his diaper. The wet shirt had been a surprise, but the kid had a darned good aim.

He placed the wriggling infant in Gib's big hands. "He's strong, but you've still got to support his head."

Gib's mouth dropped open, a look of wonder crossing his face. "I can hardly tell I'm holding anything. How much does he weigh?"

"Just under six pounds."

Tony removed his eyes from Christopher long enough to glance at his friend. Gib's blond hair looked freshly washed and was secured at the back of his head in a stubby little ponytail. His face was clean-shaven. The man had seen horrors he wasn't at liberty to discuss. Right now, his hazel eyes, eyes that were as changeable as the seasons, were trained on Chris. "He's got a lot of cry for a six-pounder."

Tony told himself there was absolutely no reason he should suddenly feel taller, broader, stronger. No reason why he should feel so, so proud. But he straightened his shoulders and fought the urge to ruffle Gib's hair, anyway. "Yeah. He's always been a fighter. He's an amazing little kid."

Feeling strangely uncomfortable with his new set of emotions, he reached for Chris, saying, "Here. He's a baby, not a live grenade."

Gib handed the baby over willingly. "Then, I guess throwing myself on top of him is out of the question."

Tony laughed, the sound rumbling and burgeoning from deep inside. Whether it was the sound or the vibration or the feeling that he was safe, Christopher stopped crying. Just like that, the room became quiet.

Silence. Hell, it was golden. Silver, bronze and platinum all rolled into one.

"What happened?" Gib whispered incredulously.

Making a sound that was half sigh, half moan, all feeling, Tony said, "I think my son and I just reached a little understanding. Come on downstairs, Malone. Something tells me he'll drink his bottle now. And then he'll probably sleep for a couple of hours."

"That's good," Gib answered, following more slowly. "Maybe that will give you enough time to explain why your wife had a marriage contract drawn up, and why you look frustrated enough to bite somebody's head off."

Autumn was in the air, and so was blessed silence.

Tony and Gib were sitting on the patio on the wicker furniture Martin Smith had helped move from Beth's place less than two weeks ago. Now that Chris was sound asleep in his crib upstairs, the night was infinitely quiet, beautifully, amazingly, wonderfully quiet. Lights were coming on in houses up and down the street. The stars weren't out yet, but the moon was full, and lights twinkled from the windows of the cabins sparsely dotting the face of the mountain.

"Whew," Gib whispered, propping his left leg on a low stool. "It only took one six-pound baby to do what it usually takes a tall, voluptuous blonde to do. That kid of yours wiped me out. Wore me down. Turned me weak in the knees. If you're lucky, I might have enough energy left to listen to what's bothering you. So why don't you tell me what's going on, why you look ready to hit somebody, and what it all has to do with that marriage contract I happened to leaf through when I first arrived."

Running a hand through his hair, Tony took a deep breath and eyed his friend. He hadn't planned to confide in anyone about this, but suddenly he wanted to tell Gib. He didn't really know where to start, so he started at the beginning. "I don't know how to explain it, but something strange happened to me the night Christopher was born...."

Gib nodded every once in a while and asked the occasional question. For the most part, he listened, taking it all in, piecing it all together. Tony told him about the zing that had gone through him immediately after he and Bethany had helped Annie Moore bring Christopher into the world. He explained how Beth had asked him to marry her and why, and everything else that had happened since. When he'd finished the entire, sordid story, neither man said anything for several minutes.

Finally, Gib spoke. "You've gotta find a way to tell her you're sorry, man. You *are* sorry, aren't you?"

Tony was leaning ahead in his chair, his elbows on his thighs, his chin propped on his hands. Staring out into the darkness of his backyard, he said, "I'm sorry as hell. I'm just not sure what for."

Gib shook his head and reached for the drink he'd been nursing for the past hour. "It looks to me as if Beth's Achilles heel is her inability to have biological children. You found her most tender area and stomped on it."

"I didn't mean to."

Tony was glad Chris was upstairs, too far away to hear

Gib's reply, because he'd really hate his son's first word to be the four-letter one Gib had just pieced together and spit out so eloquently.

"That's probably what Roosevelt said right after the A-bomb blew a hundred thousand innocent people to smith-ereens," Gib declared.

Analogies such as that one were what had gotten Gib in trouble with the Marine Corps years ago. It was one of the reasons he'd gone to work for a private agency. Although Tony didn't appreciate the analogy any more than the armed services would have, he couldn't fault Gib for his insight.

Heaving a huge sigh, Tony leaned back in his chair, deep in thought. Things had been a little crazy lately. He grimaced at the understatement. Hell, marrying a woman he barely knew was more than a little crazy. He'd followed his instincts, and look where it had gotten him. He was beginning to realize it was going to take more than gut instinct to get him out of the stalemate he'd reached with Beth.

He'd hurt her, plain and simple. And Gib was right. He was going to have to tell her he was sorry, in words, or in deeds, or in any way it took.

"What are you going to do?" Gib asked.

Tony scrubbed a hand over his eyes. "I'm going to take your advice."

Gib finished his drink and rose to his feet with the help of his cane. "No need to thank me. Just make me Christopher's godfather and we'll be even. How long before the kid wakes up again, anyway?"

"It's hard to say, but it'll probably be soon."

"This goes on all day and all night? The feeding and the diapers and the feeding and the diapers?"

When Tony nodded, Gib shook his head. "That's why I *always* carry protection."

"One of these days you're going to meet someone who

can resist you, Malone. And you know what they say. The mightier they are, the harder they fall.''

Gib flashed his thousand-watt smile. ''I fall all the time. For tall blondes, and tall brunettes, and tall redheads.''

Tony ran his hand across his face and on down his bare chest. ''Spare me the details, will you? I'm having a hard enough time keeping my hormones in check these days. Now, go on, get out of here, so I can work on my apology to my wife. Oh, and Malone? I'll talk to Beth about Christopher's baptism, but I'd be honored if you'd be his godfather.''

Placing a fist to his own chest, Gib swallowed, hard, then slowly made his way around the back of the sprawling old house to the driveway where he'd parked his Jeep. Tony watched him go. In all the years he'd known Gibson Malone, he'd never seen him speechless. Until now.

When Tony smiled this time, he noticed it didn't feel half bad.

Beth let herself in the back door, unsure of what she would find. The house was dark, except for the light over the stove. Dishes were stacked in the sink; a soggy kitchen towel was balled up on the counter. The place looked a little messy, but no worse for wear.

Although she'd thought about Tony and Christopher a hundred times, she was amazed at how little she'd worried. She'd seen Tony with his nieces and nephews, and she knew Christopher was in good hands. Of course, the fact that the emergency room had been crawling with patients had helped pass her time. Although Jenna always claimed it was obvious, Beth didn't know why so many people did so many dangerous things when the moon was full.

There were no lights on in the living room or in the foyer, but the moon was bright enough to light her way. Anxious to find out how things had gone for Tony and

Christopher, she slipped out of her shoes, and her footsteps on the stairs were quick and light.

She stood in the center of the hall, their bedroom on her left, Christopher's on her right. She glanced into the room lit up by the faint glow of a night-light first. Finding the room empty, she padded to the doorway of the room she shared with Tony. She paused, her head tilting automatically, her arms gliding around her waist.

Tony was sprawled out in the easy chair that was tucked into one of the many nooks in this big house. Christopher was nestled on Tony's chest, his only blanket the weight of his new father's hand. They were both scantily dressed—the baby in a diaper and T-shirt, the man in navy boxers and nothing else. Both looked blessedly warm, and relaxed, and peaceful.

Soft-touched thoughts shaped Beth's smile. Something shifted in her chest, spreading outward like waves on a quiet shore. The lamp near the bed was turned to its lowest setting, casting a faint glow over everything it touched. She strode farther into the room, stopping only when her right foot came into contact with the cold, wet dress shirt lying on the floor. She reached down, smiling to herself at the probable cause.

Now that she looked around, she saw that the place was a mess. Sleepers littered the floor, a baby blanket dangled from the bed, and what looked like a torn, dry diaper was hanging, half on, half off the dresser. Two partially empty baby bottles and a half-full one were lying on the floor near Tony's chair. It looked like a cyclone had swept through the room. Poor baby, she thought, glancing at Christopher's puckered little mouth. Staring at the shadows Tony's lashes cast on his cheeks, she whispered, "Poor babies."

Drawing in a deep breath, she felt a lingering vibration, like emotions tugging on her heartstrings.

Uncertain of her growing feelings and reluctant to disturb

Tony and Christopher's sleep, she tiptoed to the closet for her robe, then headed for the shower.

She stripped out of her clothes, tucked her hair into a shower cap and raised her face to the soft shower spray. The warm water washed away the last remnants of the evening's work, but it didn't lessen the fullness in her chest or take away the flutter in her heartbeat.

When she was finished, she turned off the shower, dried herself with a clean towel and donned her long robe before padding back to the bedroom. With the gentlest of movements, she lifted Tony's hand from Christopher's back. Instead of dropping easily to his side, his hand closed around hers. Her breath caught in her throat, her gaze on his face.

"I thought you were asleep," she whispered.

"I was."

His eyes opened, and she was almost sure she could feel herself slipping right in. "Rough night?"

He shook his head. "Rough week."

He made no move to release her hand, but his gaze strayed to her lips, down to her throat and on to the V-neckline of her robe. Leaning over him as she was, Beth knew he had a clear view of her breasts. Her throat convulsed as she tried to swallow, and Tony's gaze followed the movement back to her eyes.

"I thought I'd put Christopher in his bed. I didn't mean to wake you," she whispered.

"I've been waiting for you."

"You have?"

"I'm sorry."

She closed her eyes against the tears swimming there. Opening them again, she stared into his eyes. She knew Tony Petrocelli was a private man, a man who wasn't comfortable with people traipsing thought his thought processes. And yet his eyes were open wide, letting her look her fill.

Jenna had told her it was impossible to guard her heart

from being broken, impossible to guard against falling in love. Even while she was drowning in the dark, murky desire in Tony's eyes, even while they somehow managed to walk into Chris's room and tuck him into his crib and lovingly cover him with a soft blanket, even when Tony took her hand once again, she told herself Jenna was wrong. She could guard her heart. She could.

She'd never remember exactly how they came to be standing at the foot of the big bed. Perhaps they'd walked, or maybe they'd floated there. All she knew was that Tony hadn't stopped looking at her, and she had to remind herself, every couple of minutes or so, to breathe.

He put his arms around her, and she let him. She knew she shouldn't, not if she wanted to keep the tenacious hold she had on her emotions, not to mention on her heart. But she let him, anyway, for the plain and simple reason that it felt good. She wasn't going to turn all poetic and imagine that she'd found heaven in his arms and a haven in the little nook between his neck and shoulder where she rested her cheek. There was nothing heavenly or poetic about any of this. He didn't love her. And she didn't love him. He was just a man, and she was just a woman. That's all they were, a man and a woman, holding each other in a dimly lit room.

He shifted away from her slightly so that he could bring his hand up to her face. "I've missed you, and I'm so sorry I hurt you. I signed the contract you left for me, although I have no intention of holding you to it. In fact, there's only one thing I intend to hold you to."

He moved against her so there was no question in her mind about his meaning. She closed her eyes. See? she told herself. She was safe, her heart, her mind, her emotions. She could have sex with her husband without turning poetic and falling in love, even when the moon was full.

He removed the clasp from her hair, the heavy tendrils falling around her shoulders. "Beautiful," he whispered. "So beautiful."

The tenderness in his voice sent a sweet ache all the way through her, the yearning in his dark eyes shaping her lips around a soft smile. Her eyes fluttered down in direct response to the brush of his lips along her cheek, her ear, her neck.

"Is it okay with you if we ask Gib to be Chris's godfather?"

Beth heard the words, really she did. She even felt the tickle of his breath on her skin. But in her hazy state, she couldn't seem to understand their meaning. "Gib?"

"He came over tonight. And I sort of already asked him."

Beth laughed, the release it brought her infinitely sweet. They could do this, she thought. They could have a real marriage based on their mutual love for Christopher, and on respect, and passion, without pretending that the wind was singing through the cottonwoods or that there was magic in the moonbeams spilling onto the bed.

He drew her face up, one finger beneath her chin, lowering his head at the same time. "Ah, Beth," he murmured so close to her mouth she felt the words on her own lips. "I want you. Only you."

In that instant before his mouth covered hers, the wind sang through the trees, the breeze teasing the curtain at the window. Somewhere, an owl hooted in the moonlight. Far, far away, another owl answered. It was magical, as magical as the sound Tony made against her lips, half moan, half impatience. Beth sighed in return, parting her lips, deepening the kiss.

His fingers worked her sash free, parting her robe. She gasped at the first brush of his fingers on her breast, her gasp turning into a moan when he took them both into his hands. Her gown fell to the floor with a quiet swish, his shorts following in one sure swipe.

"Tony?" she whispered, crawling to the center of the bed.

Half sitting, half lying in the moonlight spilling across the quilt, he looked up at her. Slowly raising his head, he kissed her, sighing against her mouth. "Hmm?" His lips moved down to her chin, then farther, and farther.

Her head lolled back, her eyes opening to the moonbeams slanting through the window. "Never mind. I'll tell you later."

His laughter rumbled from deep inside him. "Later, we're going to do this again."

Beth smiled, but what he did next replaced her smile with a deep, earthy moan.

"I've been waiting all week to hear you make that sound," he whispered huskily. "But I can't wait another minute to do this."

Ten

Tony didn't know whether to whistle or grin. He breathed in the rich aroma of piping-hot coffee and let his mouth make the decision for him. Placing two mugs of coffee, two glasses of orange juice, two bagels and—because it had been a couple of hours since Chris had eaten—one warm bottle of formula on a tray, he started for the stairs, his lips shaped to a mellow whistle.

Oh, what a difference a day could make. He woke up smiling a little over an hour ago. He'd thought about waking Beth, had in fact already lifted a hand to do just that, but she'd looked so relaxed and serene and peaceful, he'd decided not to. He hadn't always been so thoughtful. At least he hadn't been when he'd awakened her at 2:00 a.m.

Beth didn't appear to have moved in his absence. He placed the tray on the stand on his side of the bed. Being careful not to do a lot of jostling, he stacked some pillows behind him, reached for one of the many medical journals that had a way of piling up and settled down to drink his coffee and do a little catching up. Hot coffee, great sex and interesting reading. Life was definitely good.

Beth felt as if she was floating, coming awake a layer at a time. She became aware of the scent of fresh coffee first, and then of the sound of papers rustling. Her pillow felt blessedly soft, the sheets warm and smooth. She opened her eyes slowly and smiled the same way, enjoying the opportunity to look at the man she'd married.

Tony appeared to be lost in some magazine, alternately

turning pages and sipping his coffee. He had broad shoulders, strong arms and a washboard stomach. She knew, because she'd kissed every single ridge last night. His chest was bare, and although he was covered to his waist, she doubted he was wearing anything beneath the sheets. Barry had slept in monogrammed pajamas. Tony Petrocelli slept in the nude. If she'd had any doubts regarding the vast differences between the only two men she'd ever slept with, she didn't anymore. She'd loved Barry, but their life together had been sedate, organized, and so had their sex life. There was nothing organized about the things Tony had done to her, or about the things she'd done in return.

If she'd ever known she had a penchant for wild sex, it had been squashed in her formative years and forgotten in her quest to conceive a child. Last night, Tony had brought it out into the open, and Lord, she was still amazed. She didn't know if he'd harbored any thoughts about protection last night. She'd been beyond caring, lost in a world of touch and texture, of whispers and sighs. *She* certainly hadn't given any thought to becoming pregnant. For that she was so grateful. He'd given something to her last night and again in the wee hours of the morning, something she hadn't realized she'd been missing. He'd drawn a wildness from deep inside her, then proceeded to ignite it, stoke it, take it, only to give it back again with more feeling than she'd dreamed was possible.

The man had been incredible. *She'd* been incredible.

She moved ever so slowly, arching her back and stretching her legs, the slight tenderness in her muscles testimony to a night to remember. She'd promised herself she wouldn't become poetic, but somewhere around midnight, she was certain she'd known how heaven sounded, and tasted, and felt.

Tony put his paper down and smiled. "Good morning, beautiful."

Silently, Beth could admit that she'd been incredible last

night, but she drew the line at the slightest possibility that she looked beautiful first thing in the morning with her hair tangled and her face lacking makeup. Since she'd learned how futile arguing with Tony Petrocelli could be, she fluffed her pillows and accepted the mug he handed to her.

They sipped their coffee in companionable silence, although Tony's hand seemed to be inching closer and closer to her thigh. He stilled at the first squeak from Christopher's room. They both straightened, but Tony was the first to swing his feet off the bed. "You finish your coffee and leave everything else to me."

She'd been right about what he *hadn't* been wearing. Naked, he moved with an easy grace and a maleness she'd never witnessed before, strolling from the room without a backward glance. The man really didn't have a self-conscious cell in his body.

He must have bumped the musical mobile on Christopher's crib, because it jingled for a few seconds. He said something to the baby, who answered with a couple of squawks, which was followed up with a series of thunks that made Beth wonder what in the world was going on in there. Minutes later, Tony was back, a freshly diapered, wide-eyed baby tucked into the crook of one arm.

"You know," she said, watching as he strolled around to his side of the bed, "for a man who grew up in a family of women, you're awfully uninhibited."

He shrugged one shoulder. "It's a gift."

She wasn't surprised he hadn't said, "If you've got it, flaunt it." Bragging wasn't Tony Petrocelli's style.

Their gazes met, their smiles hovering on their lips long after they looked away. Accepting Christopher from his outstretched arms, Beth thought it felt right, it felt good to be sharing with this man.

"By the way," he said, handing her the bottle he'd warmed ten minutes earlier, "you're looking at the new head of obstetrics of Vanderbilt Memorial. Noah told me about the board's decision yesterday.''

Beth looked up from Christopher, who had clamped onto his breakfast with gusto. ''Tony, that's wonderful. Congratulations. You found a godfather for the baby and were promoted to a new position, all in one day. I'd say you had a very busy day yesterday.''

''It was nothing compared to last night.''

She closed her eyes dreamily, breathing in Christopher's clean scent. Mmm, he smelled sweet, part talcum powder, part natural sweetness, all baby innocence. Glancing from the child in her arms to the man at her side, she smiled.

Tony returned her smile and settled back into bed, reaching for his medical journal with one hand, his coffee with the other, seeming completely and utterly comfortable with himself and their situation. Beth had tried not to plan too far into the future, but it was so easy to imagine the three of them living together, loving together, laughing together for years and years to come. She and Tony would grow closer, and Christopher would slowly grow into a happy, bright, energetic child.

Smiling down at the baby, everything felt right with the world.

''Beth? Have you seen my flowered tie?''

Bethany felt her forehead furrow slightly. *His flowered tie?*

''You'd better go up there,'' her sister said, reaching for Christopher. ''Evidently it's ties with Tony. MacKenzie could never seem to find his favorite cuff links.''

Beth nodded before setting off in the direction of the stairs, but her brow was still furrowed when she paused in the doorway of their bedroom. Crossing her arms, she said, ''I didn't know you had a flowered tie.''

Tony stopped fumbling around in the closet and turned to face her. ''I don't.''

Beth closed her mouth, only to open it again in order to draw a breath into lungs that were suddenly in dire need of oxygen. Tony was looking at her, a vaguely sensuous light in his eyes, a smile of pure masculine intent on his mouth. Just as he had two weeks ago, he'd watched Christopher while she'd worked last night and had risen early to attend a meeting with the head of obstetrics at the hospital in Vail this morning. He'd arrived home fifteen minutes ago, saying he'd only stopped in long enough to change his clothes before making afternoon rounds at Vanderbilt Memorial. The man had every reason to be exhausted, yet he didn't appear to be suffering from lack of sleep.

"You don't have a flowered tie," she repeated.

He shook his head, his eyes taking on a sleepy glint that didn't necessarily mean he was tired. "It was just a ploy to lure you into our bedroom."

"Then, you admit that your motives were less than honorable," she whispered, doing everything in her power not to smile.

He nodded, slowly moving closer. He might have admitted to earthy intentions, but there was no remorse in his expression. His lips were parted slightly, his features as striking and strong as ever, but it was his eyes that held her spellbound. There was warmth in those dark brown eyes, and a lazy, seductive gleam that sent an answering heat all the way through her.

Tony wondered if Beth was aware of the smile that stole across her face. He wondered if she was aware of what that smile of hers was doing to him. He noticed a movement at the corner of her lips and saw the light in her eyes. Oh, she knew what she was doing, all right. And she was enjoying it very, very much. But then, so was he.

He breathed through his mouth and bent one knee in an attempt to ease the fit of his pants. It didn't really help, but he hadn't really expected it to. He didn't mind the desire coursing through him, unspent though it might be, because he knew it was only a matter of time before he had Beth in bed all over again.

This was fun. Hell, it was damned invigorating, this new twist on their old pause, ponder and parley tactics. It had been this way since the night Beth had come home from the hospital two weeks ago. These past few weeks had been like a slow dance of advances and kisses, of warm, secret smiles that led to long, dreamy sessions of making love. Tony had considered himself experienced, yet he'd never experienced anything like it. No matter what he tried, he couldn't seem to get enough.

Beth watched Tony's advance, almost certain her eyes had a mind of their own, drifting partway closed, only to flutter open again. "My sister's right downstairs," she whispered.

"That's too bad." He angled his head toward hers and began the slow descent to her mouth.

Her eyelashes fluttered down again in anticipation of his kiss, only to open when his mouth hovered an inch away from hers. Knowing full well what he was doing, she rose up on tiptoe and took the kiss she wanted.

His hands came around her all at once, hers gliding beneath his open shirt, up his chest where his heart was beating a heavy rhythm. He pulled her hard against him, letting her know without words exactly what she was doing to him.

The kiss broke on a stifled moan from both of them. Pressing a smile along the base of his neck, she whispered, "I'm afraid you're too much man for me, Tony Petrocelli. Half the time I don't know what to do with you."

He took a small step backward, lowering his chin slightly and settling his hands on his hips in that smooth, masculine way he had. He smiled, his eyes growing darker, leaving little doubt what he was thinking. "I have to say I'm partial to the way you're figuring it all out, because whether you know it or not, what you give back is pretty damn powerful.

If your sister wasn't downstairs, I'd show you what I mean, and then you could show me that I'm right.''

"That's what I like about you," she said, tongue in cheek. "You're always so willing to let me show you things."

His advance had little forewarning, the descent of his mouth on hers swift, his kiss possessive and sure. She let her head fall back, her lips open, her arms twining around his neck. She let him kiss her, and hold her, and work her blood into a slow simmer. And when he made a sound deep in his throat, letting her know how much it was costing him to break the kiss, she let him go, although it was far from easy.

"If you don't stop looking at me like that," he said, reaching up to button his shirt, "I'm not going to be held accountable for my actions. I just think you should know that, what with your sister being right downstairs and all."

"What's the matter?" she asked from the doorway. "Don't you think Janet could take it?"

"I'd rather take you."

"Later," she said softly. "Maybe I'll take you up on that gracious offer then."

"Believe me, Beth," he said, working his way down the buttons on his shirt. "There's no maybe about it."

Beth took a calming breath at the bottom of the stairs. By the time she reached the kitchen, she'd smoothed her hair off her forehead and had removed the telltale smile from her face.

Tony popped into the room a few minutes later, only staying long enough to say goodbye and give Beth a long, searing look and a promising sort of kiss. When Beth finally pulled her gaze from the back door, she found Janet watching her, an unreadable expression on her face.

Looking strangely uncertain, Janet visibly pulled herself together and returned to the task of preparing a sandwich for her youngest child. Twisting the lid on the mayonnaise, she said, "Chaz would like to know if you'd mind if he eats his sandwich outdoors. I think he's a little bored with us and the baby."

Glancing from Christopher, who was watching from his infant seat on the counter, to her six-year-old nephew, whose eyes were trained on the toe of his shoe, Beth said, "Of course I don't mind, Chaz. There's a neat old bench next to the driveway that would be a perfect place for an autumn picnic."

Chaz accepted his diagonally sliced sandwiches and headed for the door. "Don't go near the street," his mother called.

"Yes, ma'am."

Beth reached into the refrigerator for the chilled plates of chicken and pineapple salad she'd prepared earlier. Following her to the table with two glasses of ice water containing wedges of lemon, Janet asked, "Did you find Tony's flowered tie?"

Beth shook her head and placed the first plate on the table in her sunny new kitchen.

"He doesn't have a flowered tie, does he?"

The second plate slipped out of Beth's hand, clanking to the table a few inches below. Staring at her sister in amazement, she asked, "How did you know?"

"Because MacKenzie never wore shirts that required cuff links, either. And you have the dreamy look of a woman who's recently been thoroughly kissed."

Sensing an underlying note of sadness in Janet's statement, Bethany gazed across the room at her only sister. Janet's appearance was as impeccable as always, her blouse feminine and soft, the scarf at her neck picking up the auburn streaks in her hair and the warm tone of her skin. Her diamond ring was large, her hands perfectly manicured. Although Janet's features were carefully schooled, Beth was certain she saw tension in her fingers and sadness in her hazel eyes.

This was the second time Beth had seen Janet these past two weeks. The first time she'd brought all three of her children over to see Christopher. Today, she'd suggested meeting Beth for lunch. Since Bethany wasn't comfortable leaving Christopher, she'd invited her sister here. They'd never fought, had rarely argued, even as children, but they'd never been close enough to trade secrets, either. As a result, Beth didn't know how to broach a personal subject now.

Obviously, Janet didn't, either, because she began to talk about her fourteen-year-old son, Mark, her twelve-year-old daughter, Danielle, and six-year-old Charles, or Chaz, as everyone called him. After relaying her children's progress in school, violin lessons and ballet class, she said, "Mother called me a few days ago. She seemed quite taken with Tony."

Lowering her voice to a careful, neutral tone, Beth said, "I'm a bit surprised. Money and social status have never mattered to me, but they matter to Mother. Although Tony's a very respected doctor, he comes from a large, working-class family. I didn't expect Mother to like him."

"You know Mother," Janet said matter-of-factly. "She's a very gracious snob."

Beth knew her mouth was gaping, but she couldn't help it. Staring at the glint of mischief in her sister's eyes, she burst out laughing. When Janet smiled, too, something went warm in Beth's throat, and she realized that they were sharing a rare moment of camaraderie.

Janet checked on her younger son, who was sitting on the bench out front, and Beth carried Christopher's infant seat to the table. Taking her chair, she found Janet looking at her.

"Janet, is something wrong?"

Janet lowered her gaze to her plate. Tracing a pattern on

her linen napkin, she said, "I'm thinking about asking MacKenzie for a divorce."

Beth's hand flew to her throat. Of all the things she'd thought Janet might have said, she hadn't expected this. "No wonder MacKenzie looked so tense and tired when I saw him in his office a few weeks ago."

"MacKenzie doesn't know," Janet said, slowly meeting Beth's gaze.

"Has something happened?" Beth asked.

"Do you mean an extramarital affair or abuse? No, nothing like that."

"Then, what is it, Janet? I always thought you and Mac had the perfect marriage. I envied you for that."

The surprise on Janet's face was too stark to be anything but real. "I've always envied you."

"Me?" Beth's croak startled Christopher. Being careful to keep her voice low, she said, "But you've always been the perfect sister. You walk the right way, talk the right way. You've always been the perfect hostess, the perfect wife, the perfect mother, while I've struggled to get any of those things right. Why would you possibly envy me?"

Janet's hand shook as she raised her water to her lips. Returning the glass to the table, she said, "Because you've never allowed Mother and Father to dictate your life, while I always followed the exact course they set for me, attending the university of their choice, marrying the kind of man they wanted me to marry. The only thing I've ever done to deviate from the plan was to have a third child. Chaz is my one claim to independent thinking."

"Are you sorry?" Beth whispered, trying to understand this depth in the sister she barely knew.

"That I married Mac and had three beautiful children with him? No, I'm not sorry. But I'm sad that he doesn't look at me the way Tony looks at you. I'm sad that he doesn't look into my eyes when he talks to me anymore.

Half the time I don't think he knows I'm alive. And I haven't been number one in his life in a long, long time."

"Then, restake your claim." Beth felt nearly as surprised as Janet looked. Who was she to give marital advice? After all, she'd gone through a painful divorce little more than a year ago. And her marriage to Tony wasn't exactly conventional.

"What do you mean?" Janet asked.

"I'm not sure," Beth answered truthfully. "I think too many people give up too easily these days. If you're still committed to the marriage, and neither of you has done anything unforgivable, it seems to me there must be something worth fighting for."

"Then, you think I should fight for my rightful place in Mac's life?"

"I think you should fight for your rightful place in *your* life," Beth answered. "Shake Mac up. Make him see you, really and truly see you."

"How do I do that?"

"You have to find the answer to that, but tell me something, Janet. How did Mac react to your wish to have a third child?"

For the first time all day, Janet's smile looked smug. "He was very—shall I say—excited about the prospect."

So, Beth thought to herself, her demure sister had a wild side, too, a side that Mac had liked. She wondered how long it had been since Janet had been completely spontaneous with her husband. "Perhaps that's where you should start."

"Do you think I should try to open his eyes by suggesting a fourth child?" Janet asked incredulously.

"I was thinking more along the lines of opening his eyes with great sex."

Janet blushed. In a voice barely above a whisper, she said, "MacKenzie is working so hard to become a full partner in the firm he spends most of his time at the office. It's been a long time since he's called me upstairs to help him find his favorite cuff links, if you know what I mean.''

Touching a drop of condensation on the outside of her glass, Beth nodded. ''Nobody ever said you had to limit your search for those cuff links to your bedroom. If Mac has been spending most of his time at the office, you might have to search there.''

Janet's gasp reminded Beth of their mother's, but there was nothing motherly about the glint in her eyes. ''Are you suggesting I...we...at the office?''

Beth shrugged, and Janet picked up her fork, moving a piece of lettuce around on her plate. ''I once saw a segment on a daytime talk show about women who strolled into their husbands' offices wearing a fur coat and nothing else.''

''There you go.''

Spearing a piece of grilled chicken, Janet said, ''It's much too warm for a fur coat.''

''A trench coat would work just as well.''

''I don't own a trench coat.''

Reaching for her own fork, Beth said, ''Then, it looks as if you have a little shopping to do.''

They shared a long look, then burst out laughing. For what was quite possibly the first time in their lives, they continued to talk over a companionable, sisterly lunch. Janet seemed more relaxed, and Beth was very nearly brimming with happiness and joy. She still felt the glow of Tony's passion, Christopher's adoption was progressing right on schedule, and she and her sister were working their way toward a closer relationship. With just a little more time, she would have everything she wanted, everything she needed, everything that made her whole.

''Hey, kid. Whatcha doin'?''

The pebble Charles Alexander Nelson—Chaz—had been kicking down the driveway rolled out of his reach. Instead of walking toward it, he stopped in his tracks. He was extremely intelligent. Grandmother Katherine had told him so. He wasn't supposed to talk to strangers, but he'd always thought of strangers as adults. The girl who'd spoken was a kid. A little older than Mark, maybe, but a kid just the same. Still, he didn't know her. He wondered if kids could be strangers, too.

"You live around here?" the girl asked.

Chaz shook his head, studying her. She seemed tall, but then, most everybody seemed tall to him. Her dark hair was in a ponytail, and her blue jeans had holes in them. They were the kind Danielle wanted to wear, but Mother wouldn't allow it.

"No," he said, finally deciding it was okay to talk to her as long as he kept a safe distance. "My mother and I are visiting my Aunt Beth."

"You're kinda formal, aren't you?"

"So what if I am?"

Chaz watched the girl's eyes widen, then settle back to normal. Her eyes were blue, her skin awfully pale. She was skinny, too. It made him wonder if she got enough to eat, which in turn made him glance at the sandwich halves in his hands. He'd taken two bites out of the one in his right hand, but the other one was as good as new. Holding out his left hand, he said, "Would you care for a turkey sandwich?"

She glanced all around her the way he did when he was thinking about going into Mark's room. "Don't you want it?" she asked, staring at his left hand.

"I can get another one if I want."

Chaz felt like smiling when she accepted his gift. "Do you have a name?" he asked.

"Everybody has a name."

She'd answered with her mouth full, but Chaz didn't mind because he forgot sometimes, too. Still, he noticed that she hadn't answered his question. "My name's Chaz.

My real name is Charles, after my grandfather on my mother's side. That name is even dumber than Chaz.''

She smiled for the first time, and suddenly Chaz felt sort of weird.

"I don't think Chaz or Charles are dumb names.''

"You don't?''

"Uh-uh,'' she said, shaking her head. "They're kind of like Christie and Christopher. And those are my two favorite names in the whole wide world.''

"Really?'' Chaz asked, his young voice full of amazement. "Christopher is my new cousin's name.''

"That right?'' the girl asked, taking the last bite of her sandwich.

"Yes. He's very small. Too small to do much except eat and sleep and cry. He wears pajamas most of the time, except they're not called pajamas. They're called sleepers. Anyway, Aunt Beth sure loves him. So does my mother. They couldn't stop making goo-goo eyes at him. That's why I came out here.''

"Do you like your Aunt Beth?''

He shrugged, because a kid could get into trouble admitting he loved his aunt. "She smells nice. And she never says I'm clumsy if I break something or spill my milk at dinner. And she never, ever calls me a baby.''

"She sounds smart. I'll bet you take after her in a lot of ways.''

Chaz felt himself blushing and was awfully glad that the girl was bending down to tie her shoe so she wouldn't notice. He saw something sticking out of her back pocket. "Is that a baseball cap?'' he asked.

She took it from her pocket and smoothed it into shape. "Yep. It used to be my sister's. She gave it to me a coupla years ago. You can try it on, but you've gotta give it back, cuz it's my lucky hat. Do you understand?''

Chaz nodded, although he didn't really understand completely. He'd never heard of a lucky hat, but he had heard of lucky rabbits' feet and horseshoes and lucky numbers. His older brother said all the luck ran out of horseshoes that were pointing down. Chaz wondered if the luck ran out of a lucky hat if somebody else wore it. Since he didn't want the girl to run out of luck, he declined her offer. "No, thanks. You'd better hold on to it if it's lucky."

"Maybe you're right."

Chaz knew it wasn't polite to stare, but he couldn't help it. He simply was not accustomed to being told he was right. Suddenly, he wanted to know everything about this girl with the lucky hat and the serious blue eyes. "Do you live around here?" he asked.

She nodded. "I got me my own place down in the Downs." She laughed. "Get it? Down in the Downs?"

Chaz had heard his grandparents talk about a place called the Downs. Although he'd never actually been there, he understood enough about the way they said it to know that it wasn't a part of town they cared to live in. "My grandmother said the Downs are on the wrong side of the tracks."

"Yeah?" she asked. "Well, sometimes the tracks run in circles, ya know?"

Chaz didn't have any idea what she'd meant by that. How in the world could train tracks run in circles? Still, if the girl was old enough to have a place of her own, even if it was in the Downs, wherever that was, she must have been older than she looked.

Sighing over his perpetual youngness, he said, "It must be cool to have your own place."

"It's cool in some ways, hard in others. You'll see when you get a little older."

"It's taking forever to get older."

She laughed. Chaz didn't know what was happening to him, but his throat felt funny and he practically squashed his sandwich.

"It's not taking forever," she said. "You're getting older every minute of every day."

"I am?" he asked.

She nodded. "Everyone is."

He gave that a considerable amount of thought before saying, "I suppose you're right. I'm almost seven." He didn't tell her his birthday wasn't until February. As far as he was concerned, he'd been going on seven since the day he'd turned six.

"Almost seven is pretty old," the girl said quietly. "Think it's old enough to keep a secret?"

"What kind of secret?" he asked, feeling at once important and afraid because the last time Danielle had asked him to keep a secret, he'd told. She'd been so upset she'd slammed the door in his face, but not before he'd seen the tears in her eyes. He couldn't remember what the secret had been, but he sure remembered those tears.

"It's no big deal, really," the girl with the lucky hat answered. "It's just that I'm not really supposed to be here right now, and I don't want to get in trouble. So I'd appreciate it if you wouldn't tell anybody you talked to me. Deal?"

It took Chaz a minute to realize that she'd held her hand out to him because she wanted to shake on it. Feeling ten feet tall, he juggled his sandwich into his other hand and placed his fingers in hers.

"Be extra nice to Christopher, will ya?" she asked.

He nodded.

She smiled again, stuffed her hat on her head, then turned around. He watched until she'd disappeared around the corner at the end of the block. Then, because he wasn't a baby at all, he ate his sandwich, even though it was smashed and dry. Rubbing the crumbs from his hands, he strolled back up the driveway and on into the house Aunt Beth lived in with her new husband and their new baby boy.

He heard his mother and Aunt Beth laughing as soon as

he opened the door. Chaz paused at the sound, not entirely sure why he felt like laughing, too. Maybe it was because it had been a long time since he'd heard his mother laugh that way, or maybe it was because he'd made a new friend. Whatever the reason, he walked right up to the table and looked at his new cousin much more closely than he ever had before.

"He's cute, isn't he?" he asked his mother.

"Almost as cute as you," his mother answered.

Feeling strangely important, Chaz said, "I'm too big to be cute. I'm getting older every day, you know."

"Yes, I know," his mother said affectionately. "Before you know it, you'll be as big as Mark and Danielle. Your brother and sister will be home soon. We should go, too."

For as long as Chaz could remember, he'd wanted to be big like Mark and Danielle. But suddenly, there was somebody else he wanted to be like. "Okay," he answered. "But could we do something on the way home?"

"Do you want to stop at the park to play?" his mother asked.

Christopher was looking at him with serious blue eyes that somehow made Chaz feel older, taller, wiser. Grinning, he held his finger out the way he'd seen Aunt Beth do, and laughed out loud when the baby clamped onto it with his own tiny hand. Mesmerized, Chaz shook his head, being careful not to pull his finger out of his new cousin's grasp. "I want to go shopping for a baseball cap like my friend's."

"What friend?" his mother asked.

"A baseball cap?" Aunt Beth asked at the same time.

He stopped suddenly, his breath catching in his throat. He wasn't supposed to tell anybody about his new friend. He'd promised. Why were secrets always so hard for him to keep?

Chaz glanced up at the grown-ups. He recognized the look of curiosity on his mother's face, but he didn't understand the worry on Aunt Beth's. Since a promise was a promise, he pulled his finger out of Christopher's grasp and tucked his hand into his mother's. "All the guys in school wear them."

Beth tried to tell herself there was no reason for the chill running down her spine. Surely there was no connection between Chaz's sudden desire to own a baseball cap and the person several witnesses had seen near the nursery, a person whose most outstanding feature seemed to be a baseball cap.

Chaz had said it himself. All the kids wore them. Hundreds of thousands of people wore them. Why, then, did goose bumps skitter along her arms when she glanced out the window where Chaz had eaten his lunch? The bench was empty, the early autumn afternoon sunny and clear. There was nothing amiss. It was just a normal Thursday afternoon. The leaves were beginning to change colors, the mountains rising in the west like ever-watchful friends. Why, then, did she suddenly feel as if her chance for happiness was hovering dangerously close to the edge of a treacherous cliff?

She didn't have an answer, but she strode directly to the table, unstrapped Christopher and lifted him into her arms. His warmth seeped into her chest, her love for this child gradually chasing away all but the faintest traces of fear.

She walked Janet and Chaz out to their car. Waving goodbye, she felt her eyes close dreamily. She held the baby away from her face and cooed, half in English, half in gibberish. "I love you, Christopher, yes I do."

He looked up at her. And smiled for the very first time.

Wrapping her arms around him, she cradled him close and pressed her cheek to his, wondering if all mothers felt as if their time with their babies was slipping away. She scanned the driveway and the mountains, and everything in between. Blaming her lingering sense of unease on an overactive imagination, she turned and carried Christopher inside.

Eleven

"Taste this, Anthony," Tony's mother said, holding a spoon to his lips. "Does it need more oregano?"

"It's perfect, Ma," Tony answered, licking his lips. "But you've gotta stop feeding me or I won't be able to eat a bite at the dinner party the board of directors is throwing tonight."

His mother made a grunting sound that was all but impossible to imitate. "That's hours away. You'll have worked up an appetite by then. What about your Grandma Rosa's sauce? I think there's a little too much basil, don't you?"

Tony backed away, holding up both hands. "I'm not tasting that sauce, and I'm sure not taking sides when it comes to you and Grandma Rosa's opinions on basil. Have Maria taste it. Where is she, anyway?"

"Your sister's running the register up front, not that she'd come near you after the way you practically bit her head off a little while ago."

Shrugging sheepishly, Tony glanced out the doorway that separated the kitchen from the rest of the store. Mario's Grocery was in a midafternoon lull. In fact, there were more Petrocellis wandering around than there were customers. But his mother was right. He *had* been a little short with Maria earlier when she'd teased him about all the stops he and Beth had made before coming here.

He'd only been making conversation when he'd told her he'd gone to the gas station, the car wash and the dry cleaners to pick up his best black suit, and Maria had only been making conversation when she'd joked that he sounded like an old married man. He wasn't sure why it had rankled, but it had.

"Don't worry about Maria," Elena said, stirring the big pot of homemade Italian sauce the store was noted for selling. "She's just jealous because you asked Carmelina to baby-sit tonight instead of her."

He shrugged, breathing in the heavy scent of garlic, tomato, onion and oregano. The store always smelled the same. Like home. For some reason, it didn't make him feel better today.

Two dark-haired children streaked around the corner of aisle five. Leaving his mother to her cooking, Tony headed his nephew and niece off at the pass, lifting the smallest of the two off his feet. "You'd better not let your mama catch you running in this store. She'll tan your hides for sure."

Four-year-old Gabe Bulgarelli and his six-year-old sister, Robin, looked at each other, then glanced around nervously. Ruffling both dark heads, Tony said, "I think you're safe for now. What do you say we go find your Aunt Beth?"

Turning dark brown eyes rimmed with curling black lashes to his uncle, Gabe said, "Grandma Rosa has her cornered in the freezer section."

"Then, we don't have much time. We have to get to her and save her before it's too late." Tony settled Gabe on his hip and took Robin's hand, all three of them setting off for the back of the store.

They hadn't gone far when they came across Tony's sister, Gina, who was stocking shelves. Looking up from a display of canned green beans, two for a dollar, Gina swiped her hands on her short apron, looked at Gabe and exclaimed, "The older that son of mine gets, the more he becomes the spittin' image of you, Tony."

Gabe wiggled to get down. Tony obliged him, his gaze

settling on Bethany about the same time Gabe's feet touched the floor. Just as the kids had said, Grandma Rosa was talking to her in the freezer section. Beth was nodding at the old woman, her hand patting Christopher's back in a steady rhythm. The baby was strong enough to hold his head up now and seemed to be mesmerized by all the bright colors. His hair was as dark as Gabe's, but it was becoming apparent that Christopher's eyes were going to be light blue.

"Beth tells me Christopher is beginning to smile," Gina said conversationally.

"Yeah," Tony answered absently. Then, coming to his senses, he said, "Yes, he is. It's the darnedest thing, too. I swear his whole body lights up every time it happens. Beth can lure a grin out of him all the time, but he's only done it twice for me."

"He's with Beth a lot more of the time," Gina answered, returning to her task.

"I'll have you know I spend time with my son, too."

Gina's head came up and around with a snap. "I didn't say you don't. For crying out loud, Tony, there's no need to bite my head off. Maria's right. You are a crank."

Tony wouldn't have needed to see the look in his sister's brown eyes to feel like a heel. He scowled. Gina and Maria were both right. He was cranky. He wasn't sure why.

"Tony?"

"Hmm?" he asked, his sister's voice drawing his gaze away from Christopher's dark little head and mesmerizing blue eyes.

"If you hurry, you might be able to rescue Bethany before Grandma Rosa reaches the war years."

Her wink was part of the standing family joke. Just like that, Tony knew all was forgiven. "Thanks, Gina. I think I'll do that."

"Oh, and Tony?" she called to his back.

His answer was a raised eyebrow and a "what" sort of look over his shoulder.

"Break a leg tonight. The hospital board made a good choice."

Swallowing the lump that had come out of nowhere, he nodded. "I'll do my best."

"You always do."

Tony was glad Gina didn't wait around for his response, because he would have been hard-pressed to come up with one. Of all his sisters, she was the one he'd always argued with the most. Their mother claimed it was because they were too close in age and too much alike. Until now, it hadn't felt like a compliment. Maybe that was the reason behind the dull ache in his chest.

Making his way toward Beth and Chris, he wished he felt a little more convinced.

Bethany studied her reflection in the mirror. She'd applied her makeup with a light hand, placing more emphasis on her eyes than on the rest of her face. As a result, her lashes looked long and thick, her lids tinted a pale brown, her brows darkened just enough to call attention to their delicate arch. She applied a bit of translucent powder to the rest of her face, and followed that up with a hint of blush on her cheekbones and a coat of deep red lipstick on her lips. She liked the effect when she was finished, but she knew that it wasn't makeup that was responsible for the healthy glow on her cheeks and the glimmer of happiness in her eyes.

Always one to give credit where credit was due, she had to admit that Christopher was responsible for her more rested appearance. Tipping the scales at six-and-three-quarter pounds, he was growing like a weed, eating more at each feeding and sleeping longer in between. As a result, Beth was able to sleep for four hours at a time. When Tony didn't wake her, that is. That brought her to the other reason for her glowing appearance, another reason who just happened to be lounging in the doorway, watching.

"Tell me more about your sisters," she said, brushing her hair.

Ready except for his jacket, Tony strolled farther into the room, stopping near the foot of the bed. From this angle he could see the back of Beth's head as well as her reflection in the big oval mirror over the makeup table. She reached up with her hands, winsomely twisting her hair into some sort of knot on top of her head. His heart thudded, then settled back into its normal rhythm. "I've already told you everything there is to know about my sisters."

"All right," she said, securing her hair with a wide rhinestone clasp. Several strands were already falling around her ears and neck. Catching some up with strategically placed pins, she said, "Then why don't you tell me why you were snapping at them earlier this afternoon."

With his eyes trained on the length of neck she'd exposed, he said, "Me? Snap?"

Meeting her gaze through the mirror, he shrugged, because he didn't want to talk about what had been bothering him earlier. What he wanted to do was remove those well-placed pins and watch that mane of long hair fall around Beth's shoulders. And then he wanted to reach for her hands, drawing her to her feet.

As if reading his mind, she stood and slowly turned around. "Aren't you curious about what your grandmother and I talked about?"

The lift of his shoulders was as automatic as his answer. "She told you, in broken English, about the day she met my grandfather, Mario, how he swept her off her feet and married her two months later, and how proud she was to present him with their first and only child—my father."

Tony enjoyed the smug feeling of satisfaction that settled over him as her eyes widened, indicating that he'd hit the nail on the head where his Grandma Rosa was concerned. "Did she bore you to death?" he asked.

"Actually, I enjoyed it. Especially her references to you."

He knew she was aware of his slow advance, because the closer he got, the warmer the glint in her eyes became. "You should know better than to believe everything an eighty-year-old woman tells you," he said quietly.

"Then she didn't chase you around the house from time to time with a wooden spoon?"

He shrugged. "Oh, that part's true enough."

"Did she ever catch you?"

He nodded, watching the flick of her tongue across her lips and the movement of her neck as she swallowed.

"How often?" she whispered.

"How does twice a day sound to you?"

Beth's hands stilled at the sash at her waist. She'd been referring to him getting spanked as a child, but in the span of one heartbeat, his answer took on an entirely different meaning. She untied the sash, letting the robe fall from her shoulders, revealing the dress she was wearing underneath. Certain that no man had ever looked at her with so much open longing, she tipped her head slightly and smoothed her hands down the royal blue fabric of her dress. "Twice a day sounds like a tall order, even for you."

She'd expected a lightning-quick comeback, but all she heard was Tony's sharply drawn breath. Glancing up, she found his gaze trained slightly to the right, where her back was reflected in the mirror. The next time his eyes met hers, her breathing had deepened and a familiar sensation had taken hold of her body.

"Yoo-hoo. I'm here!"

They both jumped at the shrill voice coming from the bottom of the stairs, their surprise slowly giving way to grins.

"Tony? Bethany? Are you up there?"

"We'll be right down," Beth called to her sister-in-law.

Tony heaved a sigh. "We've got to start locking that door."

"Do you really think that would keep your family out?"

Making a sound deep in his throat, he ran a hand over his face. "Probably not. There is one thing I forgot to mention about my sisters. They all have rotten timing."

"Oh, I don't know," Beth said, sliding her feet into her evening shoes. "If Carmelina hadn't shown up, you might have been late for your own party."

"Bethany? If Carmelina hadn't shown up, we wouldn't have made it to the party at all."

"You sound awfully sure of yourself," she whispered.

"You make me very, very sure."

It was all Beth could do to look away. While she put the finishing touches on her appearance, Tony strode across the hall to get Christopher. Carmelina was waiting for them when they reached the bottom of the stairs.

"When he's sleeping," Carmelina said, eyeing Christopher shrewdly, "he looks just like you, Tony."

Of Tony's four sisters, Carmelina, the oldest at thirty-eight, looked the most like Elena and acted the most like Rosa. Beth thought it was quite a combination, even for a Petrocelli. But the other woman was right. Christopher's coloring was very similar to Tony's. With pride filling her chest, she slipped her hand into the crook of Tony's elbow, and paused. If she hadn't felt the muscles flex beneath her palm, she wouldn't have known he'd tensed. She glanced up at him and found his eyes hooded.

"How long since this little trooper's eaten?" Carmelina asked.

"Almost three hours," Beth answered, automatically striding to the refrigerator for a bottle, trying to understand the reason for Tony's tension at the same time. Long before she could make sense of it, Carmelina exclaimed, "*Mama mia!* What a dress!"

Tony was smiling the next time Beth's eyes met his. Handing the baby into his sister's capable hands, he said, "If you'd waited two more minutes to call up the stairs, I would have had it off her."

"Aye-yi-yi. Sex and supper. That's all you men think about. Now, tell me what this baby needs so I can shoo you out of here and spoil him rotten."

"Actually," Tony said, running a hand down his tie, "I haven't thought about supper in days. Perhaps you could help me talk Beth out of going tonight."

Tony watched Beth's emotions play across her face. Quirking her eyebrows in that engaging way he was coming to recognize, she said, "Oh, no you don't, Doctor. Tonight you have to dazzle the board of directors so they have no doubt that they made the right choice."

"Uh, Bethany?" Carmelina crowed. "Something tells me that in that dress, you'll be the one doing the dazzling tonight."

Randolph's restaurant was much more impressive than its name. It was perhaps the most elegant restaurant in all of Grand Springs and its surrounding area. How had Beth put it? Opulent grandeur at its finest. Waiters in black ties and tails served champagne from sterling silver trays. The room was flanked by Victorian-era sofas and flute-edged tables, the light from gleaming chandeliers casting a golden hue over everything it touched.

Located a few miles out of town, on the road toward Squaw Creek Lodge, the structure had been built more than a hundred years ago by a miner who'd struck it rich in the silver mines nearby. He'd designed the house for his young wife, who had been born out East and was accustomed to the finer things in life. The young woman was reportedly friends with the Unsinkable Molly Brown, who became notorious for her bravery and heroism on the maiden voyage of the *Titanic*. Tony had always been more interested in the folklore surrounding the shack where Doc Holliday, of OK Corral fame, had holed up one entire winter after reportedly shooting two men over in Leadville. But as far as Tony was concerned, Bethany could have lit up either place.

He nodded at a waiter and, with a glass of champagne in each hand, headed back the way he'd come. The crowd parted, awarding him a clear view of his wife. She was talking to Oliver Witherbee, who'd been sitting on the hospital's board for so long he had a permanent Vanderbilt imprint on the seat of his pants. Oliver laughed at something Beth said, and Tony smiled to himself. She had the old stuffed shirt eating right out of her hand.

His sister had been right about who would be dazzling whom tonight. There wasn't a man in the place who could take his eyes off Beth. Her only jewelry was a fine gold watch and delicate rhinestone earrings that caught the light with the slightest movement of her head. Her dress had a high, slightly rounded neckline, long tapered sleeves and a straight skirt with a slit that stopped several inches short of being provocative. It looked very demure from the front, befitting the new wife of the newly appointed head of obstetrics of Vanderbilt Memorial. From the front, every hot-blooded man from eighteen to eighty appreciated the color, the fit, the style. One glimpse at the sweep of royal blue material that bared her back all the way to her waist had every one of those men practically gnawing on their fists.

While Mr. Witherbee moved on to talk to someone else, Beth gave the entire room a sweeping glance. Tony didn't know how she knew where to look, or how her gaze unerringly picked him out of the crowd, but the smile she bestowed on him kicked his libido into high gear. Holding her gaze even after he'd reached her side, he said, "You seemed to hit it off with Oliver Witherbee."

She smiled up at him. "His wife and my mother go way back. I'm telling you, Tony, it really is all who you know."

Tony doubted he'd ever tire of listening for the wry humor, subtle though it might be, in Bethany's voice. Placing a glass of champagne in her hand, he bent his head close to her ear, all ready to tell her exactly what she was doing to him.

"Hello, Beth."

Tony turned his head an instant later than Beth, what he'd been about to say never making it past his lips. He didn't recognize the man who was smiling at Beth as if he'd known her all his life, but he didn't appreciate the interruption.

"Barry. Hello."

Barry? Hell. Tony felt his eyes narrow, his jaw firm, and he was barely able to force himself to loosen the arm he'd wrapped possessively around Beth's back.

"You're looking well," Barry said.

"Thank you. How's Chelsea?" Beth asked.

For a second Tony thought Barry was going to say "Who?" but evidently the man came to his senses in time to form a more intelligent answer. "She's fine, thanks. I heard you remarried."

Something about the way he'd said *remarried* went over like fingernails on a chalkboard, the sound clashing with the four-piece orchestra playing nearby. Until now, Tony had pictured Barry Kent with a pocket protector and Coke-bottle glasses. He sure as hell hadn't pictured him so tall. So tanned. So muscular. Big or not, if Barry didn't stop looking at Beth as if she was dessert and he hadn't had sweets in months, Tony was going to flatten that arrogant, well-bred nose.

"As a matter of fact, I have," Beth was saying. "This is my husband, Tony Petrocelli. Tony, Barry Kent."

"Nice to meet you, Tony."

Tony had enough social grace to shake the other man's

hand, but he hadn't been born with a silver spoon in his mouth. As far as he was concerned, that meant that he didn't have to lie just to be polite. He did nod, though. Luckily, ole Barry took the hint and ambled on back to the table he was sharing with his very pregnant wife.

Watching him go, Tony said, "So that was your ex-husband."

Something in Tony's voice drew Beth's gaze. His dark suit had cost a pretty penny and fit him to perfection. It wouldn't have made any difference if it had been three sizes too small. What he was wearing didn't matter. He was by far the most attractive man in the room. His white shirt was in stark contrast to the rich color of his skin, but if she wasn't mistaken, his tan was taking on a greenish hue.

"Are you jealous?" she whispered incredulously.

"Should I be?"

It wasn't the answer she'd expected. Cocking her head slightly and crossing her arms, she said, "So lawyers aren't the only ones who answer questions with questions."

"You were saying?" he prodded.

Looking up at him, she lost the battle not to smile. "Should you be jealous?" she repeated softly. "Not in a million years. I'm over him. Completely. Unequivocally. Permanently."

He made a sound deep in his throat, half moan, half impatience. Placing their untouched glasses on a passing waiter's tray, he took her hand, leading the way to the small dance floor nearby. He turned her into his arms for a slow dance, letting the orchestra set the pace, letting the slow burn deep inside him set the mood. "I have to say your taste has improved, Mrs. Petrocelli."

"Success has gone to your head, Dr. Petrocelli."

Several guests turned at the sound of his deep chuckle, the action awarding them a clear view of his smooth turn in one direction, their gentle sway in another. The board of directors were very pleased with the amorous attention their new head of obstetrics was paying to his wife. Tony didn't give a rip about the board of directors. No matter what Beth said, success hadn't gone to his head. Bethany had.

He placed his hand in the small of her back, sucking in a deep breath at the feel of her soft skin beneath his palm. "I hate to say this," he whispered, letting his lips move against the delicate arch of her ear, "but your *ex*-husband can't take his eyes off you."

There was a little catch in her breathing as his hand slowly moved lower. "I highly doubt that."

"Fine," he murmured, dipping her in the opposite direction. "But *Chelsea* is sulking at that table right over there, just beyond the area the hospital reserved for this little celebration."

"Then, I feel sorry for her. Because I've been exactly where she is right now."

Tony wasn't normally a man who gave in to public outbursts, but he wanted to tip his head back and laugh out loud. "Trust me," he said instead, "there isn't a man in this room who isn't watching you."

"Are you *trying* to make me step on your foot?"

"I'm bragging."

Beth pulled away far enough to be able to look up into his eyes. Thoroughly enjoying the feelings slowly thrumming through her body, she gave him an arched look and quietly said, "I've always heard that talk is cheap."

He missed a step and didn't even try to take another. "Are you telling me to put my money where my mouth is?"

"Actually, I was hoping you'd take me home."

She didn't say, "And have your way with me," but it was there between them. And they both knew it.

They stopped at their table for her evening bag, said their goodbyes to the members of the board, then hurried toward the door like children playing hooky.

"Dr. and Mrs. Petrocelli. Wait!"

They both turned around, but neither of them recognized the man who had thwarted their retreat. Something about him made Beth glad they were in a lighted foyer and not a dark alley.

"Can we help you?" Tony asked, placing himself in front of Beth.

The man's expression was cynical, but his smile seemed genuine enough. He held up one hand and reached into the inside pocket of his sport coat with the other. "I didn't mean to startle either of you," he said, drawing a badge into the light. "I'm Detective Jack Stryker. I've been working with the Department of Social Services in trying to locate Annie Moore."

Beth stepped out into the open. "Do you know where she is?"

"A girl matching her description has been seen in the area."

"When?" Beth asked.

"Where?" Tony said at the same time.

"A few days ago in a park over on Valley View."

"But why?" Beth asked. "Why would Annie still be here?"

"I don't know," the blond-haired detective said in a "the facts, ma'am, just the facts" monotone. "I understand you're going through the process of adopting the baby she abandoned a few months ago. I also understand the two of you were there the night she had the child. Have either of you seen her since that night?"

Tony thought about the person Martin Smith had thought he'd seen out of the corner of his eye just over a month ago, and about the owl it had turned out to be. In answer to the detective's question, he shook his head.

Beth thought about the goose bumps that had danced along her arms when her nephew had asked for a baseball cap, and the times she'd felt as if she were being watched.

But had she *seen* anyone matching Annie's description? "No, Detective, I haven't."

"I see," the man answered.

"Does the department always make such a great effort to locate a runaway?" Tony asked.

"I'm afraid not. It seems her mother and new stepfather in Detroit want her back pretty bad."

Something in the detective's expression made Tony pause. If he wasn't mistaken, the other man didn't much care for Annie Moore's mother and stepfather.

"You've spoken to her parents?" Tony asked.

"Over the phone." Tucking his badge back into his pocket, Detective Stryker said, "I just wanted you to be aware of the situation, so you can be on the lookout."

"Be on the lookout for what?" Tony cut in. "Do you think she's going to try to do something, maybe take Christopher?"

Beth gasped. "Why would she do that?"

The detective shrugged. "Why did she abandon him in the first place? Everybody's got reasons for doing the things they do. Look, it might not be her. Like you said, why would she stay in the same town as the kid without making arrangements to see him? I don't want to scare you. I just want to keep you abreast of the situation."

The detective pulled a business card from between his fingers the way a magician might produce a coin. "If you see anything, or have any questions, don't hesitate to contact me."

Without another word, he disappeared into the next room. Beth and Tony were left standing in the lobby, staring at the card in her hand. Much more subdued than they'd been minutes ago, they made their way to Tony's Lexus.

They spoke during the drive down the mountain, asking questions that had no real answers. Was it possible that Annie Moore was still in Grand Springs? If so, what was she doing here? Was she capable of stealing back her own baby? And the most important question of all.

Whose baby was Christopher?

Beth couldn't have loved him more if he'd been born to her. But did that make him hers? Yes, she screamed inside her head. Her heart thudded a much more painful answer.

"Look at those lights."

The low strum of Tony's deep voice drew her from her dark thoughts. From their vantage point they could see the entire city of Grand Springs in the valley below. The pale yellow glow of streetlights and porch lights gave the town an ethereal quality, a peacefulness that reached inside Beth, relaxing her, calming her.

Tony reached for her hand, one by one twining his fingers with hers. Something about the gesture, the unity of that one small act, sent Beth's worries far away and brought back the hazy sensuality she'd felt in his arms on the dance floor earlier.

"It's been quite an evening," she whispered.

"It's not over."

She hummed her answer, her emotions shimmering in her chest in a similar fashion. It had been five weeks since she and Tony had exchanged wedding vows in the old house where he and his sisters had grown up, five weeks since she'd assured herself that she could guard her heart against falling in love. Little by little, Tony was obliterating the lines she'd drawn to protect her heart against heartache. It wasn't any one thing, but a combination of small things. The sight of Christopher asleep on Tony's bare chest. The excitement and wonder she'd seen in Tony's eyes a few nights ago when he'd come back to bed in the wee hours of the morning after delivering a baby. The laughter in his voice, the sounds he made in his sleep, the way he watched her when she was getting dressed.

Her husband wasn't perfect. There was a side of him he kept hidden. But he gave her free rein to the rest of him.

She smiled to herself at the memory of a few of the things he gave her free rein to. Desire uncurled in her belly like the smoke of a wood fire on a cool autumn day.

"What are you thinking about?"

Beth very nearly jumped, but smiled, instead. "Oh, wood smoke, and autumn, and, I suppose, you."

He took his eyes from the street long enough to look into her eyes. "I like the sound of that."

"I figured you would."

The car had pulled into the driveway and had inched its way toward the garage before either of them noticed the extra vehicles parked near the house.

"That's Gib's Jeep," Tony said, throwing the lever into Park.

"And that's Jenna's car," Beth added, pushing her door open.

"Christopher," they said as their feet hit the sidewalk, impending doom beating in their temples and lengthening their strides.

Twelve

Tony was the first one through the door, Bethany drawing to a stop two steps behind him. Carmelina glanced up from the romance novel she was reading at the kitchen table. Slowly pulling her feet off an adjacent chair, she said, "Have you two seen a ghost or are you just glad to be home?"

"We saw the extra cars outside," Tony declared.

"And we thought something might have happened," Beth cut in breathlessly.

"Oh, something's happened all right."

"Oh, my God! Christopher!" Beth cried.

"What? No. The baby's fine. He's been an angel all night. I can't exactly say the same for your friends, though."

As if on cue, Jenna entered the room, her dark eyes flashing, her bangle bracelets jangling as she planted her hands on her hips. "Tony, would you please tell that, that Neanderthal to leave so I can have a moment's peace?"

Gib limped into the room a few seconds later. "Beth, would you mind telling this short Gypsy here that I have medals bigger than she is and I'll leave when I'm good and ready?"

"Go," Jenna taunted.

"After you," Gib replied around the curl of his lip.

"See what I mean?" Carmelina asked.

Tony spared a glance at Beth, who rolled her eyes expressively before releasing a pent-up breath. Running a finger between his neck and the starched collar of his shirt, Tony asked his sister, "Have they been this way all night?"

"Pretty much. They both stopped in to visit the baby. I tried to referee at first. That went over like a lead balloon, so when I tucked Christopher into his crib after his last feeding, I decided it was safer to stay in here, out of their way. They've been pretty quiet this past half hour. I thought they might have kissed and made up."

Jenna gasped. "I wouldn't kiss this arrogant jerk if he were the last man on earth."

Tony recognized the shrewd look in Gib's eyes. After all, his friend hadn't won those medals he'd mentioned by being stupid. Tactical maneuvers were Gibson Malone's specialty. Tactical maneuvers and women, that is. He claimed there wasn't a woman on the planet he couldn't lure into bed. Staring at the hostility flashing in Jenna's exotic brown eyes, Gib obviously realized he had finally met one.

In an effort to defuse the situation, Beth slipped out of her shoes and padded over to Jenna. Before she could say a word, a wolf whistle rent the air. Three pairs of eyes turned to Gib. It seemed to require a considerable amount of effort on his part to tear his gaze from Beth's bare back, but he lifted his hands and smiled with equal parts innocence and male appreciation. "Sorry. It was a reflex action."

Bethany shook her head, Tony offered to break Gib's other ankle, and Jenna sputtered a curse straight out of one of the books in her store, ending the tirade with "Obnoxious swine."

Gib's hazel eyes twinkled. "Sweetheart, I thought you said you didn't care."

"Oaf."

"Why don't you come here and say that?"

Although nobody else spoke the language Jenna used during her next tirade, the translation was universal.

"I love it when a woman talks dirty to me."

"Fool."

"Seductress."

"Ox."

"Tigress."

"Jack—"

"I'd love to stick around and see how this ends," Carmelina declared, tucking a strand of her short dark hair behind her ear. "But I have a husband and four kids who'll be up early wanting a big Sunday breakfast."

While the insults were still being flung back and forth behind them, Beth said, "Thanks for staying with Christopher."

Beth caught a glimpse of Tony in Carmelina's wink. "Anytime. Let me know how World War III turns out, will you?" Grabbing her purse and her paperback, she hurried out the door.

Beth and Tony had hardly had time to exchange a "what do we do now" sort of look before Jenna clamped her mouth shut and stalked toward the door. Without bothering with a farewell, she flicked her hair behind her shoulders and said, "Tony, your taste in friends concerns me."

A second later, she was gone.

In the ensuing silence, Beth glanced at the two men in the room. Tony was staring at the door in amazement the way a person might gaze at a violent storm that had somehow passed him by. Gib had a much more serious expression on his face. "Jenna Maria Brigante." He shook his head. "A woman with three names always spells trouble."

"Jenna's very volatile," Beth murmured softly. "But I'm sure she didn't mean everything she said."

Narrowing his eyes and lowering his chin, Gib said, "Oh, she meant what she said, all right. But she failed to mention one thing."

"What's that?" Tony asked.

"She wants me."

Tony recognized the challenge in Gib's eyes, but the wonder was brand-new. "She could have fooled me, buddy," he declared.

Gib ambled toward the door, more surefooted than he'd been before the walking cast had been removed, but still not as agile as he used to be. "That's exactly what she was trying to do. She put a hex on me. She means trouble, all right. It just so happens that she's the kind of trouble I want to get into. Which way to her mountain cabin? Never mind," he said, running his hand over the stubble on his chin. "I have a better idea."

Like Jenna had before him, he left without saying good-bye.

Beth turned in a half circle after he was gone, making a sweeping glance at the quiet room. "Do you think Jenna stands a chance against him?"

Tony's eyebrows went up a notch at a time, his smile slow in coming, and all male. "If she wanted to, I think she could eat him alive."

"He called her short."

"She called him an obnoxious swine."

Beth smiled. "So she did. Do you really think there's a chance they might get together?"

"I'd rather think about you and I getting together. If you know what I mean."

Beth felt her heart tilt as warmth slid all the way to her stomach. "I always know what you mean."

"That's what I like about you."

She would have liked to ask what else he liked about her. Instead, she said, "We overreacted, you know."

"About Christopher?"

She nodded and he shrugged.

"I think we should talk to Mrs. Donahue about it at the next meeting," she whispered.

He nodded once with every forward step he took.

"That's not until Monday. This is Saturday night. And I still have to get you out of that dress."

She met him in the middle of the kitchen, going up on tiptoe to touch her lips to his, her arms gliding around his back, his hands homing in on her zipper as if guided by radar. She kissed his mouth, his cheek, his neck, then took his hand, leading him up the stairs where, like the enchantress he'd called her hours earlier, she—slowly, seductively, wantonly—took him to bed.

"Rita," Mrs. Donahue said into an old black telephone that took up one small corner on her cluttered desk, "hold my calls until I finish this session with Dr. and Mrs. Petrocelli."

Making herself comfortable in her chair, Beth felt a new respect for the way the social worker made sense out of the confusion and interruptions that had occurred every few minutes since she and Tony had arrived at her office. The older woman released a breath that stirred the overpermed bangs sticking out on her forehead. Removing her reading glasses, she looked from Beth to Tony and back again, tapping the business card Beth had given her all the while.

"This detective came right out and told you that someone has seen Annie Moore in Grand Springs?"

Tony's chair squeaked as he leaned forward and shook his head. "He said someone matching Annie Moore's description has been seen in Grand Springs."

"What if it's Annie?" Beth asked quietly.

Although Beth's taste tended to run toward pastels and more classic styles, she was beginning to understand why Florence Donahue wore those brightly flowered dresses with her black hose and thick-soled shoes. They certainly brightened up what was otherwise a dismal room. However, a clown's clothing couldn't have detracted from the integrity in her steady gaze.

"If you're asking me what legal right the birth mother

has to Christopher, the answer is none. Her parental rights were terminated in a court of law when she failed to come forward following the publication of the supplemental petition in the *Grand Springs Herald*. Unlike those tragic cases that made national news headlines a few years ago, Annie Moore hasn't contacted us, nor has she made her presence or her intentions known in any way, shape or form. Legally, Christopher is no longer her son.''

''And morally?'' Beth asked.

Mrs. Donahue adjusted the oversize collar at her neck. ''People have been grappling with that issue since King Solomon's time. Since cutting the child in half wouldn't work any better now than it would have back then, you have to be the ones to answer that question. What would you do if Annie came back tomorrow and told you she wanted Christopher?''

Beth's hands flew to her face, and her heart thudded painfully in her chest. What would she do? She would surely die.

''I can't imagine any reason Annie would have for waiting this long to come forward to claim the child. And she couldn't take him. Not legally,'' Mrs. Donahue pointed out. ''Grand Springs has a population of sixty-some thousand people. There must be a hundred girls matching Annie's description. I don't believe she's here.''

''Then, we're free to adopt him?'' Tony asked.

Florence nodded. ''I'm filing my report and making my recommendation today.''

Tony came to his feet with a loud whoop, pulling Beth with him on his way up. She laughed out loud when he swung her around, then he moved to the other side of the desk to do the same to Mrs. Donahue, that brightly flowered dress fluttering in the wake of the breeze he created.

''Dr. Petrocelli, please. I have a reputation of sternness and grouchiness to uphold.'' Florence's voice was as clipped as always, but there was no disguising the twinkle in her eyes.

Beth met Tony's gaze over Mrs. Donahue's curly head. His eyelids dropped down slightly, his expression changing in the most subtle of ways. Something went warm inside Beth. And she knew. She was in love.

It had been on the tip of her heart for a long time. *Love.* She'd been afraid of it, and had worried because of it. She shouldn't have bothered, because with the worry, came the wonder, and with the wonder, blessed joy. She was in love with the man she'd married. It was incredible. Love was incredible. Tony was the most incredible of all.

He could go from aloof to playful in the blink of an eye, from arrogant to daring just as quickly. He was a very virile man and had the reputation to prove it. As far as Beth was concerned, his reputation didn't do him justice. It didn't touch upon his gentleness, his curiosity and sense of humor, or his earnestness when she caught him talking to Christopher when he thought she wasn't listening. It didn't even come close to the things that made him the man he was, his humanness, his strength of character, his quick temper. He was exactly the kind of man she would have chosen to be the father of her biological children, exactly the kind of man she had been fortuitous enough to have chosen to be a father to Christopher.

"Take care of him for me," Annie had said before Beth had whisked Christopher upstairs to the neonatal nursery four-and-a-half months ago.

Tears filled Beth's eyes, blurring her vision, thickening her throat. Smiling tremulously, she offered up a silent prayer of thanksgiving for Christopher, and for Tony, and last but not least, for Annie Moore's strength and bravery to give life to a tiny, innocent, beautiful child.

It was one of those rare autumn afternoons when the sky was a vivid blue and the air carried the earthy scent of dry leaves. Wood smoke rose from the bonfire Tony and his brother-in-law Rocky had built. What had started as an idea for a simple hot dog roast with a few of Tony's family members had turned into a full-scale party. Beth was coming to realize that the Petrocellis did everything in a big way.

Tony's sisters and their husbands and children had arrived en masse, transforming the quiet meadow into a place where voices rang out with raucous laughter and children darted around adults, where marshmallows and hot dogs were roasted side by side and plates were heaped with chips and pickles and brownies and fat chunks of Colby cheese.

Nearly a week had passed since Beth had realized she was in love with Tony, although now that she'd thought about it she realized she'd been falling in love with him almost from the beginning. She hadn't been able to help it, but she wasn't sorry. These feelings welling up inside her were intoxicating, heavenly.

"Bethany," Maria exclaimed, walking over to the fallen log Beth had perched on to feed Christopher, "that baby is growing before my very eyes. His outfit is adorable."

Beth smoothed her hand down the baby's powder blue overalls and the butter yellow shirt adorned with ducks and blocks. Christopher was four-and-a-half months old, but because of his premature birth and medical problems early on, he wasn't as big as other babies his age. Actually, he was closer to the size of an eight-week-old, which was exactly how old he would have been had he not come into this world two-and-a-half months early. As far as his doctors were concerned, he was right on schedule, and Maria was right, he was quickly making up for lost time.

"Isn't Andreanna's and Rocky's news exciting?" Gina exclaimed, joining the little huddle.

"I can't say I'm surprised," Maria declared. "She always said she wanted three children close in age, and Ricky is a year-and-a-half old."

Bethany shifted Christopher to her shoulder and began to pat his back, listening to the conversation with only one ear. She couldn't help it, she'd been feeling as if she were floating on a cloud all week. She was in love, and life was full of mystery and wonder.

"So," Maria said, "when are you and Tony going to start working on a baby brother or sister for this little tyke?"

Beth's hand missed a beat against Christopher's back. She floundered for an answer. *A little brother or sister for Christopher?*

The sound he made against her shoulder gave her someplace else to look. Tucking him into the curve of one arm in order to give him the rest of his bottle gave her something to do with her hands. Despite those things, Beth was at a complete and utter loss for something to say.

"Nice going," Maria declared. "Now you've gone and embarrassed her."

"I didn't mean to."

"Yeah, well some people have more class than others, and Beth undoubtedly isn't used to being grilled about her sex life."

"I wasn't grilling her about her sex life. At least I didn't mean to make it sound that way."

"Of course you didn't," Beth murmured, recovering slightly. "You just caught me off guard, that's all. Actually, Tony and I haven't discussed Christopher's future siblings."

"Of course you haven't," Maria said. "You're still newlyweds."

"There's plenty of time for the two of you to have a baby," Gina agreed.

Doing her best to cast her sisters-in-law a semblance of a smile, Beth glanced to the right and found Tony watching her from the other side of the fire. He was close enough to have heard Gina and Maria, and must have read the sorrow and disappointment in Beth's eyes. They faced each other, silent and uncertain, gray smoke curling toward the sky between them. Her heart broke a little at the expression on his face. With great effort, she turned her attention back to the baby that had brought her and Tony together, but the joy and wonder of the past week was gone.

It was dark. Thankfully everyone had finally left.

After tucking Christopher into bed, Beth strode down the stairs and on into the living room, somehow knowing she'd find Tony on the deck outside. He was leaning over slightly, one knee bent, his forearms resting on the railing, his hands dangling over the edge.

She walked toward him, stopping close to him but not quite touching. They both stared out into the darkness, neither of them knowing what to say. An owl hooted, a lonely sound that matched the ache in Beth's chest. Crossing her arms against the chill of the autumn night, she said, "Neither Andreanna nor Maria knows that I can't have children, do they?"

His only response was a slight shake of his head.

"Does anyone in your family know?"

His eyes flickered to hers, then shied away. Beth knew without asking. She asked, anyway. "Why haven't you told them?"

He straightened but didn't turn to face her. "I couldn't bring myself to tell them. I'm sorry." There was a current in his voice, like a taut rope being strummed with one finger. It was a sad sound, a sad declaration, a sad truth.

Beth closed her eyes against the tears threatening to roll down her face. "Don't be sorry, Tony. You're bright and ambitious and good-looking. You have strong family ties, strong family values, high ideals. You have so much to give, so many wonderful traits to pass on to a child. There's nothing wrong with yearning to see reflections of those traits in your sons' and daughters' faces, or with wanting to see bits and pieces of your personality in theirs.''

He faced her stiffly, as if it required effort to look her in the eye. ''Then, you understand?''

She nodded.

''You're an incredible woman.''

An incredible, infertile woman, she added to herself.

Tony watched a tear slowly roll down Beth's face. He felt like a heel. Worse, so much worse. The last thing he'd wanted to do was hurt her. But he couldn't help it. He'd been dodging these feelings for weeks. Somehow, they'd caught up with him. Now he found himself looking for family traits in every one of his sisters' kids. He loved Christopher, dammit, but he wished the baby had his eye color, his blood, his...something. Anything.

There. He'd allowed himself to think it. And lightning hadn't struck him down. He almost wished it would. What kind of a father was he?

''I'm sorry,'' he said again, his voice heavy with pain.

She held up her hand to silence him. Tony took it, drawing her into his arms. He kissed her, heard her gasp and kissed her again, hoping to convey in actions what he couldn't put into words. ''I'm sorry, Beth.''

''So am I.''

''You have nothing to be sorry for. You didn't do this. It was an act of fate.'' He kissed her again, hard, swift, then more gently, drawing a response from her. She relaxed against him, her sigh of sorrow slowly turning to need.

He didn't deserve her, but he kissed her again, anyway, and touched her. He swung her into his arms and carried her inside, through the dimly lighted living room and on up the stairs. He didn't stop until he'd reached their bedroom, and then only to unbutton her shirt and peel away the rest of her clothes.

She whimpered when he stepped away to remove his own shirt and jeans, and clung to him as he lowered her to the bed. What followed wasn't a profound performance. Such things required forethought and planning. And Tony didn't plan, he only reacted to the need pulsing through him, the need to give something to her, and the knowledge that he couldn't give her the one thing she wanted and deserved.

His fingers stroked, parting her most private flesh. She gasped and moaned deep in her throat. Her head lolled back and her eyelids slipped down, and he could wait no longer. He made them one, their hips finding that age-old rhythm. They moved together until the blood pounding in their ears obliterated her hurt and his regret, and the fact that neither of them knew how to make things right. And then, when it was over, they wrapped their arms around each other and silently told themselves that everything would be all right.

"Has Tony apologized?"

Beth's gaze climbed from the water spot she'd been staring at in the center of the cafeteria table to Karen Sloane, who was looking at her from the other side. Trying on a faint smile, Beth said, "Why do you ask?"

"Does that mean you don't want to talk about it?"

Beth stopped drawing figure eights on her tray. "Is it really so obvious?"

Karen pushed her fingers through her short light brown hair and shook her head. "That's questions—four, answers—zero."

For the first time all night, Bethany's smile was genuine. "You're something else, do you know that?"

"Yes, I'm afraid I do." Karen's sense of humor was only one of the things that made her one of the most popular doctors at Vanderbilt Memorial, even though she was only a second-year resident. The two women had been little more than friendly acquaintances until Karen's eight-year-old daughter had been trapped in a cave during the mud slide in June. In the ensuing months, a deep friendship had formed between them. Beth knew Karen would listen, but she didn't know what to say. Tony *had* apologized for failing to tell his family about her inability to have biological children. As far as apologies went, Beth had never received anything like Tony's. He *was* sorry for hurting her, so sorry that nearly everything in their lives had taken on a kind of desperation. Even their lovemaking had changed, becoming more intense, more instinctive, more powerful.

"It's all right," Karen said quietly. "I know firsthand that sometimes apologies are enough, and sometimes they're not."

Beth empathized with her friend. When Detective Stryker had stopped her and Tony to tell them that a girl matching Annie Moore's description had been seen in Grand Springs, Beth had had a tiny inkling of what Karen and her husband, Cassidy, had gone through while waiting for their child to be pulled safely from a cold, dark cave. She and Karen had had heart-to-heart talks since that night, but tonight, Beth didn't know what to say.

"Are you okay?" Karen asked.

Beth's nod was automatic, and a little sad.

"All newlyweds go through a period of adjustment," Karen said, reaching for her coffee.

Beth nodded, but no matter what Karen said, few husbands had to adjust to something as life-altering as his wife's inability to conceive his child. Beth knew Karen had enough problems in her life right now. They showed in the circles beneath her eyes and in the expression deep inside them. "Are things any better between you and Cassidy?"

Beth didn't know how a person as petite as Karen could release such a huge sigh. Her gray eyes were trained on her coffee, her voice strangely tired as she said, "I know tragedy sometimes brings couples closer, but it hasn't worked that way for Cassidy and me. We thank God every day that Vicky was saved, but he and I have grown more distant than ever. Our little girl was the reason we got married, and I've never regretted her or anything about her for even an instant. But I'm not sure it's going to be enough to hold Cassidy and me together forever."

Beth's heart went out to her friend. "Oh, Karen, I'm so sorry."

Blowing on her steaming coffee, Karen said, "So am I, Beth. So am I."

Since there was nothing left to say, they changed the subject to more pleasant topics such as Vicky's new colt and Christopher's first belly laugh. Karen and Beth parted, laughing, but their eyes reflected their private worries. They went their separate ways at the elevators, Karen heading to surgery, Bethany to the emergency room on the first floor.

Time passed slowly. The only patients to wander into the ER were a handful of rain-soaked trick-or-treaters with tummy aches, and one man who'd sprained his ankle when he fell off the roof of a haunted house. With too much time on her hands, Beth could do little except think. About Tony. And Christopher. And what Karen had said about whether or not Vicky was enough to hold her and Cassidy's marriage together.

She was still lost in thought when her shift ended and she was finally able to go home, her mind still in turmoil when she fit her key into the door they now kept locked, tiptoeing into the dimly lit kitchen. There was an open jar of Grandma Rosa's Italian sauce near the stove, and an empty baby bottle near the sink. Dropping her purse on the table, she reached up and slowly began to loosen her braid while making her way up the stairs.

"There, there, that's my boy. Shh. You're a tired guy, just look at those heavy eyelids. Yeah, there you go. That's it. Go to sleep. Shh."

She followed the soft murmur of Tony's voice down the hall. By the time she reached the doorway to Christopher's room her hair was loose around her shoulders and her heart had lodged in her throat.

Tony was leaning over the crib, his feet bare, his shirttail out, his shirt unbuttoned. Noticing her presence, he placed a finger to his lips, cast one last look at the child who appeared to be sleeping peacefully, then motioned for her to meet him out in the hall. Once there, she whispered, "Has he been crying?"

Tony nodded. "He rolled over for the first time tonight and scared himself."

Beth melted a little inside at the depth of wonder in Tony's voice. "He rolled over?" she asked.

This time Tony grinned. "I was talking to him from the doorway. In order to see me, he had to pick his head up so far he lost his balance and tipped over. I think he's going to be a holy terror when he's two, but I'm telling you, that kid's gifted. Just wait. He'll be a linebacker someday, or maybe a rocket scientist or a business tycoon. Our son is going to be anything he wants to be."

Beth melted the rest of the way, a piece of her heart sliding all the way into her stomach before spreading outward through her body. It happened every time she and Tony talked about Christopher, every time she heard the wonder in his voice and saw the pride in his eyes. Tony hadn't come to terms with her infertility, at least not completely, but he loved Christopher as much as she did. It was as if that baby was the link between them, their mutual ground, the tie that bound them together.

Tony's cheeks and jaw bore the evidence of how long it had been since he'd shaved. His eyes and cheeks were drawn with fatigue. The past month had been hard on her, but it had been harder on him. He knew he'd hurt her, and Anthony Petrocelli wasn't a man who lived easily with that knowledge. It only made her love him more.

"What are you thinking about?"

Smiling past the emotions threatening to make her lips tremble, she said, "Oh, that you're the only man I know who can look exhausted and sexy at the same time, for one thing.''

''That a fact?''

He was also the only man who could deliver such a question with just enough insolence to make it sound like a statement. She smiled tiredly, and he went utterly still for a moment, then slowly reached out to cup her cheek with the palm of his hand.

She felt a tightening in her throat and a flutter someplace lower. She covered his hand with hers, slowly gliding her fingers along his arm, on up his shoulder, to the back of his neck, where it took no persuading whatsoever to draw his face to hers.

As if her kiss was all the invitation he'd needed, he took over from there. He back-walked her into their bedroom, half lifting her the last remaining steps to the bed.

His kisses had taken on a new urgency these past few weeks, his lovemaking reaching a new level of intensity. Her nurse's uniform came off so easily she should have gasped, her white nylons and slip following close behind. As if too impatient to wait for her to ease him out of his clothes, he whisked them off, then came to her, joining his mouth to hers even though they both knew kissing would never be enough.

She twined her arms around his strong back because she loved him, and because the things he did to her, with her, for her, made her forget about everything except this moment with this man. She sighed when he worked his own brand of magic on her body. He groaned when she worked her brand on his. They came together with so much passion, so much feeling, so much need, it made Beth's head spin and her heart fill to bursting. She almost blurted out her love for him. At the last minute, she kissed him, instead.

Listening to the thud of his heart beneath her ear a short time later, she tried to move to her own side of the bed. His arms tightened around her, even in sleep. It seemed he needed this closeness as much as she did. In time, he'd come to terms with her infertility. Meanwhile, they had this, and they had Christopher. For now, that was enough. Closing her eyes, she drifted off to sleep.

"Just look at you. You're so-o-o big," Beth crooned, lifting Christopher's arms over his head.

He kicked his feet and flailed his arms, screeching and cooing with obvious glee. Fastening the second tab on the fresh diaper, she couldn't resist planting a kiss on his soft, round tummy. He giggled out loud, and Beth did, too.

She whisked him into her arms, breathing in his clean scent. She'd just finished giving him his bath, and he smelled so sweet she couldn't resist nuzzling his neck and dancing him around the room. She took him with her down the stairs, stopping in the laundry room for an armful of his clean sleepers and little shirts.

They'd had a very busy day. They'd met Janet and Chaz at the newly reopened Grand Springs Diner for lunch. Although Beth hadn't been able to ask a lot of questions with Chaz hanging on her every word, Janet had *happened* to mention how much MacKenzie had liked her new coat. The comment went over her six-year-old nephew's head, but Beth shared a knowing smile with her sister. After lunch, she and Christopher had dropped in on Jenna at the Silver Gypsy. Jenna had muttered something in Romany when Beth had asked about Gib, which led her to believe that Tony's best friend hadn't made much progress with one petite Gypsy.

Tony had been waiting for them when they'd arrived back home. While Christopher napped, they sat out on the deck dressed in fleecy jackets to ward off the chill in the air, and sipped hot coffee. Tony had been called to the hospital around five. Now it was almost six o'clock, and the sun was low in the sky.

"Just look at that view," she said to Christopher, stopping at a window overlooking the backyard.

Spring was supposed to be the time of hope and renewal. It was fall, and Beth had never felt a stronger promise of fulfillment. The air was full of it, rife with its sweet scent. The leaves had reached their peak weeks ago, but the days were sunny and the nights crisp and clear.

As far as she was concerned, she had good reason to feel so jubilant. She loved staying home with Christopher, loved watching him change and grow every day. The adoption proceedings were almost final, and she was married to a wonderful man who happened to be incredible in bed. She couldn't give him biological children, but she'd given him Christopher, and he already loved this baby beyond words. Everything was going to work out. She felt giddy with hope and possibilities.

The phone jangled from the kitchen. She moved Christopher to her other shoulder and reached for the telephone with her right hand. "Petrocelli residence."

"Beth. This is Florence Donahue."

"Hi, Florence. What are you doing working on a Saturday? Don't you know it's a glorious day outside?"

The silence on the other end of the line made Beth stiffen. She could picture the older woman sitting behind her cluttered desk, wearing one of her many flowered dresses, chewing nervously on her lower lip. "Florence, is something wrong?"

"I came into the office to catch up on some paperwork this afternoon. Someone stopped in a few hours ago. Someone who wants to see you."

Beth couldn't move, couldn't breathe.

Mrs. Donahue's voice shook with emotion. "It's Annie, Beth. She wants Christopher."

Thirteen

Beth was dying inside, her throat so full of fear and misery she couldn't breathe. A thousand thoughts pummeled her mind, a thousand protests, but only one question formed on her lips. "Why now, Florence, after all this time?"

Mrs. Donahue sighed into the phone. "She said she's been working, saving her money so she could get a decent place for her and Christopher to live."

"She has such a place?"

"Yes."

Beth died a little more.

"Evidently, she's been waiting to come forward until she turned eighteen. It seems there's been abuse in her past, and she wanted to make sure the authorities couldn't send her back to her mother."

An invisible hand closed around Beth's heart, cutting off her blood flow. She shut her eyes and placed her fingers over her trembling lips.

Mrs. Donahue's voice grew softer, thicker, as if she were fighting tears, too. "I explained the legal process to her, how a search was conducted, what forms were filed in court and how her parental rights were terminated. She said she asked you to take care of Christopher for her. She never intended it to be forever. She said you'd understand."

Beth's first instinct was to throw the phone down and run. Someplace far away. Where Annie could never find her and Christopher. But the memory of the look on Annie's face, of the tears streaming down her young face and of the trust in her eyes when she'd asked Beth to take care of Christopher rendered Beth immobile.

"Beth. Are you there?"

Beth would never know how she managed to squeeze anything past the lump in her throat. "Yes, Florence, I'm here."

"I asked Annie to wait for me in the outer office so I could speak to you in private. As a social worker licensed with the State of Colorado, I want you to know that you have no legal obligation to return the child to his birth mother. As I said, her legal rights to Christopher were terminated in a court of law. If she chooses to pursue this it could take years, if ever, for those rights to be returned to her. There really is no telling how it would turn out. A judge could award custody to you and Tony. You can fight this, Bethany. What do you want me to tell Annie?"

Christopher wiggled at her shoulder just as a tear squeezed out of the corner of her eye. Gazing down at him, Beth thought she loved everything about this baby, from his dark, flyaway hair to his soft, round cheeks to the size and shape of each pudgy finger and toe. But she loved his blue eyes most of all.

He had Annie's blue eyes.

Beth's heart screamed in protest against being sliced wide open, but there was one thing she had to know. "How *is* Annie, Florence?"

There was a long pause on the other end of the line, followed by a slowly drawn breath. "Are you asking me if she's capable of caring for Christopher?"

A sob lodged sideways in Beth's throat, so that she could only make an affirmative sound into the telephone.

"She's thin, but she's neat and clean, and old beyond her years. She said she'd take a drug test if we wanted her to."

Beth and Tony had started locking their doors for fear that Annie, or someone who looked like her, might try to snatch Christopher while they were sleeping. How silly they'd been. Annie had never intended to steal him away in the night, just as she hadn't abandoned him, at least not in her mind, and not forever. She'd always planned to come back for him.

Annie Moore hadn't had to give Christopher life. She hadn't had to endure the pain of having him, and she hadn't had to name him after her beloved sister. Yet she had. Beth had wanted to believe that something magic had been in the air the night Christopher was born. She'd wanted to believe it had all been predestined, preordained. She'd needed a baby. Christopher had needed a mother. It had seemed so simple, so fair, so true.

Whose baby was Christopher? Beth had asked. The answer broke her heart all the way.

"Beth?"

"Yes?"

"What do you want me to do?"

"Bring her over."

"Oh, honey, I hate to make you go through this. I can hold her off, give you and Dr. Petrocelli time to talk, time to come to terms with her request, and time to make your decision."

"If we drag this out, I'll never have the strength to go through with it."

"All right. We'll be there in an hour."

An hour.

The phone fell to the floor just as Beth's knees gave out, sending her slumping into a chair. As if sensing her distress, Christopher's bottom lip pouted and quivered. Seconds later, he started to cry. Holding him close to her heart, Beth cried along with him.

Minutes flew and stood still at the same time.

She tried to reach Tony at the hospital, and nearly sobbed all over again when the woman at the switchboard informed

her that he was performing a very dangerous emergency
C-section and couldn't be disturbed. She wanted to scream
into the phone that *she* needed Tony more, and so did
Christopher. Aching for the way Tony was going to feel
when he found out what had happened, she imposed an
iron will upon herself. Praying that Tony would come home
before Annie took Christopher, she pulled herself together
and saw to the baby's needs. She warmed a bottle and fed
him, never taking her eyes off him, never laying him down.

The wind had picked up, rattling shutters and howling
through the eaves outside. Inside, the house was strangely
silent. Beth sat in the rocking chair, but she didn't rock.
She held perfectly still, memorizing the color of Christopher's skin in the dimming evening light, the curl of his
dark lashes, the bow of his little mouth, the weight of him
in her arms, and in her heart.

She didn't jump when the doorbell chimed. She'd heard
the car pull up. She just sat there, staring at the duck-shaped
night-light in Christopher's room, her thoughts screaming
inside her skull.

*I can't do this. I thought I could. But I can't. I love him.
Please. I'm not strong enough to give him up. Don't ask
me to. Please.*

The wind howled. The doorbell rang again. And Beth
rose to her feet. She descended the stairs on wooden legs.
She opened the door and came face-to-face with the girl
who was going to break her heart.

Annie's eyes were the same vivid blue that Beth remembered, but her face was thinner. The girl's hair had been
wet the last time Beth had seen her, first from the rain, and
later from sweat and tears. Today it was dry and clean and
shone with a healthiness and darkness that fleetingly made
Bethany wonder if there could have been some Italian in
Annie's ancestry—and therefore in Christopher's. Tony
would have liked that.

"He's grown so much I hardly recognize him," Annie said in a voice thick with awe.

Beth's arms tightened around the sleeping child. *Please don't take him, Annie. I'm older and more able to provide him with a stable home. There's nothing you can say to make me believe that he doesn't belong with me.*

Mrs. Donahue closed the door, then stood unobtrusively to one side. Annie looked decidedly ill at ease. She couldn't seem to take her eyes off the baby. Finally, with great effort, she raised her gaze to Beth. "I love him. He's all I have."

A sob stuck in Beth's throat. Biting her lip until it hurt, she realized she'd been wrong. There was one thing Annie could have said, after all. *I love him. He's all I have.*

When Beth had at least partially regained control of her emotions, she turned to Mrs. Donahue.

The older woman nodded sadly. "I've spoken to Annie's employer and her landlady, Beth. She has a means of support and a place to live. She's worked real hard, and she says that everything she's done, she's done for Christopher. I'm sorry. If you would like, I'll help gather his things."

"No," Beth answered. "I'll do it."

Annie felt her lips quiver, and hated herself for it. She saw a tear roll down Beth's face. And hated herself for that, too.

She may have been young, but she'd seen a lot of houses, and none of them had looked more inviting than this one did. She followed Beth up the stairs, into a pale yellow room decorated with clowns and ducks. The rocking chair looked well used, the crib expensive, the mobile brightly colored. There was a quilt in one corner, a rocking horse in another. Hardening her heart against it all, she said, "All this stuff is nice, but he's mine."

She almost wished Beth would scream at her, yell obscenities at the top of her lungs, rant and rave. The other woman's silent pain was much more difficult to endure, the tremble in her fingertips impossible to ignore.

"He'll need all these diapers. And these sleepers, too. Oh, and he always sleeps with this blanket."

Bethany had moved Christopher, who was still sound asleep, to one arm, placing his things into a cloth bag with the other. Annie yearned to hold her baby. She almost cried out with the need to snatch him into her own arms. But she didn't want to hurt Beth any more than she was already hurting. So Annie listened as Beth told her about Christopher's schedule, how he liked to have his back rubbed in soft half circles after he ate, how long he slept, how he was beginning to like his bath, and how much formula he drank at each feeding.

Flexing her fingers at the end of her empty arms, Annie said, "I woulda breast-fed him, but my milk's gone."

Beth turned around, her cotton skirt swishing into place around her legs, her hand flying to her trembling lips. Giving up on the tears rolling down her cheeks, she said, "I always wished I could have had that connection with him, too."

They stared at each other for interminable moments, these adversaries who might have been friends under different circumstances, soul mates in another lifetime. They both turned at the sound of footsteps in the doorway. Mrs. Donahue stood there, her face mirroring their own sadness.

Taking a deep breath, she bustled into the room, filling her arms with Christopher's favorite things. "I took the liberty of gathering the bottles of formula from your refrigerator. Is that all right with you, Bethany?"

Beth stared at the other woman, wishing there was something she could say, something she could do to keep this from happening.

"Beth?" Mrs. Donahue repeated. "Is that all right?"

"That's fine, Florence."

Too soon, a lifetime too soon, Annie held out her hands. "I'll take him now."

Beth closed her eyes, praying for strength. A sob wrenched from a place deep in her chest. Tears coursed down her face. Her entire body shook as she kissed Christopher, then slowly placed him in Annie's arms.

Annie sobbed, too, but she held him to her, soaking up his warmth and sweet baby smell. Turning, she hurried, surefooted and agile, down the stairs and through the old house.

"Annie, wait!"

All Annie wanted to do was escape this place, flee from this feeling of guilt and inadequacy. All she wanted to do was take her baby and make a life for the two of them. Somehow, she managed to hold her head high and turn around, but there wasn't anything she could do about the distrust narrowing her eyes. She was all ready to say "Yeah?" in that snide way that rankled people in authority, but she saw the way Beth was shaking, and the comment died on her lips.

"It's November."

Annie lifted one shoulder. "So?"

Through narrowed eyes, she watched Beth stride to the closet. Bethany Kent's auburn hair had been in a braid the night Christopher was born. Today her hair was long and loose around her shoulders. Her hands had been calm that night. Today they shook as she reached inside the closet, taking a plain, expensive-looking brown coat from a hanger.

"What are you doing?" Annie asked.

"It's November," Beth whispered again, tucking the coat around Annie's slender shoulders. "I don't want you to be cold."

Annie Moore had always considered herself tough. She wasn't afraid to run, and she wasn't afraid to fight. She'd seen horrors most kids her age only glimpsed in the movies.

She'd seen the bruises on her dying sister's slender body, and she'd known what the leers her mother's latest boyfriend used to give *her* had meant. She'd been beaten up a time or two, and had accepted the fact that her boyfriend hadn't wanted anything to do with being a father. She'd born the pain of childbirth alone, but Annie didn't know what to do about the shaking in her knees right now, or the warmth seeping into her shoulders beneath Beth's coat.

In that instant, she knew what people meant when they said they were being killed with kindness. Before she slid into a heap on the floor, she nodded at Beth, covered Christopher with a warm blanket and motioned for the middle-aged lady with the frizzy hair to open the door. "Thanks," she mumbled, without meeting anybody's eyes.

Beth watched them walk away, across the porch and down the steps and on out to the car. The wind pressed the coat against Annie's back, the outside light penetrating the darkness. Florence looked up at her before getting in on the driver's side, but as far as Beth could tell, Annie never looked back.

The car inched its way down the driveway, then slowly pulled out onto the quiet street. When it had disappeared from sight, Beth turned and walked aimlessly back into the house. Leaning against the door, she listened to the sound of silence. The sound of her world falling apart.

Tony fit his key into the lock on the side door. The whistle died on his lips when the door opened before he'd turned the key. He strode inside, his eyes automatically taking in the uncharacteristic messiness. Water dripped from the tap that hadn't been thoroughly turned off, cupboard doors hung open. There was a pile of unfolded baby items on the table. Reaching for a little shirt Beth had had specially made, Tony smiled to himself, reading the words printed across the front. My Daddy's a Doctor. What's Yours?

A low, beeping sound drew his eyes to the floor where

the telephone had been dropped. An ominous sense of fore-boding lengthened his stride.

"Beth?"

Silence.

"Beth? Where are you?"

He took the stairs three at a time, bursting into Christopher's room on a run. Drawers were open there, too, blankets hanging half in, half out. The musical mobile Chris loved to watch was gone. The crib was empty.

"Bethany, where are you?"

"I'm here, Tony."

Beth's voice had come from the other side of the hall, and she had spoken so softly he'd barely heard her. He spun on his heel and was across the hall in an instant.

She looked up at him from the other side of the bed. Her eyes were red-rimmed, swollen by tears.

"Where's Christopher?"

The way her throat convulsed on a swallow caused the knot in his gut to tighten. She finished folding a blouse and had placed it in a suitcase before answering. "He's gone, Tony."

Her voice had been as soft as tears and so full of dashed hopes that dread dropped to his stomach like lead. "What do you mean?"

She took a shuddering breath. "Annie came for him. More than two hours ago."

"And you let her take him?" he shouted.

He saw the instant squeezing hurt in her eyes and wanted to call back his words. He saw the desolation in her every feature, and he wanted to hit something.

"Annie and her sister Christie had been abused as children. Christie died, and Annie ran away. Her mother wants her back. Today is Annie's eighteenth birthday. She's an adult, free of her mother, and free to claim her child. I tried to reach you, Tony. You were in surgery."

The entire explanation took ten seconds. It said more

than he'd ever wanted to hear. Weariness washed over him. And desolation. While he'd been bringing someone else's child into the world, Christopher was being taken from his. The horrible, twisted irony nearly buckled his knees.

So Annie had been here in Grand Springs all this time. He remembered the night he'd first seen her. He'd introduced himself and asked her how old she was. Her face had been contorted in pain, but she'd still found the strength to say, "I'm seventeen. How old are you?"

The girl had spunk. She'd been too young to have a baby—she was just a kid herself—but she'd had Christopher, and now she'd come for him.

God, Tony couldn't breathe. He couldn't think. He couldn't move. It was his heart. There was something wrong with it, and with his lungs, and with his mind. There was something terribly wrong with his life.

What would he do without his son? He hadn't even been able to say goodbye.

Gradually, he became aware of movements on the other side of the room. His vision cleared, and he saw that Beth was walking from the closet to the bed, carefully folding blouses and skirts before tucking them into a suitcase.

"What are you doing?" It was an inane question, but he couldn't help it. He wasn't thinking clearly.

"We married because of Christopher. There's no reason for me to stay."

Tony's shoulders shook from the effort to hold himself together. He stared across the room at Beth; he on one side of the bed, she on the other, a whole chasm of pain and sorrow stretching between them in the dimly lit room.

She was so achingly beautiful he couldn't take his eyes off her. Her face was pale, her lashes brimming with tears. She loved Christopher so much.

God. Christopher. His son. His boy was gone.

Gone.

It was amazing how blood and genetics and eye color

made no difference when a man's heart was breaking. If he could have his son back, he swore to God it would never make a difference again.

He didn't remember walking closer, didn't recall skirting the edge of the bed or turning Beth to face him, but he'd never forget the wariness and the sadness on her face as she raised those watery eyes to his. There wasn't anything he wouldn't give to take her sorrow away.

"Don't go. Please, Beth. It's going to take both of us to get through the night." He opened his arms, holding his breath as she closed her eyes.

Beth didn't know how much more of this she could stand. She'd thought she'd lived through the worst kind of pain imaginable when Barry had left her because she couldn't conceive his child. At the time, she'd mourned the passing of their marriage. She'd mourned her chance of ever becoming a mother, too. Then she'd believed it was possible to miss something you never had, to mourn it as you would someone who had died. She'd been wrong. Realizing that she would never give birth to a child had been a horrible sadness. Barry's departure had added insult to injury. But losing Christopher was so much worse. She didn't know how she was ever going to survive it, let alone recover with her heart even partially intact.

Tony was waiting for her answer, waiting with open arms. There were a dozen reasons, all of them good, why she should finish packing and go. There was only one reason she didn't. She loved this man who was hurting as she was hurting. She knew she would have to face the fact that their marriage was no longer necessary. But she didn't have to face it tonight.

She opened her eyes and walked into his arms.

They held each other for a long time, not moving, not talking. There was nothing to say, nothing to think about except the past, which was filled with too many achingly sweet memories, and the future, which was filled with too much sadness and loneliness to fully comprehend or contemplate.

When they both felt strong enough to stand alone, she said, "We have to tell our families."

"I know."

"Do you want to call them tonight?"

He shook his head. "They'll all be here as soon as I call. They'll all want to help in any way they can. I don't think I'm ready for that."

"Then, you want to wait until morning?" she asked quietly.

He covered his eyes with his hand and took a deep breath. "Yeah. I'll call them in the morning."

Tony and Beth looked at each other. Neither of them said it, but neither of them knew how they were going to get through the long, lonely night.

Fourteen

Time passed slowly. The house was too quiet, and so was the night. Tony turned the television on in the living room. Beth turned the radio on in the kitchen. The sound covered the quiet, but it couldn't quiet their thoughts.

Around midnight, Tony switched off the night-light in Christopher's room. At two o'clock he found Beth standing in the dark doorway, tears streaming down her face. Her shoulders were stiff as he drew her away.

Her voice raw with grief, she said, "I should have fought for him. I shouldn't have let him go."

Tony had been plagued with the same thoughts, the same doubts, the same regrets, but in his heart he knew there had been no other way. "Would you really have been able to make Annie fight for him? Because if we had, the media would have turned our lives and Christopher's into a three-ring circus. No matter how it turned out, we would have grown bitter. Nobody wins in those situations. Everyone loses. You said yourself that Annie had good reason for waiting to come forward. She's been through so much, and whether we like it or not, blood is thicker than water. A judge very well could have granted custody to her. And then someday we'd open a magazine or turn on the television and see Christopher being asked how it all had affected his life. Is that what you think we should have done, Beth? Is it?"

She shook her head and allowed him to lead her away

from the room she'd so lovingly prepared for the child she'd so desperately wanted.

At 4:00 a.m. he finally talked her into lying down. "Not to sleep," he said, his voice becoming coaxing and soft. "But you need to rest. We both do."

He placed her suitcase on the floor and slipped her shoes off her feet. Together, they lay down on top of the covers, staring at the ceiling, not talking, not touching, not sleeping. Waiting for morning.

The distant hoot of an owl carried through the darkness. Beth listened, straining to hear an answering call. As the minutes ticked slowly by, the events of the past twenty-four hours played through her mind. She stared at the dark ceiling, her eyes burning from weariness and from her earlier tears. Beside her, Tony's breathing became deep and even.

She knew he'd wake up if she needed to talk to him. But her grief was beyond words. He'd asked her not to go. So she'd stayed. And she wasn't sorry. She didn't know how she would have gotten through this long, bleak night alone. She'd stayed, but nothing had been settled between them. She knew the day of reckoning couldn't be postponed forever. But it could wait. At least until morning came.

The clock ticked. The wind moaned through the branches of the bare cottonwood trees. In the meadow, the lonely owl called again. Some place farther away, another owl answered. And Beth's eyes finally drifted closed.

Waaa-waaaa.

Beth tried to open her eyes, but she was so tired and her eyelids were so heavy.

The cry came again. It was Christopher's cry. But it sounded muffled, as if it was coming from someplace far away.

"I'm coming, Christopher. I'm coming." Her feet hit the

floor in the same instant her eyes opened. She was halfway across the hall before she remembered.

Christopher was gone.

But his night-light was on. Hope sprang to her chest. Maybe he was back. Maybe he'd never gone. Maybe it had all been a horrible nightmare.

One look at the empty crib, the missing mobile and the open drawers squashed her hopes where she stood. Christopher was gone. It was a nightmare. But it was real.

Tony, who must have come into the room while she'd been asleep, looked up from the miniature baseball glove in his hand. His face looked haggard, his eyes as ravaged as hers.

"I heard Christopher," she whispered. "He was crying."

"It was a dream, Beth."

She wanted to shout that he was wrong. But she couldn't have heard Christopher, because Christopher wasn't there.

She trudged to the crib, where she ran her hand along the rail, burying her fingers in an airy blanket Jenna had brought weeks ago. "What time is it?"

"Almost five in the morning."

The night would soon be over. In an hour, or two, they would call their families, and Gib, and Jenna. And somehow they'd get through the day, the week, the rest of their lives.

Bringing the blanket to her face, she whispered, "What if he's really crying, Tony? What if he's scared? We're all he knows. What if he needs us?"

Tony stared into the nothingness beyond the dark window. The house was quiet. Eerily quiet. He remembered how terrified, how utterly incapable he'd felt when he'd been faced with Christopher's wails. As the days, weeks, months had passed, the sound of the baby's cries had changed along with the way Tony felt about them. They'd become a beautiful symphony, surprisingly robust, achingly sweet. Painfully short.

What if Christopher was crying? Beth had asked. What if he needed them?

Tony shook his head. He had no answer.

Annie saw the door open, but the only thing she could hear was Christopher's wails so close to her ear. Cora trudged in looking tired and older than ever. Her overalls were tattered and torn, her complexion was ruddy, her steel gray hair sticking out in every direction. Annie had never been more relieved to see anybody in her life.

"He's still goin' at it, huh?"

Annie nodded, so tired she could hardly hold her eyes open.

"He's got good lungs, I'll give him that. He's makin' my cats howl."

Jiggling Christopher, Annie paced to the opposite end of the small room. "Sorry. I know how much you love your cats."

"Don't you be sorry. Those cats will curl up in a patch of sunshine tomorrow and sleep the day away. The little one still won't eat?"

Annie shook her head. Christopher wouldn't eat, he wouldn't burp, he wouldn't sleep. He wasn't wet. She'd checked a hundred times. She tried to pull him closer, but he arched his little back and screamed all the louder. "Do you think he has colic, Cora?"

Cora narrowed her eyes and shook her head. "My Willie had colic. The cry was different. I don't think this baby's sick. He's mad as a wet hornet, that's what he is. But he'll get over it. Don'cha worry. He just has to get used to you, that's all."

Humming a tune that was lost to everyone else, she ambled stiffly out of the room.

Left on her own, Annie felt more afraid than she'd ever

been in her life, and she'd been scared plenty. "Don't cry. Please?" she said in Christopher's ear. "I worked so hard to fix this place up for us. See? I mended that torn shade. Looks almost as good as new, doesn't it?"

Although Christopher took a shuddering breath, he was obviously unimpressed, because he cried all the harder. Trying not to cry herself, she told him how she'd washed and scrubbed the floor until her arms ached and the skin on her hands had been raw.

"The place might not be gleaming, but it's clean, and it doesn't smell bad anymore. I rearranged the furniture, what there is of it. I even put some dried flowers from Cora's garden in a Coke bottle on the table underneath the window. See?" she said, her voice shaking. "Don't they look pretty?"

She showed him her baseball cap, and told him all about his Aunt Christie, who would have been sixteen next month. She even took an old photo out of her wallet. She tried not to let her hands shake as she propped him up so he could see.

Staring at the blurry snapshot, Christopher started to relax. Little by little, he stopped crying. She turned him around so she could look into his face. His eyes were red, but he looked up at her, and she swore her heart melted.

"Hi, there. Do you remember me? You used to kick me so hard in the middle of the night you woke me out of a sound sleep. I'm your mama, and I'm gonna take care of you from now on."

He turned his head as if searching the sparse room for something familiar. Or someone. He stiffened, a moment's panic passing through his eyes. His face turned red, his arms flailed, his whole body shaking with the renewed strength of his cries.

Annie walked with him. She tried jiggling him, she tried swaying him to and fro. When she couldn't think of anything else to do, she lay down with him on the narrow bed in the corner.

"I'm not going to let anything bad happen to you, Christopher, I promise," she whispered. "I love you so. Won'cha please love me back?"

Christopher cried on.

Tears rolled down both sides of her face, wetting her hair. Her chest ached from the effort to hold in her sobs. Eventually, the baby stilled, finally falling into a fretful sleep.

Cora was right, she thought, her eyes drifting closed. Christopher just had to get used to his real mama, that's all. Everything would to be all right. Once morning came.

Christopher had been gone for twelve hours when Tony called his family. Vince, Elena and Grandma Rosa were the first to arrive, casseroles in their hands, their hearts on their sleeves. Elena kissed Beth's cheek, Grandma Rosa muttering something in Italian before setting off toward the kitchen.

Elena stood next to her husband, seemingly at a loss for words. Watching his aging mother disappear into the kitchen, Vince slowly shook his head. "Eating is probably the last thing on your minds right now, but it's life's most basic routines that get us through times like these. Life's most basic routines, and the people who care about you."

Beth thought her tears would have run dry by now, but fresh ones spilled onto her lashes. Vincent Petrocelli was a man of few words, and he didn't waste them on flowery phrases. He said what he felt, then moved on to let someone else do the talking. Beth felt honored to have known him, to have had the opportunity to be his daughter-in-law, if only for a few short months.

She wasn't sure why her gaze went to Tony. She only knew that looking at him made her feel even more sad. His head was turned slightly, as if he was listening to whatever his mother and father were saying. Of course, there was no telling what he was really thinking; he wasn't an easy man to read. But he was hurting. She could see it around his eyes and in the deep grooves beside his mouth. He missed Christopher every bit as much as she did.

Fresh tears threatened to fall. She could have attributed them to the lump that formed in her throat every time her thoughts came close to Christopher. But she knew there was more to this ache than that.

She loved Christopher. The memory of him made her feel like crying and smiling at the same time. It made her heart hurt, because her time with him had been so sweet and so fleeting. This ache in her heart was even bigger than the loss of the baby she loved. It included the loss of the man she loved, the loss of the idyllic dream she'd been living these past few months. The loss of everything she wanted and needed.

As she blinked away tears, her vision cleared. She wasn't certain how long Tony had been looking at her. She only knew it required every ounce of strength she possessed to send him a wavering smile before pulling her gaze away so she could answer the door.

Tony was vaguely aware that his mother had headed for the kitchen to see if Grandma Rosa needed any help, and that his father had mumbled something about making himself useful someplace else. Tony couldn't seem to move, and he couldn't take his eyes off Beth.

She greeted Teddy and Gina and their four kids, accepting their tears and their condolences. She was wearing pale yellow slacks and a simple white blouse, the fabric fluttering slightly when she bent down to speak to Gina's second oldest. Beth was exhausted, with good reason, but she was achingly beautiful even now, as pliant as a willow switch, and just as strong.

Out of the blue, little Julie wrapped her pudgy arms around Beth's neck. Beth happened to glance at Tony, the expression in her eyes holding him spellbound. Before he could figure out what it was he saw, she turned away. He felt the lack of her gaze all the way from across the room.

Tony answered the door when Nick and Carmelina and their active brood arrived. After that, someone else took over. By noon, the house was noisy, food was being set out and parents were bustling after their kids who had forgotten their solemn reason for coming and were taking turns sliding down the banister.

Christopher had been gone for eighteen hours when Beth's family arrived. Although their hands didn't contain casseroles and their hearts weren't on their sleeves, their eyes held worry and sadness. Tony realized that they loved Beth very deeply and wanted to ease her pain.

Beth. He'd lost track of how many times his thoughts had strayed to her. He'd found her looking at him several times throughout the day, but he couldn't remember how long it had been since she'd touched him, or since she'd done more than cast him a wavering smile from the other side of the room. He couldn't shake the feeling that something important was staring him right in the face.

Gib and Jenna arrived together, of all things, when Christopher had been gone for twenty-three hours. Jenna went straight to Beth, and Gib, who'd been Tony's best friend for most of his life, seemed to understand that Tony wasn't up to making conversation and moved on to speak with Janet and MacKenzie and their son Chaz.

Tony appreciated everything everyone was trying to do, but the noise level was getting to him. He needed a minute to himself. He tried the kitchen first. Not only were his mother and two of his sisters there, but Nick and Frank were there, too, making themselves useful, they said, fixing his leaky faucet. The living room wasn't much better, but at least the low drone of the boxing match coming from the television in the corner kept the men who had gathered there from noticing when he took to the stairs.

He stopped in the doorway to Christopher's room first. As he ran a hand over his tired eyes, memories washed over him. He pictured Christopher kicking his feet and flailing his arms, grinning as Beth changed his diaper and talked to the baby in that lilting voice she always reserved for him.

She'd really come alive when she'd mothered that baby.

He remembered standing in this very doorway while she waltzed Christopher around the room. He'd never forget the look on her face when she'd turned and found him watching.

There it was again, that nagging sensation in the back of Tony's mind.

He strolled across the hall and on into the room he'd shared with Beth these past two months. The room was empty, the bed made, Beth's sighs and murmurs only memories now. If she'd come alive as a mother in Christopher's room, she'd come alive as a woman here.

A sound, this one real, drew his attention to the doorway. Gib looked at him, quietly on alert. "Sorry to intrude. I know how much you like your privacy, but they were talking about sending up the troops. I offered to come, instead."

Tony nodded and Gib ambled in. "Were you surprised to see me show up with Jenna?"

A shrug found its way to Tony's shoulders. "The last I knew, Jenna was boycotting anyone carrying the Y chromosome. The two of you seem to be hitting it off pretty good."

It was Gib's turn to run a hand through his hair and sigh. "Actually, Jenna and I seem to be stuck between heart-to-heart conversations and the bedroom."

Tony took a long, hard look at his friend. "I thought you only dated tall women."

"Jenna makes me feel tall. I know you've got a lot on your mind, but for months I've been feeling as if I've been treading water in a shark-infested ocean. Suddenly, it's as if someone has thrown me a lifeboat. Wouldn't you know a Gypsy would be holding the rope?''

Although it hurt, Tony smiled for the first time in nearly twenty-four hours.

"You know," Gib said, striding to the window. "I once surprised a counterintelligence guerrilla from behind. Yet Jenna anticipates my every move. I think I'm in love. Now, what are we going to do about you?"

Tony followed the course of Gib's stare, straight to the suitcase Beth had been packing last night. "I'm a lost cause."

"Then, Beth's really leaving?"

If Tony hadn't been standing directly in front of a chair, he would have sunk all the way to the floor. He ran a hand through his hair, down his forehead, across his eyes, all the way down to his chin where his palm rasped over twenty-four hours' worth of stubble. "She's hurting, Gib."

"Losing Christopher has been hard on her."

"Yes, but she's been hurting for weeks. It's my fault."

Gibson Malone had spent his formative years in combat and covert action. He could read an enemy's eyes and a prisoner's reaction to the simplest of questions. Taking in the room that had once been purely masculine but now held feminine touches, he said, "What are you going to do about it?"

Tony's chin jerked up, his eyes going from Gib to Beth's suitcase and back again. As he slowly came alive, an idea took hold in his mind. What was he going to do? Something he should have done months ago.

"Gib?"

"Yeah, buddy?"

"Would you have one of my sisters come up here?"

"Sure. Do you care which one?"

"No. Any one of them will do."

Gib nodded, then sauntered out of the room, his limp

little more than a distant memory. A couple of minutes later, Tony's youngest sister strode in. "Gib said you wanted to talk to me about something."

Tony spoke without looking up. "Come on in, Andreanna. There's something I want to tell you. And when I'm through, I want you to pass it on quietly to the rest of the family. And then I'd appreciate it if you'd all leave so Beth and I can be alone."

Andreanna gasped. "Tony, you're not dying or anything, are you?"

Tony shook his head. "I'm pretty sure I'd have to feel better to die."

Andreanna sank to the bed, her brown eyes round with concern. Tony rested his forearms on his knees, his arms crossed at the wrists, his fingers loosely folded. "There's something I should have told you months ago, but I didn't know how...."

His sister leaned closer. Sometime during the telling, she placed one hand on his forearm, the other low on her abdomen where her second child was growing. She asked a question now and then, but for the most part, she listened. When Tony was finished, she wiped her eyes and went to do as her brother had asked.

Fifteen

Beth took in the empty kitchen in one sweeping glance. Dishes had been put away, towels had been folded, counters wiped off. Someone had even taken care of the little shirts and sleepers she'd dropped on the table early yesterday evening. *When Christopher had still been here.* She closed her eyes against the jagged thought, wondering if she would ever stop measuring time in relation to how long Christopher had been gone.

Of its own volition, her gaze strayed to the window that overlooked the driveway. Tony was walking the last straggling members of his family to their van. Frank and Maria's three little girls had arrived in their Sunday best. Now the bows in their hair were askew, the sashes on their dresses undone, their voices slightly whiny as they pulled on their mother's and father's hands. Tony swung the youngest high over his head. Settling her in the crook of his left arm, he followed the rest of the family to the minivan parked next to the quaint little bench facing the side yard. Frank opened the door, then reached for his youngest daughter. While the other two children climbed inside, Maria rose up on tiptoe and kissed Tony's cheek.

Beth closed her eyes and stepped away from the window. Normally, the Petrocellis' demonstrativeness leaned more toward raised voices and laughter than hugs and kisses. Today had been an exception. She was glad Tony had his family. Their infinite caring was going to help him through this difficult time in his life.

Feeling weepy and bereft, she went upstairs to finish

packing. While she folded slips and sweaters and slacks, her mind wandered. Her family had been there for her today. And Tony's family had done everything in their power to wrap her in their warmth. For that, she would always be grateful. They had been wonderful, they truly had. Each and every one of the Petrocellis possessed a unique brand of warmth and charm and intelligence. Each and every one of them could have used a lesson or two from Gib on covert actions.

They might have thought their raised eyebrows and whispers had gone undetected, but Beth had noticed every one. A buzz had started in the kitchen, spreading from one family member to the other. Only one thing could have added to their looks of sadness. Tony had undoubtedly told them about her inability to conceive.

The Petrocellis had helped her through a day she'd thought would never end. They were all gone now. It was time she left, too.

A door closed below. Tony's steps were heavy on the stairs, the deep breath he took at the top carrying all the way to Beth's ears. After that, she heard only silence. It wasn't until she'd opened another empty suitcase and had begun to fill it that she noticed a movement near the doorway.

Her eyes met his, then slowly trailed to the baby blanket in his right hand. Her heart went out to him. She hoped he knew how grateful she was to him for giving her the opportunity to be a mother, if only for a few short months. Wishing there was some way to tell him how sorry she was that he was hurting, she tried to smile but failed.

"You're a wonderful man, Tony. The way you loved Christopher, well, few men have the capacity to love like that. Your future children are going to be very lucky."

Tony took a few steps into the room. He was so exhausted from lack of sleep and from trying to keep his emotions in check all day his head was spinning. "What makes you think I'm going to have future children?"

She looked up at him, her hair falling to the front of her shoulders. ''I know we'll both always miss Christopher, but this infertility isn't your problem, Tony, it's mine. You can still have children. Look at Barry.''

''I don't want to look at Barry, dammit.''

''I know, but, er, I mean, I'll give you a divorce, as soon as I...''

''Is that what you want, Beth? A divorce?''

She stopped stammering and raised watery eyes to his. Tony couldn't take his eyes off her. Her face was pale, her lashes brimming with tears. And there, way in the back of those eyes that could soak up everyone's troubles and bring out the wariest of smiles, he saw love. Suddenly, he knew what had been staring him in the face all these weeks. Beth loved him, and had for some time. Why hadn't he noticed its quiet presence?

He'd never know how his knees held out long enough to carry him closer, or how his hand stopped shaking enough to cover one side of her face. ''Because I don't. I don't want a divorce. And I don't want you to leave.''

''But Christopher's gone.''

''Yes. God, I loved that baby. But I love you even more.'' The last declaration was dredged from a place so deep inside him his voice shook with the effort to pull it to the surface and say it out loud.

A tear spilled down her face, rolling onto his hand. ''But I can't give you children.''

''Then, give me everything else, all your love, all your passion, all your days, and all your nights.''

She didn't answer. In the ensuing silence, his heart pounded in his ears. Powerful emotions surged inside him, making him afraid of what she might do, afraid of what she might not do. It hurt to breathe, it hurt to talk, but he had to try to convince her to stay.

''I don't know how I'm going to learn to live without Christopher, but I know I could never learn to live without you. I'll beg if I have to. And I'll badger you mercilessly.

But I won't give up. Marry me again, Beth. This time, for the right reasons.''

For a long time Beth could only stare. "Are you serious?''

His expression was more serious than she'd ever seen it. "Then, you really love me?''

"I said I did, didn't I?''

Beth didn't know whether to shake her head or tap her foot. Wasn't it just like Tony to finally tell her he loved her as if he wanted her to make something of it?

He loved her.

She closed her eyes and smiled through her tears.

His arms came around her, holding her tight, gradually molding her closer, his mouth covering hers as if he needed her kiss more than he needed to breathe. He loved her. The knowledge sang through her mind, across her senses. Passion started in a place that seemed far away, a place she couldn't name. It grew, surrounding them in their own private world.

He unfastened the buttons down her white shirt, and she unfastened his. Their lips clung, their sighs mingling with the clink of belts and the rasp of zippers.

They'd made love often these past months, but this desire was different, because it was tinged with sadness, as well as with hope and love and need. Passion built, and although nothing was forgotten, it was as if the sadness they were facing somehow allowed them to experience a greater depth of love. The pleasure they found together was a balm to their bruised and weary hearts, their unity a ray of hope for the future.

Their release was no less intense than it had ever been, but when it was all over, tears wet their smiles. They burrowed beneath the blankets and lay in the center of the bed for a long time, arms and legs entwined as they listened to the silence all around them, missing Christopher, hoping, praying that he would grow up happy and healthy and safe.

Neither planned to sleep. Yet they both did, only to wake

up again sometime later. In the wee hours of the morning, when the sky was the darkest and dawn seemed forever away, Tony murmured a term of endearment along with a kiss on the top of Beth's head. When he spoke, it was in a voice husky with sleep and emotion.

"I, Anthony Petrocelli, take you to be my wife, to have and to hold, from this day forward, in good times and bad, in sickness and in health. I promise to love you, and honor you, and cherish you all the days of my life."

Pressing first a smile, and then a kiss, just above the place where she could feel his heart beating in his chest, Bethany whispered her reply. "I, Bethany Petrocelli, take you to be my husband...."

They were both awake before the alarm. Tony headed for the shower; Beth made her way downstairs to start breakfast. Turning off his electric razor a short time later, Tony breathed in the scent of freshly perked coffee. He remembered when his father had said it was life's most basic things that helped people through difficult times. Staring at Beth over the rim of his coffee cup minutes later, he thought his father was a very wise man.

It was the beginning of November, and the grass outside the window was white with frost. Here inside, he and Beth were warm. He knew he'd always miss Christopher, but as long as Beth was at his side, he'd have a chance at happiness.

"What are you thinking about?" she asked, blowing at the steam rising from her coffee.

He let the caffeine kick in and his eyes travel over every inch of her body covered by her pale blue robe before answering. "I was just wishing I didn't have to make rounds this morning."

There were dark circles under her eyes, and hollows beneath her cheekbones, but she seemed to be doing everything in her power to try not to let her sadness show as she mimicked Carmelina. "Sex and supper. That's all you men think about."

Tony lowered his coffee cup to the table. "I never said anything about supper."

The doorbell chimed in the middle of Beth's tender smile.

"It must be your family," he said, following her to the front hall. "Mine always uses the back door."

Half expecting to see Beth's sister leaning on the doorbell, he stood to one side as she turned the handle and opened the door. Beth gasped. "Annie."

Tony froze. Fighting his way out of a daze, he took a long hard look at the girl standing on his front step. Her eyes were puffy, but her chin was raised at a belligerent angle, her arms filled with blankets and bags and the most beautiful child in the world. He wondered if she had any idea what it was costing him to keep from grabbing Christopher and never letting him go.

Annie Moore stepped over the threshold, dropping everything except the baby she wanted more than anything else in this world. Staring at Beth, she said, "He wants you. Not me. Besides, he'd only get in my way."

The girl glanced up at Tony, and he knew her toughness was only an act. With jerky movements, she handed Christopher to Beth. "I'm going to California. I heard it's nice there. I'm going back to school, too, so I can make something of my life. Maybe you could tell him that someday."

Annie tried not to look at Christopher, but she couldn't help it. He was staring up at Beth, one chubby fist tangled in her hair. Eyes bright, he opened his mouth and grinned for all he was worth. She woulda sold her soul to have him smile at her that way.

"I gotta go."

Her hand shook as she reached for the doorknob. At the last minute, she remembered the coat. She'd already pulled one arm from a sleeve when the butterfly touch of Beth's fingertips stilled her movements.

"I'd be honored if you'd keep the coat, Annie, and if you'd write to us, so we know you're safe."

"I could do that?"

Although she didn't look up, she sensed Beth's nod. No longer caring if they saw her fingers shake, she reached into her back pocket and brought out her baseball cap. "I'd like to leave this with Christopher. If it's okay with you. Christie always said it was lucky."

The doctor took the hat from her hands. "We'll give it to him, Annie. And we'll tell him how much you love him. And maybe you could write to Christopher now and then and tell him about his namesake, and about you."

She looked up at Dr. Petrocelli, and then at Beth, and finally at her baby. Not even trying to hide the quiver in her chin, she took a backward step and slowly turned around. She thought she heard Beth whisper, "I love you, Annie," but she didn't look back to make sure. She'd always wanted to do the right thing. Finally, she had.

It required all the strength Beth possessed to close that door, to keep from calling Annie back from the life she was going to make for herself. That young girl didn't deserve the pain she was going through. Staring down into Christopher's blue eyes, Beth vowed to do everything in her power to care for the precious gift Annie had given to them.

"Mrs. Donahue is going to be so surprised." Of the millions of thoughts scrambling through Beth's mind, she had no idea why she'd uttered that one.

Tony shrugged as if his thoughts were scrambling, too. "Mrs. Donahue? The phone lines between my sisters' houses are going to be red-hot."

"Janet is going to be thrilled."

"Wait until I tell Gib."

"And Jenna."

They laughed and spoke at the same time, and laughed some more. When Beth reached for the telephone, Tony covered her hand with his. "We can call everybody in a little while. First, I want to hold my son."

His hands slid under Christopher's arms, his fingers meeting in the center of the baby's sturdy back. The same man who had once felt awkward holding this child lifted him over his head as if he'd been doing it all his life.

Although Chris looked exhausted, making them both wonder just what he'd put Annie through, he kicked his feet and screeched with glee.

"I think he's grown," Tony proclaimed.

"In thirty-six hours?"

Tony lowered Christopher to his shoulder and closed his eyes. "The longest and most significant thirty-six hours of my life."

Beth reached up and kissed her husband, lingering on those features she'd always considered the most striking and strong—his chin, his cheekbones, his mouth. Sliding an arm around her waist to draw her closer, he said, "Remember when you asked me what I'd wish for if I could have anything in the whole world?"

Beth nodded, thinking of all they'd been through since that long-ago night. "I remember, Tony."

He opened his eyes, and once again she felt herself slide right in. "I want to do this again, Beth. And if we adopt a girl next, I'd like to name her Annie."

Beth was crying again, but this time she smiled through her tears. "I think Christopher would like that. And I think Annie would, too."

Christopher started to squirm. In no time at all, his lusty cries sent Beth and Tony scurrying into action. Scooping up one of the bags Annie had dropped, they raced into the kitchen to prepare a bottle for their son.

*   *   *   *   *

continues with

PARTNERS IN CRIME

by Alicia Scott
available in March 1998

Here's an exciting preview....

One

*J*osie *turned down Olivia's street and into the darkened driveway. The wind howled. No lights appeared on in the house. Black, black house. Dark, dark night.*

She got out of her car, clawed her way through the raging night and grasped the knob on the back door at last. As lightning cracked overhead, she peered through the window.

Olivia, sprawled on the elegant black-and-white kitchen floor, prostrate in a sea of teal-colored silk.

Josie fumbled with the door, then raised her fist, prepared to smash the window. When the door opened in her hand, unlocked all along, she rushed into the house.

"Olivia! Dear God, Olivia!"

Her friend, motionless. The scent of gardenias, cloying and thick. Josie was on her knees, shaking the fallen woman. But Olivia didn't move, didn't moan.

Josie searched vainly for a pulse. "Don't die on me," she whispered. "Please, please, don't die on me. You're the only person I've trusted. The only person who's believed in me..."

Another bolt of lightning seared the kitchen. She spotted Olivia's purse on the kitchen table. The cellular phone! She grabbed the purse, then turned it over and dumped out the flip phone. Dial, dial, dial.

"Please, I need an ambulance. I think she's dead."

The dispatcher asked questions. Josie fumbled through answers. She checked for noticeable injuries and began CPR and tried to will the life back into Olivia.

Live, live, live.

Sirens cut through the roaring night. The EMTs rushed into the kitchen and pushed her aside, muttering to each other. Suddenly, they had Olivia strapped to the stretcher and were rolling away, back into the horrible night. Josie wanted to go in the ambulance. She wanted to hold Olivia's hand and beg her to live.

But the EMTs left Josie behind. She stood in the rain, watching the ambulance disappear, reaching out her hands.

I didn't do it, I didn't do it, *Josie reminded herself.* Not this time....

September 5

"Uh-oh. Here comes trouble," Stone muttered.

"Damn." Detective Jack Stryker tucked the coroner's report back into the Olivia Stuart file with a last glance of frustration and longing. The answers were in there somewhere, he just knew it. He must have missed something the first time around, because it had been three months and they still had no leads on the murder case.

As Hal Stuart moved through the police station corridor in a straight beeline to Jack's desk, Jack planted his feet on the floor and summoned a last deep breath.

"I've given you three months," Hal announced, stopping in front of them. "In the beginning, everything was upside down from the power outage, I understood that. But it's September now. Why isn't my mother's case being given top priority?"

"It is," Jack said. He didn't need a lecture on his job. He already knew that the chances of solving a three-month-old murder case were slim. "We're giving the investigation everything we can."

"Didn't Randi give you a name?" Hal insisted.

"The statement's too vague," Jack said matter-of-factly. "We can't be sure they were talking about Olivia or that 'take care of the broad' means murder. And we have no idea who 'Jo' is."

They'd had this conversation before and nothing had changed.

"Then, go out and interview everyone she knew!" Hal demanded.

"We did. We asked you for a list of associates, remember, Hal? Then we talked to everyone on that list. I have the interview notes right here, and we don't have any substantial suspects. She was a good woman, Hal, and there's no one who wants to solve this case more than we do," Jack assured him. "No one."

"Yeah." Hal's expression was blatantly unconvinced. "Look, I have to get to my next meeting with Jo—"

"Mayor? Call on line one," the receptionist interrupted.

Hal grunted and took the call, then shook his head, said he'd get to it in a minute and hung up.

"You meeting with Jo?" Jack asked quietly. Was the man so dense he couldn't see the significance of his own words?

"Jo? Oh, Josie Reynolds," Hal said as he headed toward the door. Jack and Stone didn't stop him.

"Josie Reynolds, we interviewed her, right?" Jack said, pawing through the notes after Hal was out of sight. "She discovered the body and called 911. The EMTs said she'd started CPR before they arrived."

"I talked to her," Stone said. "Olivia had been the one to give Josie the job as city treasurer. Look, I have to run and meet Jessica for lunch. I'll be back in an hour."

Jack nodded as his partner walked away. Olivia had introduced Josie Reynolds to him two years ago when she'd taken the job as treasurer. His first thought had been that she was much too beautiful to be an accountant. His second thought was buyer beware—no woman with that much blond hair and such blue eyes could be good for a man. Despite all the town functions that made their paths constantly cross, he'd never really spoken to her.

He had noticed her, though. A petite, slender woman with the looks of an angel. A woman with an easy smile, but who somehow always remained alone in the room.

He would talk to her again, Jack decided, reluctantly. And he would watch her eyes. *But not so closely that she could see the nagging attraction he felt every time he saw her. His unusual response to Josie Reynolds was a complication he didn't need, not in his personal life...and not in his ongoing investigation into Olivia's murder....*

ALICIA SCOTT

**Continues the
twelve-book series—
36 Hours—in March 1998
with Book Nine**

PARTNERS IN CRIME

The storm was over, and Detective Jack Stryker finally had a prime suspect in Grand Springs' high-profile murder case. But beautiful Josie Reynolds wasn't about to admit to the crime— nor did Jack want her to. He believed in her innocence, and he teamed up with the alluring suspect to prove it. But was he playing it by the book—or merely blinded by love?

For Jack and Josie and *all* the residents of Grand Springs, Colorado, the storm-induced blackout was just the beginning of 36 Hours that changed *everything!* You won't want to miss a single book.

Available at your favorite retail outlet.

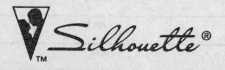

Take 4 bestselling love stories FREE

Plus get a FREE surprise gift!

Special Limited-time Offer

Mail to Silhouette Reader Service™

3010 Walden Avenue
P.O. Box 1867
Buffalo, N.Y. 14240-1867

YES! Please send me 4 free Silhouette Intimate Moments® novels and my free surprise gift. Then send me 6 brand-new novels every month, which I will receive months before they appear in bookstores. Bill me at the low price of $3.57 each plus 25¢ delivery and applicable sales tax, if any.* That's the complete price and a savings of over 10% off the cover prices—quite a bargain! I understand that accepting the books and gift places me under no obligation ever to buy any books. I can always return a shipment and cancel at any time. Even if I never buy another book from Silhouette, the 4 free books and the surprise gift are mine to keep forever.

245 SEN CF2V

Name _____ (PLEASE PRINT)

Address _____ Apt. No. _____

City _____ State _____ Zip _____

This offer is limited to one order per household and not valid to present Silhouette Intimate Moments® subscribers. *Terms and prices are subject to change without notice. Sales tax applicable in N.Y.

UMOM-696   ©1990 Harlequin Enterprises Limited

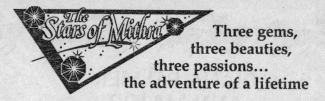

The Stars of Mithra

Three gems,
three beauties,
three passions...
the adventure of a lifetime

SILHOUETTE·INTIMATE·MOMENTS®
brings you a thrilling new series by
New York Times bestselling author

Nora Roberts

**Three mystical blue diamonds place three close
friends in jeopardy...and lead them to romance.**

In October
HIDDEN STAR (IM#811)
Bailey James can't remember a thing, but she knows
she's in big trouble. And she desperately needs private
investigator Cade Parris to help her live long enough to
find out just what kind.

In December
CAPTIVE STAR (IM#823)
Cynical bounty hunter Jack Dakota and spitfire
M. J. O'Leary are handcuffed together and on the run
from a pair of hired killers. And Jack wants to know
why—but M.J.'s not talking.

In February
SECRET STAR (IM#835)
Lieutenant Seth Buchanan's murder investigation takes
a strange turn when Grace Fontaine turns up alive. But
as the mystery unfolds, he soon discovers the notorious
heiress is the biggest mystery of all.

Available at your favorite retail outlet.

Look us up on-line at: http://www.romance.net   MITHRA

DIANA PALMER
ANN MAJOR
SUSAN MALLERY

MONTANA MAVERICKS Weddings

RETURN TO WHITEHORN

In **April 1998** get ready to catch the bouquet. Join in the excitement as these bestselling authors lead us down the aisle with three heartwarming tales of love and matrimony in Big Sky country.

A very engaged lady is having second thoughts about her intended; a pregnant librarian is wooed by the town bad boy; a cowgirl meets up with her first love. Which Maverick will be the next one to get hitched?

Available in **April 1998.**

Silhouette's beloved **MONTANA MAVERICKS** returns in Special Edition and Harlequin Historicals starting in February 1998, with brand-new stories from your favorite authors.

Round up these great new stories at your favorite retail outlet.

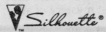

Look us up on-line at: http://www.romance.net   PSMMWEDS

ATTENTION ALL
SANDRA STEFFEN
FANS!

Silhouette Books proudly presents four
brand-new titles by award-winning author
Sandra Steffen for your reading pleasure.

Look for these upcoming titles in 1998:

In February
MARRIAGE BY CONTRACT (*36 Hours* Book #8)
Sandra Steffen's contribution to Silhouette's latest
continuity series is a marriage-of-convenience story you
won't forget.

In April
NICK'S LONG-AWAITED HONEYMOON
(SR#1290, 4/98)
The popular *Bachelor Gulch* series continues with a tale
of reunited lovers.

In July
THE BOUNTY HUNTER'S BRIDE (SR#1306, 7/98)
This contribution to Silhouette's newest promotion,
Virgin Brides, is a story of a shotgun marriage that leads
to the most romantic kind of love.

And coming your way in December from
Silhouette Romance, *Bachelor Gulch's* most famous
bachelorette, Louetta, finally gets the man of her dreams!

Don't miss any of these delightful stories...
Only from Silhouette Books.

Available at your favorite retail outlet.

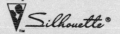

Look us up on-line at: http://www.romance.net   SRSSTITLES

Return to the Towers!

In March
New York Times bestselling author

NORA ROBERTS

brings us to the Calhouns' fabulous
Maine coast mansion and reveals the
tragic secrets hidden there for generations.

For all his degrees, Professor Max Quartermain has a
lot to learn about love—and luscious Lilah Calhoun is
just the woman to teach him. Ex-cop Holt Bradford is
as prickly as a thornbush—until Suzanna Calhoun's
special touch makes love blossom in his heart.
And all of them are caught in the race to solve
the generations-old mystery of a priceless
lost necklace...and a timeless love.

Lilah and Suzanna
THE
Calhoun Women

A special 2-in-1 edition containing
FOR THE LOVE OF LILAH and
SUZANNA'S SURRENDER

Available at your favorite retail outlet.

Silhouette®